Find Me
Falling

FIONA VIGO MARSHALL

FAIRLIGHT BOOKS

First published by Fairlight Books 2019

Fairlight Books
Summertown Pavilion,
18–24 Middle Way,
Oxford, OX2 7LG

A CIP catalogue record for this book is available from the British Library

1 2 3 4 5 6 7 8 9 10

ISBN   978-1-912054-22-0

www.fairlightbooks.co.uk

Printed and bound in Great Britain by Clays Ltd

To the illusory, magical beings who conjured

this book from the depths

This morning I visited the place where the street cleaners dump the rubbish. My God, it was beautiful! Tomorrow they are bringing me a couple of interesting pieces from that garbage pile, including some broken street lamps, for me to admire or use as models... It would make a fine subject for an Andersen fairy tale, that mass of garbage cans, baskets, pots, serving bowls, metal pitchers, wires, lanterns, pipes and flues that people have thrown away... I really believe I shall dream about it tonight, and in winter it will form a large part of my work... places that are a real paradise for the artist, however unsightly they may be.

Vincent van Gogh

FISH

The fish lies stiff in the gutter, staring into the sun rising silver beyond the bandstand. Silver scales reflecting the rays. A lone dropout from the night catch, hauled past in gleaming nets two hours since. One that the fisherman overlooked. Bearer of hidden treasure. Left to lie on this English esplanade until the early morning road sweeper comes to tidy it away.

Slit open the belly to retrieve the ring, Finder. Yours for the taking. Dig deep; no need to be squeamish. Fear not the rip of fawn flesh against your great thumb, nor the dark globules of blood under your nail, nor the splinters pricking your skin. Strive to touch silver. Beyond the slide of mucus and the squirm of soft tissue, beyond the slither of entrails, rive your thumb along the groove between the bones. Press into the bulges of yielding flesh, the tearing of whisker ribs; delve into every crevice of that hollow. Finger the deep. Let it swallow your hand, as the ring was swallowed. Don't be afraid to lose yourself in fish. Fan your fist out. Grope as far as you can go. Nudge with your knuckles against the soft inner walls where there is barely room to move. Feel in the mouth, make fish recoil and quiver; push down further and further until that hard little cervical os dilates, until the spine snaps, until the entire slippery body convulses in your fist and the ring slips onto your finger.

*

Dominic's out early: 7.10am, along the esplanade opposite the Plains of Waterloo. Between the sea and the sea, between the silver sun-path and the scatter of silver scales by the bandstand. Picking up trash along the cliff-top, between the white swoop of gulls to his barrow, and their harsh cries whose messages he can't understand. He's the finder; picks up all that's lost and thrown away by the heedless. Old news blown against railings, bottles with no messages, dead ends of chips, soiled condoms, discarded jewellery, clothes abandoned on the fugue to God knows where. On the lookout for coins, treasure of all kinds. Picking up the fish, that travels from sea to sea. That leapt off the van taking the night catch to market, to wait for him. His for the taking. With his bare hand he grabs the slippery form, the one that didn't make it, that washed up in the gutter; strides forwards, looking out from this English bandstand with its peeling benches, so far from home. The barrow parked beneath, stuck with its three brushes that vibrate as the wind catches their heads. Silhouetted in the dazzle of early light, he stares from sea to shining sea, clutching the fish. The light strobes into his brain; the shadows cast by the bandstand pillars are photosensitivity in slow motion. A sigh from the water below arrests him, like a woman arriving unheard at his side.

He looks down, his mouth brutal, twitching slightly. A sigh, a song. Music upon the waters, sweet airs from the briny deep. The elements in harmony before him, a harp that changes rhythm while keeping its own silver tone. In those depths earthly beings become aquatic, and sea creatures return to the land. Tides and timings, mersongs, church bells chiming from beneath the waves. The heaving dazzle of water, the flicker of the waves, grip his attention. His fingers close on the fish, whose harsh scream goes unheard. Sounding in shimmers to the world's edge, the water's splits of light hold and travel his eyes, which can't let go. The water's insistent rhythms travel his brain in waves, transporting him. He extends his arm towards the sea, the source of sound; his fingers are a fist of fish. Endless wavelets of light, taking him with them, on, and on. He passes into them, into that glittering vista; can't do otherwise. Into those loomings of sound, taking him with them, on, and on. Music coming to him from across the ocean, that has the power to take him to far-off lands. His entire body stiffens. His outstretched arm, his hand strangling the fish, are rigid. From sea to sea he stares, fixed, motionless. His mouth trembles; a suggestion of spittle bulges at one corner. From the river to the ends of the earth, he's gone.

Don't call him back. He's had a lifetime of people calling him back; parents, schoolteachers, doctors, lovers. Authority in every shape and form. With everything from tenderness to threats, punishments and procedures of all kinds, isolation, imprisonment, kisses, intensive care, resuscitation, strange drugs, stranger treatments. He's been seized, struck, strapped down; sat on by frightened co-workers, fucked by nurses, brutalised by paramedics. Let him stand there, a street cleaner in a blue short-sleeved shirt, deeply frayed at the neck. His face impassive; his hair, a dark blond, lifting a little in the breeze. Arms tanned and strong, like any workman; hairs glinting gold down his extended forearm. Rough, impermeable, the fluorescent waistcoat creased across the back, the prison trousers and reinforced shoes, the pink-grey squelch of fish between his knuckles. Much safer to let him stand. You don't want to know where he is, where he's gone. Let him stand staring at the sea.

'Excuse me, can you tell me where...'

The initials of the council are stamped across his back, like a prison number or warning: do not approach. But Bonnie can't read those hieroglyphics, the woman spinning towards him in her light steps and summer dress along the promenade, like a bird spun sideways. Nearly cannons into that high-visibility back, jerked upright with unnatural stiffness.

'Excuse me... Hello?'

He swings round, recalled, takes two steps up to her; she steps back. Realises she should have asked someone else, anyone else. His face deadpan, putty, the colour of old sand, the shock of the thumbed-in eyes, and the dead fish in his hand. Her own face, arrested in flight, wings of blonde hair halted mid-beat. Stepping up to her from some immense distance. For this is a man bewitched, by rare drugs, or by a stepmother who changed him so that he goes like this by day, can only be a man by night. His daily matutinal transmutation must be something to watch; just like he's changing now, returning swiftly from that other world. Face resuming colour, the yellow blench receding from his street tan. Lighting up, eyes snapping sparks in the early morning. Like the endlessly sparking sea below. One hand clutching the fish, the other fumbling at his pocket, looking for something. But before he's found it he's back, completely, eyes agleam.

'Lost, this early? Been walking round all night maybe, eh?'

It's a shock to realise he can speak, and so promptly. Voice like a gravel beach, with the drag of some accent she can't place.

'I'm glad you think it's funny. There's just no one around!'

'What – when you've found me?'

'Well, that's great, of course. But where is everyone?'

'The people here don't come out until the shops open. And then they drive. No one would dream of walking, on this island.'

'They're missing a treat, an early morning walk along the cliff-tops.'

'Like me. I start early, 6am, now that's early enough to start walking, eh, wouldn't you say?'

An outright cadging for sympathy. So she's asking him for directions, for the way back home. What a person to pick. The man in the street, his fish in his hand. Why, he's homeless himself, been an exile a long time now. Lost on this island, like her; wandering the streets all day. She strayed on to a stretch of cliff-line she doesn't recognise, doesn't know whether to go east or west. Doesn't she realise that's the way it is here? This isle's made up of garbage, floated off the edge of England and melded together by the sea. He should know; none better. Might look solid, but it's all a mass delusion, a Marian vision, a Fatima winking at the crowd. Place shifts and changes all the time. Shorelines rise and vanish, sidewalks buckle, roads that were straight one day, gone all twisted and lead someplace else the next. It's a dangerous venture, leaving home, here; might never get back again.

'Where you after, Ville-Marie? You need the other side of the harbour. See the top of Mount Royal over the way there, with the big cross? Go on down the road until you reach the roundabout...'

Directs with brusque eagerness. Raises the fish, whose nose points down the road. Who knows the way, and could have warned anyone not to take it. Its mouth stuck wide open, each side fanned out to an overlay of transparent scales. Drinking air as we drink seawater. The pink mash of roe between his brown fingers and signet rings, dark entrails spilt over his knuckles and veins. Of all the strange people she's met in this strange town, he's the strangest. She landed beside him like the wild goose touching down en route to Arctic Canada. What led her foolish footsteps to this man? Why not stay in her element, London? But London's the untenable zone, spilling over with humanity. The sparrows leaving it in droves. Now the weary, bloodied fish eye keeps catching hers. She glances round for other people, alone with this man in the early morning.

'...and then up the other side, till you come to the tide ball, can't miss it...'

'Oh, that's fine. Thanks very much.'

'OK, sweetheart. Now if you get lost again, just get someone to send you back to Dominic. Dominic the road sweeper, ask for. You come straight back and find me. And I'll set you right again.'

'No, that's great. I can see our house, actually.'

'Oh yeah?'

'The big one at the top of Mount Royal there, with all the creeper. Concordia, they call it.'

That was wilful of her. When she finds him more than a little frightening. But she's always been wilful. And in so insular a place, he's bound to find out sometime. He knows these streets and their inhabitants so well. At some point, she might even learn where he lives.

'Concordia, eh? You don't say. The old lady's house. Used to be an old watch-house, you know that? Looking out for wrecks out to sea.'

Maybe keeps an eye on him too as he sweeps. Got a far range.

'Met the ghost yet?'

'Our house is haunted? No one told me that.'

'Well, I'm telling you now. So they say. Been on the market a long time.'

He probably knows the sold price and all. Let no one underestimate him. He's the eyes and ears of this town, sees everyone without appearing to note a thing. Sweeping under benches, emptying bins, lounging down the precinct, litter grab in hand, sunk into casual intentness on cigarette packs, petrol tokens, sweet wrappers, he knows all what's going on. He's acquainted with every ghost on this isle; and then some. But when she asks, he won't say.

'Haunted by—?'

'Couldn't tell ya. You'd have to ask the locals.'

He's not from here; he's an expatriate, like she is. Waste Island, they call it, has she heard that name for it yet? No one calls it West Island like they're supposed to. This is Ariosto's lunar land, where everything lost on earth comes to rest just because it can't go any further. Ghosts, talents, lives. Squandered passions, damaged brains. Broken promises, unanswered prayers. His job to collect and bin it all. And the people here are real careless. Littering bits of themselves everywhere. Surely she's noted? How the indigenous population are all of them driven somewhat crazy by living on this bit of moon over-jutting the sea, how one day it's going to break off and fall in, and the water will come and swamp the land, drowning the memory of all who once grew weed on its edges. They won't make friends, the locals, so she better be friends with him.

'So: just moved here?'

The gleam of London gold to her hair. And her eyes see everything city-size, bigger than it is. She won't last here.

'Yes, and I've got to get back. They're delivering my piano this morning.'

'Your piano? Now that reminds me. I seen you before...' Pulls at his ear, as if for the memory.

'Have you?'

He's looking at her, eyes almost swimming with mildness. Warm, familiar. That dreamy feeling.

'We've met before.'

'Where? The town centre?'

'You shouldn't go down there, sweetheart.'

Where did they meet before, London or Montreal? By silver streaming Thames? It certainly wasn't here, this isle of the dead, with its salt-stunted trees, its reclaimed flat sea-fields, its end-of-the-world seaside towns. It's all right up here, on the esplanade. Here the air is clear and you have time to think.

If he'd met her up here before, he'd have remembered. Down in the precinct things get muddied; he's afraid that one day they're going to change his route, put him down there for good and then his life will be over.

'Do you play professionally?'

'Kind of.'

He sighs, looking up over her shoulder as if a big fist were squeezing him, squeezing it all out of him, then to her again. By asking enough questions, he knows to ground himself.

'There: said I recognised you. Saw your photo in the local paper, now I think of it, when the house was sold. So you're the maestra, hey? Plays the piano like a dream – eh?'

'Well, I...'

'They said you were relocating down here, for your health.'

'Bloody hell, you're well informed. Did they put that in?'

'Didn't you read it?'

'Of course not.'

He regards her, in slight bafflement.

'Going to play for us some time?'

'Might do. Some time.'

'When you're better, eh? Well, there's lots of people down here for their health. Some incurable.'

He tosses the herring finally into his dustcart, realising. She's relieved to see it go.

'Catch many of those round here?' Maybe too emboldened by relief.

He looks at the barrow as if he's going to pretend it hasn't happened; wipes his hand down the side of his trousers, regards her steadily. Blue eyes with a green sea gleam. The distance gathering in them again.

'Oh… well, yeah… maybe… One or two. You'd be surprised…'

He wants to tell her it's nothing for a girl to come across a man throttling a fish with his bare hand on this isle. Hooking a ring from the deep. How he already knew it was going to be this kind of day. How he always knew she'd be along. After the fish gave him warning. If she only knew what he'd already seen this morning. First the sign of the mask as he left the house, stuck atop the park railings, bare and pink, uncannily like a real face. Was it looking at him? Who put it there? It eyeballed him with its smiling uncertainty, its non-eyes following him as he cycled past, boring into his back all down the street. Then the sign of the snowy owl, down by the harbour, weighting down the kid's black-leathered wrist, cream-white and gold, an abomination of night in a daytime place. What was an owl doing here at 5.45am? Its large yellow eyes could not hunt over the glittering blue field of sea. No trees in the ocean. And surely early morning sun, reflected off a thousand yachts, was a torment for a night bird. As he cycled nearer, the sun caught it from behind, a blaze of golden feathers, eyes flaring gold. Encircled and edged with sun. Perched there in regal disdain of all things human, it turned its head after him as he rode by. The kid, fourteen or so, stood solemn and silent before the clanking masts and did not respond to his greeting.

And then the fish, the throb of its disintegration still on his fingers. And now her. Hair spun golden against the sun, eyes gold and unseeing, skin etched with a thousand fine sun-hairs, a ball of down. Toenails painted gold, in her sandals. Even in his trance of fish, he saw her approach. Blazing her way along the promenade, as if against her fate, edged with sun-fire. He's seen her before; recognises her from somewhere, even if only from the morning signs. She has the sweet, eerie smile of the mask; she's predatory like the owl; out of water like the fish. She's come for the ring. He knew it. He recognised her. He always knew she'd be along. He always knew there'd be a morning like this, choking ring out of fish in the sparkling sun. He wants to tell her. No, the fish is nothing, nothing. You wouldn't believe what I see around this town.

Just as well he can't explain, that he's almost totally inarticulate beyond the everyday. Dazed, gazing at her, from some faraway land, some special place in his brain. Déjà vu has him in its grip. And there's the mash of innards between his fingers, and the bloodied ring gripped in his palm. Instead, he smiles.

'Could you use a ring?'

   'What?'

He holds it out to her on his palm, fish guts smeared into the cracked lines of his wide mitt.

   'You could wash it. I guess it'd polish up.'

   'Where did you get it?'

   'Found it.'

   'But where?'

He's cleaning the ring on the end of his shirt, with a slight, private smile.

   'Picked it up.'

   'Maybe it belongs to someone.'

'Not where I found it. Belongs to the finder.'

'But surely you want it for your—'

She gestures at the gold band he wears, lined up in a fist of signet rings. Nothing like facing facts.

'My wife – she doesn't really care for this kind of thing. She's got her own rings.'

Still she hesitates. She likes him very much, now the first shock of meeting is over. He's got smiling blue eyes going deep into her and a nice line in cool irony. Wind creases round his eyes; just weather-beaten enough. Iroquois cheekbones. He's passionately lonely; always a terrific appeal. An engaged, maybe over-engaged, way of asking questions. He smells of home, eau de cologne. But there's a strange shadow across his face she's never seen before in another man; like drugs but not like drugs, like age but he's only forty, and fit, he's telling her that, along with all the other facts you have to list in that relentless initial catechism. Only forty, and a good catch.

'I've got rings of my own, too.'

She holds out her hand to show him her famous, magic, pearl-of-great-price hand; he takes it, without an inkling of its value, fumbles with his ring.

'See if it fits.'

It does, of course; the fish would hardly have brought it otherwise. He slips it onto her finger with the lightest of touches. Her hair puffs out, gold feathers on her exotic neck. She barely realises he took her own wedding ring off first, in one swift, light filch. She's a ringed bird now; now he'll know her again whenever he sees her.

'There you go. Maybe it'll help you play again.'

'You mean a kind of talisman?'

'Eh?'

'A lucky charm, magic ring.'

'Kind of, yeah. Why not.'

'Great. And now let me go.'

He's delighted with himself. Sea-light scatters from his eyes, he's brimming with it, his own secret humour. She should run. But he's got her hand, he's got her wedding ring, and her hair's all billowed out as in a sea breeze. Still she stands, not so much aghast at being given the ring in this cavalier manner, as troubled at being excluded from the joke. His odd insistence, as if he were visiting some private amusement or meaning on her. They stand framed in the shadow of the bandstand, he bent over her hand.

'Now mind you wear it. Keep it on, eh? I went through a lot to get that.'

His gleaming eyes, full of sea-sun; he couldn't be more pleased with himself. She dare not pull away. There's an equilibrium here she mustn't upset. Her fine white London hand resting in his, like a slim fish. Every finger worth a fortune. Perfect buffed, short oval nails. The ring is slender and glinting, sea-silver. And her hair is still spiralling out round her head, in her piloerectile state.

'Mermaid nails,' he says; their exquisite, subtle, pinky gleam. They're made for the ring. 'No surprise you play, with those fingers.'

Another restless flash of her hair.

'I must go. Can I have my wedding ring back, please?'

She'd never get into this kind of situation in London; never.

He turns her hand over to admire from the other side, her palm with its mass of unknown, fine lines, a whole life laid out for him to read. As if he'd just casually tipped her life out of her cupped palm. Her life resting in his clasp, the soilings smeared deep into his hand with its cracked lines and blunt, broad fingers, brown-grained spatulas splayed with manual work; fingernails almost unnaturally wide, much-chipped. Her first sight of him is burnt into her brain; man crushing fish, his predecessor. But surely he's a lamb; his blue eyes. And his yellow straitjacket; he's a public functionary. Even in this kind of job, the council wouldn't employ him if he was too outré, surely. The weary flop of his eyes on the ID card hung round his neck confirms his status. She's afraid of something else. He's got a long scar on his forearm, from the wrist to a curve just before the elbow, a whitish question mark wrinkling against the brown skin. Her eyes fill with tears.

'I want to go now, Dominic. Give me my ring back.'

He startles at the use of his name, as she hoped he would, releases her. Tips her own ring clumsily back into her open palm.

'I should be getting on, too. That's my break gone, really.'

She stands shaky, hair subsiding.

'Your break? Oh dear. You should have said.'

'No, no. No problem.'

'How long do you get?'

'We get half an hour in the morning.'

'Do you get a lunch break?'

'An hour at noon. And another half hour in the afternoon.'

'How do they tell if you've done your job?'

'The supervisor, he goes round in the van in the evenings, checks on the state of the streets.'

The whole conversation's been like that.

'And do you always do the same streets?'

'I get around. You can always find me.'

'I must go. I'm really late.'

'Well, like I say, next time you get lost, remember, come find me!'

She spins off, a golden bird of paradise, a ball of gold light, too fast. Always too fast. Takes her warm golden glowing face with her. Her footsteps echoing off, too definite. He stands electrified, calls after her when she's well down the esplanade.

'I'll see ya!'

*

Between the sea and the sea he wanders, dizzy with the change of sky, the change of woman. Too fast, too sudden. The way she came spinning sideways into his life, out of nowhere, like a seizure. Sick and giddy with the message of the mask, the owl. Too much, too many messages, travelling his neurons, rampaging his synapses. The excitability of the brain is too much. Fish head and squashy skeleton eye him from within the barrow, sickening. What he's just done, sickening. What he is, sickening. Stench of fish on his hand. He gropes his way to a bench at the bandstand. A place of safety; just in time. He sits, staring out to sea. Here it comes. This is it. Spinning towards him from the blue horizon. His mouth twitches; progresses across his face, his hand flickers, secondary shuddering up his arm. He always knew there'd be a morning like this, sky spinning into sea, fish spinning into sky.

Fish lies stiff on the concrete, forgetting the silver wave that washed it there. As it soared onto land, it began twitching and the air was forced out of the lungs with a harsh scream; *le cri épileptique*, that makes a strong man chill down the backbone. A rising bark like *No*: no, *not the land, no!* Its seizures were partial, focal, temporal. The cliffs inverted, spun upside down, pulsating fish up at a rate of four to five slow spiked waves per second. Fish denied the land as long as it could: no, no, no. Held down by helpful hands, staring at the sky, until it catapulted through them, staring, still. Spinning through the sky, it made complex movements of turning, searching. Its clonic curvetting imprinted its essence on the air; its irregular leaping caught the light, silver on silver belly. Its inter-ichthal fugue was prolonged. Sent its shedding scales along the esplanade silver distances, what ways went, what sights saw. Paroxysmal, irregular discharges of activity; shedding silver sparks of sun, silver belly jumping to silver sun, spiralling into silver signalling, firing. Silver waves turn round and round, fish spun 500 times a second with the greatest velocity in the tremendous vortex of a sea of silver fire.

The jumping fish stiffened. With its last jerkings, spat all its air out. He lies cheek to cheek with fish.

Rip open the belly and pull out the ring, Finder.

SEA HOUSE: CONCORDIA

She bought a house where you can hear the sea, murmuring on the edges of consciousness, night and early morning when it's quiet, the balcony door ajar. She and her husband, Austin John Ogilvy, the critic and littérateur, whose chatter can be heard likewise, always sounding in the background. A three-storey Regency house standing like a huge silence on the cliff-top, Mount Royal, that dominates the town. Panopticonic views across the sea. Almost hidden by ivy and creeper, the name just visible above the front door: *Concordia*. They're smitten, sit in the car outside, can't drive back home. It's a classic love buy. Because for sure the house wants them, too; they felt it the moment they saw it, gazing after them down the street. It's been looking out for them, the way an old watch-house should. And when they tug the iron bell pull, up those four worn steps with a sea view at the top, they feel like they're coming home. The owner refuses to show it despite their appointment – a two-hour drive with the child for nothing, Finbar, three and a half and already seasick. Makes all kinds of trouble, backs in and out of the deal, a slippery, twisty, money-grabbing old sea-witch, been there for fifty years and more, deeply in debt and with five stinky cats. Lost in the chandelier shadows of her hall. Sold off part of the garden to pay some of her debts. Should you buy a house from a person like that? They persist; buy it. See the old lady off, vengeful, muttering curses, saying the land has no dominion over the sea. Left the rusty horseshoe upside down over the front door. And a ram's head in a corner of the garden, skeletal in the sea-winds. But it's theirs. Concordia. A dream house, from the outside.

Inside. A house without ghosts but where the doors don't close, and you never really want to have your back to them. A wind lyre onto that eastern coast; a cave from which the tide has withdrawn, leaving it scattered with sand, at-home shells inching along, seaweed fronds, the ribbings of waves along its wood floors. Sea sprites whispering from every corner. A place where books swiftly sag and paper goes too limp to write on. Great for a literary journalist and musician. Bonnie's piano slides out of tune, her music sighs and fades down the stand. Austin sighs, too, talks about damp-proofing: his library, the collection of a lifetime, still in boxes at his mother's flat in Chelsea; thinks he'll leave them there for a bit, if Sally can bear it. Sit in the bath too long here and you might well start to grow a fin. Here it's possible to believe that humankind will soon return to its original element, the sea.

So they move in. Rip up the cat-soaked carpets, so they can actually sleep in the place; find what they find, such as a lot of dust. A lot of work to be done. A cellar full of the old witch's victims, dead chairs, dismembered bedsteads; the forlorn remains of a rosewood spinet. All of which they lay reverently to rest in the local dump. Discover that the real inhabitants are the woodlice, an army breathing through its gills in the attic, scuttling round as if on a perpetual quest to find the path back to the sea, whose hush can be heard whenever they stop talking. They shovel up the shrivelled, eyelash corpses with the living by the dustpan load, marvelling at these adaptive prehistoric amphibians. They can't adapt. Feel they're not of land, sea or air. They all have the same, repeated dream of flying there, father, mother, son: floating down the stairs, hand light above the rail, again and again. And the electricity won't work on one side of the house, three electricians on. Keeps giving out altogether on the top two floors. Some phantom fault they can't track. They say this was the last house in town to have electricity installed, that the old witch disapproved of it, within living memory lit the house with the gas lamps they found still in the walls when they moved in. Nor can they get rid of the uneasy smell of iodine. Maybe the house is haunted after all. What can you do with a house that goes in and out with the tides every few hours?

There's a red room to the left as you step in, a snug sea-box onto the harbour. It's locked, without a key. Takes the grumpy local locksmith a long time to break in. Completely furnished, with red velvet sofa and chairs, huge gilt mirrors hazy and spotted with grey, floor-length red velvet curtains, the mother of all chandeliers slung low over it all. A tattered red carpet that gives out in shreds at the door. Yellowed music scores, newspapers and magazines, all piled up by the marble fireplace.

'A real fire risk,' says Austin, tugging at a copy of *Vogue*.

'My God. 1964. Probably worth a small fortune. Why on earth didn't she sell these, instead of the garden?'

An attic bedroom piled with junk, a battered birdcage, a child's wooden trolley with a wheel missing, fringed lampshades and skirts, faded Christmas decorations, books and blankets smelling of mould, a model theatre with velvet curtains, long-limbed puppets splayed on top, staring and smiling at the ceiling. The past all piled up in one living, breathing heap, which should have spontaneously combusted and flared into oblivion years ago. And from the chimney, stuffed with carrier bags against wind and rain, out tumbles a bird skeleton and ash and a little knitted witch doll, sooty green, which Bonnie appropriates. Otherwise, they leave it untouched. Shut the door on that one, for another day.

'We should have made it a condition of exchange, that she clear the place of all her rubbish,' says Austin.

She left other things, too. The top floor landing rail all overhung with dresses, lace and tulle, black and pink, dull green-gold, a spray of silk cherry blossom. The old witch, who once wore these as a young witch, not contactable for their return. Bonnie tries them on instead by candlelight, frightens her husband and child with how well they fit, bodice snug as a glove. How well they suit her. Hair and night eyes glowing just the way they used to after a concert. They both stare at her like foxes; Austin's hair a dark red quiff, Finbar, a soft ginger spray. Both in Austin's typical pose, lips parted as if about to burst into speech, both of them of a freckled, loquacious indoor tribe. As if, voluble as they are, they could say so much more than they do.

'Don't you miss it? How can you so look the part and not perform?' says Austin. 'Get into the living room there and give us a tune.'

'Shall I? Do you think the house would like some music?'

'I'm sure it would listen most attentively.'

'Play *Alouette*,' says Finbar.

'In the style of Schubert.'

And she goes to the piano, dress sweeping the length of the floor, a candlelit recital for two, and anyone else who wants to listen out in the street. It sounds grand, grand, says Austin. Just like old times. And she surely hears the house applaud.

It's a house you want to please. Always straining at the wind, as if it too would be happier released into the other element. An attic always swaying with sea-breezes. It's got winged wallpaper that's alive, swooping all up the stairs, a pattern of wild geese. The trapped entities of the house, waiting for Bonnie to release them. Finbar trails them up and down with his fingers, talking to each one. But they don't move yet.

They bought it as an investment, like the good Londoners they are, to mop up a little inheritance from Austin's grandmother, who died last year. Haven't severed their links with London yet. No way; far too astute. Rented out their house in Hammersmith at a good let. Got time to play before Finbar starts school and they need to be rooted. A six-month let, just in case. Bonnie doesn't care. She'd have sold the house, walked away from London, and no looking back. But Austin would sooner sell his soul. Meanwhile, of course, true to form, they're going to do Concordia up. It'll be a labour of love. And if ever a house needed love, this is it.

They bought it for the outside; it so looked the part. For the pink light that comes off the water late afternoon. For the Regency crescent behind, that smiles round a dark green lawn, and the address, Ville-Marie, that sounds like a town in a faraway land. The huge front door with its fabulous stained glass and interwoven motto: *Je me souviens*; I remember. He's always wanted to live in a house with a massive entrance hall like that, says Austin. The price, absurd compared with London. The size: six bedrooms. Open fires. A conservatory. The style and charm of the place, the stairwell twisting the length of the house, its many landings and doors, leading out onto other domains. There's room to spare for her piano, and a music shop down the hill. It was obviously meant to be, as they say down here.

'And to think they threw in a ghost as well!'

'The one thing it isn't is haunted. Can't you feel it, that there's nothing here?'

Beyond a slight sense of watchfulness. But that surely goes with having been a watch-house.

'It is haunted,' she says proudly. 'The road sweeper told me.'

'Did he give you the winning number for the lottery as well?' says Austin. 'Seeing as he's gifted with infallibility and can't tell a lie?'

'He wouldn't lie to me. He's a poppet. He's my friend.'

But hey, who needs friends, with a house like this?

*

Bonnie and the house quickly establish a rapport. Sunlight dancing on the walls, the soft clunking of window frames, shadows whisking away in a *clin d'œil*, all that. But it only works when they're alone together. When she can play very softly to its listening silence, feel her fingers start to unfreeze. Just the two of them; in harmony like the name says, Concordia; with one heart. Once the redheads are there too, father and son, the sense of maternal attentiveness vanishes. Banished by Austin's constant talking and Finbar's manly chatter. Anyway, Austin's the type dislikes bumping into shadows on his way up the stairs, and Finbar's plain spooked. Says he can hear the piano playing late at night when everyone's asleep, saw an old lady on the landings with a face that's horribly like Mum's. Says the blackened little witch doll surely walks when no one's looking; it's never where you left it. And another thing: this house wanders the streets at night. He's woken more than once to feel its gentle lurch, the bed sliding from side to side of the room, even smelt the raw earth where it's torn itself out by the roots. It goes down to the front and looks out to sea. One morning they're all going to wake to find themselves on the other side of the world. At which Bonnie smiles. Father and son both look at her in dismay. It's a bore they don't like the entities here, cramps her style, spoils her fun a little, when she can hear so plainly what the house is whispering, dreams from some faraway land. *Je me souviens.* Creaks from the attic, wind down the chimneys, pages of an open book turning in a draught no one can feel, footfalls down the corridors, the sense of scrutiny from the high ceilings. But Bonnie feels protected.

'This house must be glad we moved in.'

'It might show its appreciation by allowing the electricity to function.'

'It's early days yet. We've got to remember we're new in town. Give it time to get used to us.'

'I hope it's not going to take *too* long. You can get tired of going to bed by candlelight. A bore if one wants to read. Can't you persuade that spook of yours to use some influence with the fuse box?'

In that middle-class way, they were deceived by the notion of getting out of London; naïve, spoilt, provincial Londoners, even at thirty-four and thirty-three, had no real idea what the provinces were like; thought everywhere in England was like London, that other island, that doesn't even remember it was once under the sea. Thought the sea air would be good for the child, good for Bonnie, who's been kind of run down since his birth; developed almost a kind of phobia about London, says she can't breathe there. Or, more importantly, play there; says the place gives her stage fright. On that impossible UK quest for better quality of life. Don't they know, even Dominic could have told them, you've got to go to somewhere like Canada for that? The air is indeed different down here, its cold breezes, the light's different. The whole isle has that blue light, like a dome. A forlorn light. And it's black at night. Not the warm orange lamp post glow of London. Time's different; it's five minutes and forty-one seconds ahead of Greenwich Mean Time on this east coast. What can happen in an extra five minutes? You can come round a corner and meet someone, have a seizure, conceive a child, face your execution and have it reprieved. Anything can happen in five minutes.

In five minutes Bonnie's career vanished down a crevasse in time. The five minutes it took to deliver Finbar, ripped out by caesarean to save both their lives. The first five minutes when she came round afterwards, and realised she was mortal. Saw the void she'd been playing against, faltered, fell, from a great height. Tumbled to earth, lost her world of air. Lost the beat, lost her ability to read music; signs and symbols of all kinds; can't even read street names, useless at maps, worse at people. Can't keep time any more, in any shape or form. Doesn't know when to come in, how slowly to play. Her famous perfect timing gone, as well as her perfect pitch. Maybe she'll find it again in the strange sea rhythms of this place.

So now she's out of time, Bonnie's full of whims and fancies. Reckons that something happens to time in this house, that those extra five minutes expand and spiral inwards. That the hands of her bedside clock start running backwards at night. Just like the night she was in labour, time counting down from the other side. The pangs coming like clockwork, Bonnie picking up the clock to time them, but unable to comprehend the hands or the numbers. The rhythm of birth overriding hers. And now it's the same, midnight on this isle, when she goes to bed. It doesn't matter what type of clock she looks at, it won't keep time, whatever that is. So often she's wondered. Wondered where time was going the night she had Finbar, spiralling backwards. Now she knows. It went down here, and stopped.

Dominic could have told them. Not like Austin, that proud, tetchy Oxbridge chieftain, who grew up at the end of Bonnie's bed, spent his teenage years lolling there, talking, talking about education, literature, poetry, bore her off down the road still talking, to the register office, hasn't stopped talking seven years on. They were brought up together, after his mother Sally inherited Bonnie at thirteen, when her parents died in that car crash. A daughter for Sally, a listener for Austin. Neither of them could get over it, this dolly sorceress, with her fey, magic fingers, otherworldly air, blonde bob. Kind of sent by the gods as one of those magical gifts that life does sometimes throw in your way. Austin had an actual twin, Finuola, who died at birth, and now here was a replacement, a living apology from fate. They could see she was damaged, with her thousand-yard stare that had witnessed the car crash from the back seat, with her habit of leaving the flat at all hours to wander the London streets, as if searching for her lost dead. All the more reason to love her back to life. Her parents bequeathed her detachment. But Sally and Austin would overcome that. Austin, sitting at the foot of her bed that might otherwise have sailed away through the air, grounding her. They were brought up together, just too late to be brother and sister, in London, in the shade of the plane trees, whose crackly brown leaves are gathered in bin bags like cornflakes each fall, whose hard, round seedballs nod and swing in the wind regardless of the seasons. London. The flat is dry. The walls are dry.

Austin talking, glass in hand, at college parties at Oxford, literary parties in London. His film star profile, the ginger flecks on his skin like tea leaves for the initiate to read, his quivering Adam's apple a third eye. Always ready to look into the abyss, with his Scottish second sight. To say what he saw, with his Celtic chatter. Not talking about his own notability, which seems to grow even without him doing any work. His next slim volume just passing from eagerly awaited, to long awaited. Talking about hers, though, those first years of marriage. She has this mystic soul-bond with Chopin. A bit of birth trauma isn't going to interrupt that. Such a shame, just when she was about to make it, just about to break through. Just getting established on the Oxford and London circuits, of lunchtime recitals and amateur-professional concerts. Guest recitals in Sweden.

Undoubtedly it was the birth, two months premature, that touch-and-go caesarean, that seems to have left Finbar precociously aware, and Bonnie stuck in her strange clairvoyance, seeing and fearing things that aren't there. Like Chopin, who ran from his visions during a performance, terrified of what he saw emerging from the instrument. Strange beings swarming from the piano. Terrors and ghosts.

Those far-off days in Hammersmith, when golden normality still reigned, the last weeks before her upwards trajectory was interrupted. She, unincommoded by pregnancy, still able to play for hours if she sat only a little back from the piano. Proud of being visible, with her neat bump, but not gross. The pair of them so careless, so confident, attending antenatal classes ironically, as a kind of game. The type that think that pain in labour is a personal failing, and intervention during birth a moral one. And then that warm September night when she awoke to find blood pouring from her. She thought her waters had broken. Even when they saw the red sheet, they didn't hurry; sauntered over to the hospital as if they were doing it a favour. She sat up in the bed, and after twenty minutes things went black before her eyes and Austin went to get a doctor. Who sauntered up also; then he too saw the blood. For five minutes Bonnie coolly watched the medical team panicking around her, until the anaesthetist arrived.

A haemorrhage for which there was never any explanation, a birth as instant and brutal as a car crash. The groggy coming-round in the recovery room, the warm snuffle of another being close to her. She unable to move, lying giddy and still. They placed the baby by her on the stretcher, and when she gave it her first sleepy greeting, she thought she heard a sigh of relief from the doctor overhead.

She kept silent about her first sight of her baby's face, all pursed up in wrinkled fragility, with its ludicrous shades of Austin and other strangers flitting across it, like sunlight crossing a field of grass on a windy day. So many ancestors seemed crowded into this tiny being, he seemed to go back so far, taking her with him. A channel through time and space into which she felt she was falling, falling, losing herself in all the mortality that had gone before her. From then on she seemed to hear a steady rhythm that cut across all music, a multiplicity of births and deaths treading steadily and endlessly through her own passing life.

Austin's voice could no longer reach her, resounding through that first year of his son's life, when he could safely blame the birth; talking against the growing unease of the next two years, when both blamed London. Until he talked himself into believing they should move. —No, hasn't been the same, since the birth. But she'll get over it. Still has it. Still a star. They're still only too grateful that she and Finbar survived. She'll get over her stage fright some day, once Finbar's on his feet. Just needs to get her confidence back; give it time and some sea air. Still practises every day. Got that wonderful big music room for her piano now. Improvising on Finbar's nursery rhyme, *Alouette*, the poor Québécois skylark who ended up in that monotonous old Montreal voyageur chant. Fantasies of a tasty mouthful; they'd pluck it beak to tail. To keep the fur traders going over acres of snow in the 1870s, hungry paddlers into territories of the unknown. Just like them now, braving it here, this strange territory, Waste Island.

*

Austin the merciless, the one-phrase decimator. Now talking about this place, to friends, colleagues, to Sally, mother to them both. On the phone to London. Well. Here they are on an island shaped like a pig. Some 80,000 leagues from anywhere. A place to come across only by chance or after hard, long search. Only means of access: the causeway when tide's out, or the great arch of the railway bridge across the tidal flats. Waste Island: the place where time stands still. You want to get away from the London influence, this is it. Inhabited by Cro-Magnon man in a car and a few seagulls. Little hills populated by solitaries; old men and women going out to do their unrecorded shopping, walking their anonymous dogs. That Waste Island look, battered slippers and beards on both sexes. The woman who comes and puts crusts of bread out for the seagulls on a wall every morning; the man in the suit who comes along shortly afterwards and eats it all. The weather: wind, wind and more wind. A really welcoming beach if you're a dog. The front is fine, all kept spanking clean by a council badly afflicted with obsessive-compulsive disorder, not a geranium out of place and the prom all lined up with old ladies scarfing ice creams, just as it should be. A scenic harbour. A real ferry, that comes in once a day. Three really fine Regency crescents, better than Bath. One Italian café on the seafront, Barretti's, almost friendly, almost middle class. Yes, the veneer is fine.

Behind the seafront, not so good. A maze of seedy back streets, downbeat, litter all along the kerbs. Boarded-up shops, boarded-up people. A ghetto high street. You can't get a curry. Not much signal for mobiles, or the internet either, or even the radio: a lot of hissing, that's what the London influence amounts to, here. Some very deprived estates. One just opposite the swimming pool where the police won't come out at night, the St Michael estate. The kind of place where on a Tuesday morning you pass a man in woman's dress drinking vodka from the bottle. Where on a Friday night you run from the same man marching along in a swinging kilt, crooning endearments. Be careful what you wish for, because Bonnie evidently wished for solitude. But she loves it, that's the great thing; says she feels she's come home at last. Her island is surely different. Call it Atlantis. Or Cythera, windswept isle of love.

Waste Island. Restricted access. Where you needed a passport to get off during the world wars. There's just two signposts to London, the way out; the rest of the directions are local, sending you round and round in an endless loop. In any case, London's a hundred years away down that endless dual carriageway through those flat fields: no man's land, the taxi drivers call it.

Backwards? Behind the times? Actually, from what he's seen of them, the locals would probably agree with Avicenna's view that physical time doesn't exist, that it only exists in the mind, child of memory and expectation; doesn't go anywhere. Not in this time warp place. All very circular, with their endless 'See you later'. And yet they're so unfriendly, the locals. They're really, really unfriendly. But the house, the house is great.

And then Austin stops talking. From the day Bonnie came home crying, having lost her wedding ring on the cliff-top, he's gone silent. They went out together to look for it, but to no avail; even asked the road sweeper, who was on the prom doing not very much, if he'd seen it lying around. Watchful, guarded, not an easy man to approach, with his direct, vigilant stare, he just shrugged, and when Austin offered him a tenner to look out for it his eyes flashed and he refused; took their phone number and, looking at Bonnie, said he'd do it for love.

Austin reckons it's gone over the edge into the sea; she knows she flung it over, thinking it was the silver trash the bin man gave her. Rushing, always rushing. The only time she slows down is at the piano; only then is she in time. It was an heirloom bequeathed by Austin's grandmother: solid, chunky gold that's been in his family for a hundred years and more. She threw the wrong one over; the second it left her hand, she realised. Its gold spin through the air. And they both go quiet.

Now you can hear the sea all right. It's in the house the whole time, like a dying person whose breath coming and going can be heard in every room. They say the house is built atop chalk caves, that tunnels down to the beach were used within living memory, that there's an entrance via the music shop opposite, if Dudley the owner can be persuaded to show you. It's blocked by a grand piano, they say. The rooms turn to sighing sea-chambers of chalk, the rushing echo of sea against wall, air and water filling and emptying like lungs or a heart.

They say the house was the first to be built on the cliff-top, a hundred years ago. Why did they put it the wrong way round, then, back to back with the sun, if they had all that room? Facing north, it encourages wrong-way-round living, the kind of place where you have to take several steps backwards to get in. The sun watching you with pale eyes from oddball corners of rooms. The windows thin and severe to the sea. Wind coming through them from the black sea nights. The north-facing conservatory, which gets two hours of sun a day. The rooms in the mirrors look deeper, more reachable, warmer; safe. Reflect a reassuring flutter of leaf shadows from the creeper outside, even when there's no wind. They say the old lady still lives there, that she'll never leave. It's odd, but none of them can choose a bedroom, keep shifting and changing from back to front and up and down, floor to floor. And no matter where they sleep, they keep being woken by Finbar slipping into bed with them every night, saying he can hear the piano playing again.

'It's a horrible house.'
    'What, with all this space?'
    'I want to go home.'
    'But this is home.'
    'Home to London.'

*

Finbar says he can hear someone crying at night, and one night Austin wakes and hears it too. Actually sees and meets the ghost. Austin the unbeliever comes face to face with a weeping woman whose blonde hair shines silver in the moonlight, takes her frozen hand. Tells her not to grow old before her time, tries to lead her back to a bed no ghost can rest in. But she pulls away and disappears. The house is haunted after all. Bonnie's brought the ghost with her. Hers the shadow on the landings at midnight, looking out of the window down the dark street, over the harbour; hers the figure glimpsed and gone, up the stairs and vanishing at the turn. The sound of quiet sobbing from downstairs. Walking the floors at 2am, flexing her fingers and crying over her hands that won't do what she wants any more. Soft-pedalling her adored Chopin note by slow note until Austin comes down again, off his head with sleep and grief also. Tells her plainly, this move is not the answer. Sees that strange ring shine silver on her finger. That's not going to help either.

They say the couple of hundred yards between their house and the sea are where you see the ghost, a girl who went over the cliff more than a hundred years ago; pushed, they say, though it could never be proved, by the boyfriend, whom she pulled down with her. They say the girl grew into the old woman who still lives in the house, that she's the one you can sometimes hear playing the piano quietly in the dead of the night. They say she's been seen recently, that she's starting to walk again.

They say the cliff is slowly crumbling into the sea, that in fifteen years' time that house won't even be there. Concordia is heading for the sea, slowly, inexorably. Everyone knew it but them, the canny Londoners; that's why it was so cheap. They're not going to be able to sell it again, that house. And yet they had it surveyed thoroughly.

THIS TOWN HAS SOMETHING SINGULAR

This town has something singular, the sea in everything. A surprise round every corner. Surging into Harbour Street, spilling down the precinct, washing into the shops. Sucking out all the rubbish, making the street cleaners' lives easier. Take one step off the pavement and your foot's in the waves; another step, and the waters close over your head. The sea blows down all the streets, a singular grey light. Rocking the black needles of ship masts until the world's compass is set quivering. It's an early spring of thunderstorms, dark spirals down to the horizon, splits of silver lightnings, violet rainbows over a silver-black sea.

Singular gifts start turning up outside Bonnie's front door, trash from the beach. Finbar finds them, brings them in with glee, shouting. 'Look! Look what now!' A fisherman's net, hunks of salt-hardened cord, interwoven with blue rayon. A red plastic glove, still shiny wet, with the thumb cut off. Six or seven chalk skulls. A rope of mussels, their sheeny-blue insides all open, like tide-out sand reflecting sky. Mermaid's purses, cuttlefish bones taut and white, a bleached starfish splayed like a man running. A handful of marine-blue sea glass tumbled beside. The ethereal beauty of jellyfish, translucent and black-veined, drying on the tiles. A fish, a long, pale bone of sea-wood, with a round shell for eye. A sodden sunflower head. A paintbrush with its bristles washed off, a drowned water pistol, a rubber ear mutilated by the sea, all laid out on the front step and framed with white pebbles. A smooth green bottle with a note inside that Bonnie reads and quickly hides. Maybe the sea left them, maybe someone else. A shadow at the stained glass of the front door, there and gone. The neighbours can't or won't say, they're without any of the London chumminess, aren't amused by Mr and Mrs Ogilvy's piqued, middle-class intrigue at such quaint tokens. Only Finbar knows who brought them, on the watch like all kids, through any window going, watching the man sweep the street outside, working sideways across the pavement, with his big deadman's gloves and his serious air; but no one thinks to ask him, and he doesn't know to tell.

A sketch, from the top of Mount Royal, of the road winding down to the harbour on a wet evening, shining in the lamplight.

'How weird,' says Austin. 'That's the view from our top floor. Not bad, either. Someone's quite good at drawing. Bonnie! Come here and look at the latest offering!'

Seahorses.

'What the...?'

Two of them, desiccated brittle-brown, their sailing stiffened for all time. Silent messengers, whose colours died a dry death.

Their eyes blind globules. They too have forgotten their need for water; they too have amnesia for the sea. Singular lost notes from that oceanic symphony. But they mate for life.

'Bonnie! Come here! Do you know anything about this?'

Austin holds them on his nervy, red palm, an uneasy resting place for the bristle of their spines, their comical tums that used to spiral the seas. Shaped like the hippocampus, that memory organ buried deep in the sea of the brain.

She comes to look, in wonder, eyes alight. So brittle; like driftwood art. Only they're the real thing.

'These never came from Foy Beach.'

'They're a protected species, you can't get them any more. Someone round here's definitely a bit sideways. I thought we'd left your nutty fans behind. My mistake, sending that piece about you into the local paper. Who's leaving all this stuff, Bonnie? Which of the local simpletons have you been chatting up?'

'Could I have them?'

'Here, take them. They're obviously meant for you.'

They nestle in her white hand like they've come home. Singular love tokens.

'Can I have them?' says Finbar, jealous of the way her fingers close gently around them, her gentle smile.

'No, button. We'll go and find something else on the beach, you and me.'

'What are you going to do with them?' says Austin, also jealous.

'Add them to the other stuff.'

'Quite a little sea shrine you're accumulating there. You could make a mermaid.'

'A mermaid?'

'One of those Victorian things. All put together with fish bones and stuff, passed off as the real thing to the credulous. Very gullible, the Victorians. You'd have to be, to believe in science the way they did.'

A stick of rock with *I love you* all the way through. A pack of sherbet love hearts, opened and laid out on the front step: *Guess who. For ever. Find me.* They agree that someone has a singular sense of humour; neat, if a trifle spooky. But Bonnie finds that last command really quite upsetting; it haunts her for a week.

On a singular, salt-swept morning she should go and meet him, on the front, like he asked: *Find me.* A singular game of hide and seek. And like magic he's there. Eternity and icy winds on the prom. The sun sparking steel off the waves. Eyes like shining ice, breaking up into spring, brimful of joy. He's been waiting. But he won't admit it. His yellow coat swings open in the wind, careless. His heavy, navy fleece beneath, zipped up neat to the neck and characteristically untouched by dirt. She in matching navy jacket and hat. Her eyes sparkling also.

'Icy this morning.'

'Yeah, icy.'

By the flower stall with its swathes of daffodils, cut down and laid out. He gives her a bunch, slim and cold, heads still close-wrapped in grey tissue.

'Have them,' he says to her. 'The old lady gave them to me. Gives me flowers most mornings. I don't need 'em.'

Sea-chill to the touch, the ice of winter still in them.

The sea silver-grey at the end of the precinct. They meet between the lavender paths with their brittle grey stick heads, whistling in the wind.

'The old lady?'

'The one in carpet slippers you see sitting out on benches. Lives in a beach hut in summer.'

'And in winter?'

He shrugs. 'Social Security been after her a long time. Trying to persuade her to come into the warm. But if you look, the council don't take her hut down with the others at the end of the season.'

And she finds him, again and again. He's always around. You can't avoid bumping into him. In the little old post office off the front. Faded cards and fishing nets. Sending postcards home. Chewing his chewing gum, slowly; it helps him concentrate. Propped slow and thoughtful at the counter, his writing travelling down his arm, signature neat and considered: *Dominic Dubeau.* For he's the type to sign his last name on a postcard to his mother, who lives so far away. He's the type to spot Bonnie out the back of his head, turn around again.

'Hey, you're following me everywhere! Thought you had to spend all day practising.'

'I'm having a break. Getting some fresh air and exercise. Like you.'

'Fresh is the word.'

'Walked far this morning?'

"Bout three and a half miles so far. You seem to do a lot of walking yourself.'

Already he's concerned that she's wasting time. And he hates waste. He's very concerned that everything be in its place. That life be tidy. But she doesn't get it. She's pleased he's noticed. And he doesn't really bother to hide. Licks and stamps his letter definitely, sealing it with a gentle, rounded thump of his fist. Writes to his mum every month, who's as homesick as he is. She'd like to come back here, her native land, he tells Bonnie, and he'd sure like to go; makes sure to tell her when he writes, it's changed since she was here. But like he said: this isle won't last. Sometime soon it's all going to tilt back under the sea as if it had never been. Jules Verne's iceberg in *The Fur Country*, the northwest territories of Canada. Where you eventually realise you're not on land any more at all, but drifting south and melting every day.

'So how's the work?'

He shrugs again, smiling down at her. 'Same.'

And then, as a concession, 'The wind does most of it.' With the same secret humour, as if he's a winner.

'I got your note.'

'Oh yeah?' As if it's nothing to do with him.

'The one you left in the bottle…'

But he's looking at her, kindly, as if she's just a bereft little girl.

'Left it in a bottle, did I?'

He's so used to humouring the public. She stutters, halted. She was so sure it was him.

She comes home crying with the cold. She's never known anything like it. That icy chill off the sea. Could be Canada. Her fingers; she can't move her fingers.

*

Bonnie's got amnesia for most of her life before age thirteen, when her parents died, and later she'll feel that her memory only really began after they moved into Concordia, her first real home. That safe house, safe enough for her to remember. Already London's gone into the grey zone she always knew it was. She can recall isolated facts, such as Finbar's birth, that disassociation of blood sinking out of her and a caesarean almost swifter than permission; or facing the white blurred points of faces at the end of a concert, but there's no emotional content to them. She doesn't even recall the impact of the car crash, that mighty blow out of the unknown. Her memory freezes at that point; she's caught in frozen trauma. The airbag blew up like a ball of ice, insulating her; blocking off the danger, the past.

Before thirteen, there are flashes, conversely, more of feelings than events. Sally's her memory for that period, Austin's mother. Sally the wise and reformed Chicagoan, ex-drunk turned spiritual guru. Who adopted Bonnie according to the tenets of her parents' will and her own heart, brought her up alongside Austin as if she were her very own. Humble, restless, rich. Fellow traveller to all. Understands everything in heaven and earth. Known Bonnie for ever due to their parents' friendship, from when she was a fierce, staring small girl in a buttoned-up pink cardigan, with a ball of blonde hair, like a toy owl, and Austin an effervescent, privileged, ginger godlet kicking a football up the stairs. Sally the ever-tolerant. Been through so much herself; four husbands, as many countries, so many more psychic lands, and nine hundred and ninety-nine bottles of hooch before she got the message and sobered up. These days she feels so at home in London. Popping down the King's Road to do her shopping in her navy bodywarmer and jeans and headscarf, in that slim, long-legged American way. The tense, tanned face and the blonde hair and blue eyes.

Explaining to Bonnie in her American honey snarl that grief gripped her too like a vice at the thought of Bonnie's parents, two of her own best friends, in their evening dress, snuffed out like that. They were so white when they were pulled out of the car, so immaculate, that Bonnie, unhurt in the back, knew then. She has a visual memory for that moment, too. But no emotional one. To crash into adolescence and loss at the same time. Sure; facing the unimaginable; the utter and total shock of it; Sally understood. And you've got to feel those feelings before they'll go away. Yes, thirteen: the age at which everyone loses their parents, and has to find new ones inside, although with most of us it's a gradual, natural process. Bonnie's parents, also musicians, always departing, to concerts, tours; now left for good, emigrated to that faraway land. Taking Bonnie's memory with them. But Sally and Austin compensate; confabulate even, if need be. Between them, they provide Bonnie with a past, a kind of *ménage à trois* of memory. And her recall of music is phenomenal; she remembers every piece she's ever played. Only sometimes she feels she's never had a proper memory of her own.

And since Finbar's birth, she's really missed her memory. All the memories she ought to have, of her own early years. But now they're struggling to break loose, those memories; not so much of facts as of feelings. Her emotional heritage, now she needs it, to pass on to her son, now he's a little, articulate adult; and it isn't there. She managed when he was just an element, a seal pup washed up on the shore of time.

The bereavement of birth left her so remote. Threatens to trigger those other two bereavements. A lifetime's cascade of grieving stands poised to come crashing down, like an old house at the edge of a cliff.

*

So now she has two new illicit relationships: the man in the street, with his wind-cured skin and his aura of open spaces, and the house, Concordia. Both of them potential conduits for the emotional energy she used to put into performing. Austin sighs again; that old *de trop* feeling. Starts slipping off to sleep on the sofa again because he can't bear to be one of a threesome. Only up until now the third party has always been the music.

So why does she start hearing music in the middle of the night? Her favourite Chopin waltz, uncannily well played, too; she couldn't do better herself. Sits up alone in the double bed, goes padding through the dark house with a candle, looking for the source of the sound, which she can't find, the piano closed and silent. Finds Austin instead on the sofa, wakes him to tell him. Who's none too impressed.

'Obvious,' he mutters into the pillow. 'It's in your own head. Telling you it's time to take it up again.'

'But it was so real, so real.'

'You'd better pick up on the practice tomorrow, I'm telling you. For God's sake, Bonnie. It's 2am. I'd just got to sleep. Go back to bed.'

'You come, too.'

'No. I'm comfortable here now.'

'On that lumpy brown velvet? I doubt it.'

Glissades down otherworldly ballrooms. Chaconnes down dark corridors. Polkas along the midnight prom. *Études*, fugues, *gnossiennes*, slipping round the stained glass of the front door. Gradually the house is filling, like a sail in the wind, with some energy which is perhaps poltergeisted out from Bonnie, full of what she used to put into playing. If it wasn't haunted to start with, it is now; as if there's someone watching from the attic. Or an old lady shadowed on the stairs. Their child plays at the bottom of their sea garden, far away, like tide's right out, just a shimmer on the horizon. A gardener called Imlah, who only works when directed by the moon, turns up and starts digging in the back until Austin sends him away.

The visitations continue, come right into the house. Fish scales on the steps, seaweed in the hall; wet footprints up the stairs, but no one's up there. A whiff of eau de cologne on the landing, salt breezes in the bedroom. Finbar says the man left a mermaid in the night, but of course she's gone by morning, down the hill to the harbour, grumbling at the grit scraping her stomach all the way. Sure enough, a smell of fish in the bath, sand scattered down the greening old enamel, long blonde hair twined round the rusted plughole. And who's the mystery caller who rings up every afternoon at 4.15pm? It's a local phone box, they discover, on the other side of town, near the station; because here, when you ring back, some passer-by picks up the phone; it's that kind of place. Full of types to have a lengthy conversation with someone who dialled the wrong number. Bonnie develops an aversion to the phone, won't let Finbar rush to answer its black silence any more. Because she thinks the calls come from inside the house.

It falls to Austin to make terse work of it, with a few expletives. Says he's going to drive over there and karate the bastard. They all pile into the car at 4pm to see the fun, but when they get to the station, of course there's no one in the box. And as they get home they hear the phone ringing again, dying in classic fashion as they put the key in the door.

And Bonnie can hear music. Bagatelles, grace notes, there and gone. *Sospiros*, rhapsodies. There it is, there it is, and gone. She'll never get it back again. Nightly serenades that explode through her. She sits reared up in bed like a child; pain bursting down her legs, sweat and pounding heart. The panic ebbs away as the music does, fading with the dawn, the pain remains, sounding through her all day. She's a tune in space, held by a long, thin thread that no one can wind in. No one can reach her, put their arms round her and tell her it'll be okay. Austin has done, dutifully; his arms round her body, not her soul, that's floating loose. —Come on, Bonnie. Time's wearing on. Finbar's nearly four now. —And she looks back from where she is, eyes two moons, out in space. Knows that he just about tolerates her; that she is, indeed, barely tolerable, because barely reachable. But now she has the house, for sympathy. Its sea rhythms and silences, far out from land time. Feels it bending round her when she wakes in that seizure of pain. Maybe at Concordia she can come to rest.

She brings the house flowers, from that market like a dying fall along the last precinct in England. Ivory roses splashed with mauve, orange daisies like the stark palm of a hand. The shrivelling nipples of tiny salmon carnations. Pink roses neat as a swept street. Hears the house whisper with the tides, that it's been a long time since anyone brought home flowers, that her secret is safe, here in Concordia: the heart of her affliction; that she can't bear to listen to music any more. When all else fails, there's surely Bach, but even Bach has failed her and now the only music she can tolerate is silence.

But it isn't the house for silence. There's a constant shuffling in the attic, as of seagulls or rodents. The packing cases seem to shift here there and everywhere, with a life of their own. The dresses on the top landing all pulled down and tossed down the stairs. Sometimes she can hear a kind of muffled thumping from the floors upstairs, which she tells herself is Finbar playing. And why can't Bonnie keep the linen cupboard tidy? It's a genuine walk-in Victorian linen cupboard, and she's so proud of the linen Sally gave them for a wedding present, yet the place is a mess, her precious sheets always tumbled to the ground. She blames Austin, in exasperation at his perennially untidy ways, who in lordly disdain doesn't bother to deny it. Why didn't she marry a tidy man? Can't he just come and take a towel like everyone else?

Well, why can't he stay away from her cupboard? There are only three of them in the house – aren't there?

'Set your heart at rest,' he says, finally, from behind his newspaper. 'I don't even know which cupboard you're talking about. Why on earth are you worrying about tidiness? Manifestations of chaos are natural for this family. Blame Finbar.'

But Finbar indicates he wouldn't go in there for anything, because that's where the witch lives. Don't they know she never moved out?

And Bonnie betrays him, keeps very quiet about the swishing of skirts she can hear on the stairs at night, or maybe that's just the waves; the long black dress she glimpses out of the corner of her eye when she's practising. She pretends it's the metronome clacking, the footsteps she can hear behind her back. She's not scared of whatever's keeping time with her. Would never turn her head to look. Whatever walks this house is free to do so, unobserved.

'I'm not sure,' says Austin. 'I'm not altogether sure that this place is for me. Just a touch freaky. Maybe we acted too fast, actually moving. Maybe we should have stuck to that day trip.'

No maybe about it. Thank God they didn't sell London; that he insisted on renting out the Hammersmith house with all due caution. Not burning their boats. But the great thing is that Bonnie likes it. He's still busy telling Sally, the London friends, his colleagues, reassuring them all. Bonnie likes it down here. More colour in her cheeks, more settled. Though one still has to watch for the old restlessness, of course.

If only he knew. She's already started to walk again. What else was she doing when she met Dominic? A lone figure down the 7am pavements of the town, shoulders straight and slim, a shadow in the spring dusk, a ghost on the midnight prom. A singular streetwalker, can cover seven leagues in one pre-breakfast stroll. Feet drawing up power from the ground; just like Dominic. Only he walks for a living. No, she's a walker, been going walkabout all her life. Walked out on Austin so many times until he too got into the habit of leaving the front door unlocked all the time. Ever alert for its opening click in those early London days. It was Sally told him to leave the door be, not to hide her shoes, the way he did when they were still kind of cousins.

Walking, walking: so she thought Austin would stop her, his red Scottish feet planted firmly on the ground. Grounded in education, class, money, career; loved by the gods, his path clear before him. Sally and Austin, who vowed they'd love the restlessness of grief away, discipline it into the piano; neither of them willing to acknowledge how much deeper her wayward ways went. Right from when she was three and old enough to realise where she was. Sleepwalked when she could, a small ghost uncannily expert at undoing midnight locks and bolts, with fingers fairy-tale enough to insert directly into the keyholes. Watched at school, a five-year-old walking steadily out from the playground along the tree-lined drive, to the open road. Round eyes looking ahead. *Bonnie lives in a world of her own*, said her school reports, shaking their heads sadly. An expert in walkabout by seven, the age of decisions; when her parents started teaching her to walk her fingers sideways into that other place instead. The metronome striding through her early years, its imperious strut dominating her own rhythm. Orphaned at thirteen, the age of power; but she had been walking her own path long before. She was born restless; came feet first into the world, breech and before her time, two months premature like Finbar; just under five pounds, with tiny, sheeny, tearaway nails all ready and trimmed for the piano, doll fingers flexing, arms and legs flung out in repudiation, eyes rounded from birth, shell-shocked feet and bud toes already splayed against the swaddling sheet. Her new life one perpetual startle. Didn't have time, denied those last two months, to forget what she learnt in utero. Was born remembering those essential rhythms, a heart beating like steady footsteps. Blood swishing peremptorily from the source like the sea. That oceanic heart rocking hers. Destined to pass it on for ever, like some ghost ship of sound. Still plays what she heard then. Only then is she in time, at the piano, in time with the cosmic rhythm.

Where's she walking to? To that place she can only access in the music. And now she can't perform any more, it's here. She knows she'd never find it in London. It's here, spread out all before her, from Concordia all down the hill to the harbour. And now the place echoes with footsteps, from the bedroom floors out to the streets and sea-lanes. The footsteps of those coming into our lives, beating ahead, behind, around, footsteps echoing in hers stopping after she stops. Footsteps sounding after hers on the wood floors of Concordia, keeping time with her steady tread down the street stepping in the footsteps of the one walking ahead.

And now she's got a new town to walk. Where you just step out and the streets are home. Where you find what you thought was lost for ever. Step out and it's all there, winds that stand you on your head, call forth a symphony she can tolerate from the harbour below. An orchestra in full blast. A hydraulis or water organ thundered out by a stormy sea. Voices streaming sideways, every railing rattling, every mast whistling, the tide ball sounding, a whale call booming all round the harbour. Windsong, shanties, melodies from the deep.

*

'Why did you leave all that stuff outside the front door?'

'All what stuff would that be?'

'The shells, the bottles, the cans... all the other rubbish.'

She flourishes the note from the bottle under his nose. Meet me on the prom, in a neat sea-scroll. He takes it with his fingertips, eyes alight, reads it attentively, half-aloud. Half-leans on his broom, considering.

'Found this outside your front door, you say?'

'You should know.'

He shakes his head, smiles, to himself again. 'I tell ya, it's a strange place, Waste Island.'

'The people here, you mean?'

'Oh, they're real peculiar.'

He should know. He married into an island family. Now he has them all sitting in his house, his nice, detached, modern house tucked up against the railway line, that was so cosy when it was just him and his wife and kids. Mother-in-law, between relationships; comes and goes. Father-in-law, come to stay, with his fishing rod, ever hopeful. The pair of them drinking and quarrelling in the kitchen all night long. Getting the wife drunk along with them. The wife's long-lost, illegitimate sister, given away at birth and just rediscovered in Dartford after a lot of tracing; now she too has a seaside place to spend weekends. Some stray child of his wife's, turned up from way before they were married, seventeen and deeply into the island horticulture, weed. Shares a room with the toddler when she's nowhere else to go, then vanishes for weeks. Calls herself K and says she'd die without her friends, other young potheads pretending to be lesbian, youths sporting killer dogs. Girl power, warrior princesses, yeah! The police calling round regularly for them, like their cousins; that love-hate relationship neither side can do without. But they're too soft for any real crime. Destined for island life, let them racket while they can. Oh, and they all think the world of themselves. No wonder he's glad to get out in the mornings, rolling the garage door up at 5.45am prompt to get his bike. And off he goes, released, spinning slow down the road. He's exempt, with his solitariness that's like a spell, his air of stepping out of another world. It's certainly a spell over Bonnie, blinding her to other possibilities. She can barely believe he comes out of a house.

She shows him the sketch.

'Quite some detail. Well, there's lots of artists have visited this coast, on account of the light.'

'You didn't do it?'

Can he deny it? But he hands it back to her, still with that smile.

'Keep it. Might be worth something in years to come. The artist from the sea. You never know.'

'But who did it, if it wasn't you? Who left all that stuff?'

'What kind of stuff would you like left outside your door, then? Other than a load of old shells?'

'I...'

'A few ropes of pearls, maybe? Or do you prefer oysters?'

'I like oysters.'

'They sell them down the harbour, St Michael's fish stand there, with the yellow awning. Like me to drop you off a dozen of those, eh, now would that make you happy? Or would you complain to the council about me?'

'Oh, I'd never do that.'

'What would you do if you found a pearl in one? Dissolve it in champagne and swallow it? Should I add a bottle of bubbly to the doorstep?'

'Don't be silly.'

She puts a hand up to her throat, like pearl on pearl, uncertain. He sees her hand splayed across her neck like a separate living being, the spatula tips. That oversensitive look that musicians' hands acquire.

'It's like being on holiday here, though,' she says, dubious.

'You think so?'

And on they go together, into the wind; so good for Bonnie's health. Her cheeks are quite pink.

'Holiday, my dear?' says Austin, meeting them at the end of the prom. 'You confuse holiday with having taken early retirement from life.'

Where's Bonnie? She's out, walking the moonpath out to sea, treading water far out. She's gone down the thousand-step ladder into the harbour and is stepping sideways from boat to boat. She's walked out of town to the lighthouse and is following its beacon out to sea. She's taking soundings at the deep end of the lido, to see if love lies full fathom five. She's talking to someone on the prom, and isn't about to cut the conversation short.

On this isle, her feet don't touch the ground.

If only he knew. But Austin can see, as he always has done. Even if it weren't blindingly obvious. Comes down and finds the front door open again onto the spring dawn and the cracked tiles of the front path, the front gate wide, and Bonnie's place empty in the bed.

*

They have a quarrel about the road sweeper and how he hasn't found their ring; as if it was anything to do with him. As if Austin knows he was the last person to see her with it on. Educated? The chap can barely string a sentence together, the strange accent they have down here making him sound almost transatlantic. Depends what you mean by educated. Wouldn't romanticise some two-bit qualification from a technical college in the backwoods. Well; mustn't be too harsh; poor chap; might have islets. Not really that rough; polite enough, if brusque, when you talk to him. Probably fine if you're polite too and keep your distance, as I'd strongly advise you to do. Anyone can see he's not quite right. How? It's obvious. His eyes. Vulnerable is the word that springs to mind. You don't see it? I suggest you have another look. Frankly, he looks like a man who's given up the ghost. That shipwrecked face. Existential choice? Existential bollocks. Cut out the middle-class romanticism. Hanging round on street corners at the end of the world. —Darling, believe me, he's a road sweeper because he isn't capable of anything else. Naïve to think otherwise. I expect his wife has told him it's a nice, steady job. Cleansing executives one has to call them now, of course, or environmental hygienists. So patronising. How long has he been doing it, five years? No, no artist-in-waiting. Ask him, your savant friend. Ask him about his ideas on rubbish as art, for sure he'd have ideas about that. Would he agree with Metzger about auto-destructive art, art designed to have a strictly finite existence, art destined for annihilation? Doing his paintings in hydrochloric acid so they'd self-destruct, avoid the cupidity of the art dealer, the collector? How some of the finest works of art produced nowadays are dumped on the streets every evening in Soho? Art as a protest at our Western overconsumption, the obsession with destruction, especially of that which no longer serves us? The aggressive, finite nature of capitalism? Surplus and starvation? Go on, ask him for the bin man's view. Like the gallery cleaner who couldn't spot the difference and binned a prize exhibit that she thought really was rubbish; bin-bag art, so like the real thing she dumped it, to the embarrassment of the gallery, the amusement of the press. No, no, no. He's like all the other local yokel street cleaners down here; all picked to fulfil the council's disability discrimination policy. Probably just about able to follow a simple health and safety course. How to deal with sharps. Poor dyspraxic chap, he's so slow, wonderful he has a job. Painful to watch him trying to scoop the rubbish up; I feel like going out and giving him a hand. Look at when they spoke to him about the ring; very slow on the uptake. No, no great mystery about him. Lack of choice; I've just said. They're here for the benefits, he and his wife; part of the benefit society. You bet. Child or two, child benefit – three kids? Okay. Three kids. Bit of disabled benefit for him, probably; his pittance. Bit of online selling and childminding for her, perhaps. It all mounts up. Three kids. Ah well. No job's too menial when you've got a family to support, is it. 'Three kids, hmm,' says Austin, shaking his head, looking at her. 'Well, he's all right, isn't he? He may not be the full shilling, but he's all right.'

'Bonnie!'

'Yes?' She sits up, alone in the double bed, her hair a halo in the moonlight, uplifted profile soft with sleep. Finds she's walking along the cliff-top in the moonlight. The moonpath of beaten metal. Everywhere a heavy shushing.

'Bonnie!'

It's coming from below; she recognises his voice instantly, knowing she will always recognise it, that trail of broken stones. Again he calls, more faintly. Clinging to the railing, she looks down, in the faint, pale light, to the man who has the right to call her thus, because she's accepted his ring. He's fallen, right down the cliffside. He has a wound to the head, he's incapacitated. Out of it, smiling, dazed, he'd apologise if he could but he smiles, eyes swimming, upturned. Now, unwilling, she must scramble down the side of the cliff to go to his aid. The last thing she wants to do, with chunks of chalk breaking off and scree flying. The very last thing, to climb down in this way. But because she has his ring, she must, and does, hands sore, heart beating. Find him, slips her arm round him, like coming home. Her first dream of him. She wakes, heart beating, sitting upright in the bed, in the moonlight, alone.

*

The dustman hasn't found Austin's ring. Why should he? Of course, a forlorn hope. Police equally useless. Austin returned from the prom to report for the last time. Chap's still down there. Doesn't he have a home to go to? Thought he had three kids, though he must have begotten them in his sleep by the looks of him; none too friendly actually, monosyllabic, quite brusque; dopey sort, hanging round down there as if he's waiting for someone; what, Dominic, doing a bit of drug dealing on the side? They'll go up to London soon and look for another ring.

THE DREAMY STATE

Dominic is on drugs, but you wouldn't find these in the street. They're the sort that originate as a dream in a scientist's head, in secret, expensive labs, that take a long time to reach the real world. The names like those of exotic courtesans: phenytoin, phenobarbital, carbamazepine, valproate, lamotrigine. Not all at once, of course; they've changed over the years, as they try different combinations to gain better control, as new compounds come in and new diagnostic criteria. Whose effects even then may only be partial. May keep a man walking round in a private reverie. Look at Dominic's eyes: come to bed, but to sleep, to dream.

For control can be elusive. Even with the correct dosage, it yields to imponderables: strong emotion; alcohol; stress; lack of sleep or food. Then the brain starts billowing, like a woman's hair on a windy day. Then you might stand staring across the street, as if rapt in who's on the other side; or look right through them, with empty eyes. But the drugs are still his best and oldest friends; he's closer to them than to anybody else. He carries them round in his shirt pocket; his drugs, his familiars, his mediators. They slow him to his perseverative course. Soften his silver-split world to muted, mellow pewters and greys that he can handle. No one can live in a world of silver. His neuronal damping shows in his face for all who have eyes to see: a cast, an ash, a caution.

But his compliance can be erratic. Sometimes you miss your silver days. Your exaltation. Days when the sea is a silver sheet and even the grubby back streets wind ahead like silver rivers. Days when he knows everything there is to know, the knowledge building like a huge silver cloud over his head. Then, why not flirt with it a little. Why not dangle his condition before his wife, before other women, give them a bit of terror in their lives. Why not get out of it some days, why not slip into mental twilights, or have what he's never had, independence, on his own terms. Why not indulge in the headiness of love, take the risk of its turning his head altogether. So he might miss a dose or two, and maybe a few more, titrating his condition to a dreamy state.

Define the dreamy state. A fluctuation of consciousness, when brain patterns start to spike up hard like waves under a stiff sea breeze. A titillation of the temporal lobe, the seat of memory. A regression; a dissolution; a particular form of amnesia, in which the most developed forms of memory are lost, and there's a return to more primitive ways of remembering. *Déjà vécu*; that familiar feeling. Other years step forwards, dreams, dreaming. How they return, replay themselves across his brain; he's transported into a hallucinatory reliving. Dreamy days, dreamlets, other times, other tunes. The procedural memory remains, the episodic memory, which depends on activity in the prefrontal cortex, is in fugue. You can still do your routine jobs, maintain an organic orderliness. But unless the electrodes are on your head and the professors are there, no one knows where you are.

What is his experience of the dreamy state? Reminiscence. A simultaneous apprehension of past and future. A grasping of all those memories that go so far back and so far forwards, like grasping soft grasses or a woman's hair or the essence of time itself. The sensed presence, familiar, protective. Somewhere you've been before, many times; homecoming. A voluminous, all-knowing state. Eternity on the brink. A state where all the usual tools don't work: language, intelligence, persuasion, education, references, where everything is reduced to the elemental: memory, what happened before, what will happen. Sophistication is no safeguard. Then we have to start using signs and symbols, dreams and rings; then fish bring messages and owls their night songs. You can't be talked or shaken out of that state. Neither can you lie or pretend; you're transparent. And when the memories have finished their walking over you, they're gone, way over the horizon, out of sight, until next time. Wherever you've been, whatever you've been doing, there's no recalling those memories once normal consciousness has returned.

The dreamy state, that neuronal march across time: how often does he have it? Much more often than he's aware.

That sleepy-eyed sliding towards seizure. That doubling of consciousness, a doppelganger of the mind, where self stares at self, that pre-dates and underpins Freud, who used it to build his theory of the unconscious. That old poet and dreamer, who wove his shimmering theories out of others' elegant neurological studies, who only acknowledged Hughlings Jackson, the father of his thinking, in one slip: Find out all about dreams and you will have found out all about insanity.

*

In his dreamy state, in the dreamy summer sun, Dominic woos Bonnie with his remoteness. Inaccessible as the white triangles of yachts out on the horizon, he's on the prom every morning, early, his face with that invisible dusting, a dusky aura of alienation, that she can't read. There's the shadow of some vast country behind him, its vast crags and rocks, icy plains. Tracts of distance, snow. A rugged wilderness. There's that darkness to his eyes, that sad irony. Some other nationality looking out through him, that she can't identify. So detached, so unconnected, he appears, hair lifting a little in the breeze, shirt open, fluorescent waistcoat flapping, his careless, swinging walk. Gives the impression of freedom, some existential choice made, even if it's only the freedom totally to abandon expectations.

She sees him staring at her across the prom, not aware of how long he holds her eyes, the speculative sea burn in his. Stares at her longer than even North American manners warrant, seeing her approach along the lavender paths; freezing, brush in hand. Should she be flattered? He's undoubtedly pleased to see her. Preens, whipping off a glove to run his fingers through his hair. Welcomes her with an uncanny flash of the eyes, like green waves lighting up out at sea in uncertain weather. Invites her to go all the distance in his eyes.

She comes accompanied by the sweet drift of the wild wallflowers that spring in ragged yellow clusters out of the cliffside where they cluster in yellow bunches, her dress is the lacy spread of waves on the sands below, her eyes full of early sunlight. Now even at 8am it's warm as she arrives after dropping the child off at nursery. More of those conversations. What do they talk about for a whole hour?

'Why do you do this job?'

'For the money,' with one of his ironic glances, pulling at plastic bags in the hedge with the litter grab. 'Why do you play the piano?'

'Yes, but why this?'

'It's a healthy life.'

'Ye-es...'

'Someone's got to clear up the debris of a hundred old ladies with ice creams. Would you like to do it? Should we swap? Or would you like to go up and down telling them to be more tidy?'

'Only a hundred? There always seem to be far more.'

Thousands of them squashed along the benches like fat pigeons, all along the length of the prom, their grey chins sunk in cream blobs. He retrieves a sock from the hedge.

'That Barretti's got a lot to answer for, the ice cream parlour there... It started out as a joke with my wife, actually, we were down the job centre and she said, "Now there's a job you could do," and...'

She's getting used to his trailings-off. His swings from precise defiance to domesticity. The frequent mentions of the wife, which already bore her to tears. She gestures at the barrow, front compartment all kept neat with the box for sharps, the folded cloth, the insect bite cream, the disinfectant, the first aid kit, the lunchbox with the white slice cheese and Branston sandwiches.

'But don't you *mind*?'

'Oh... no...'

How could she? How could his wife do that to him? Bring him to this horrible isle to be near Mum and then let him do that job? She's furious that he takes so little account of himself; too incensed to listen out for the edited version. She can't hear the words omitted in his pauses. What job can he do? Who will employ him, a foreigner in a desperately deprived area, with his special sickness? Austin has warned her again.

'There's a reason that chap's a road sweeper, Bonnie. Talk to him if you must, but do me a favour: don't get involved. No meals in the kitchen.'

Her dreams have warned her, more than once. But she can't get it, like an owl in daylight sees without seeing.

'Walking round all day?'

'Why would I want to go any faster?'

Is that why she's so fast, this Bonnie? Rushing into his life. Not weighted down by her soul, which she left wandering and flickering behind her somewhere? He looks at her, hanging there like a hovering bird. Her hair tangling with the morning. Long cheekbones; the first crow-lines gentle, like time doesn't really mean it; the questing eyes, to which he'd be scared to admit that he has no quest. His own eyes blue, smiling, with a friendliness ringed deep in them. He was an architectural draftsman until he thought he'd go crazy from sitting. Now he's off his butt and he's got a whole town to walk through, away from supervisors and prying women. No past and no future. You just stroll down an alley and escape.

'Oh, no, no...' Reassures her, not himself. 'No. It's what they threaten you with – You'll wind up being a road sweeper – but it's really not so bad.'

She wonders who threatened him, and why. Who predicted such a future for him with such unerring accuracy. The hedge is curving in a circle, into a small maze; he continues to litter-pick inward.

'I really hated drafting, to be honest with you.'

How tell her, how his daydreaming got the better of him at his desk? How increasingly he couldn't wake up properly for long enough before the end of the working day?

'This is okay. It's in the open air and... oh no, this is fine.' He thinks, how to explain about the freedom. 'Worked as a roofer before this. Longer hours, worse money. This compares okay.'

Though naturally he's quick to extract all the sympathy he can; oh, the Victorian nature of the job; in constant peril of his life, the cars shaving past him – holds up a finger and thumb to show how much. His life's a series of near-misses. Everyone on the street thinks they're immortal. And that you'll move first. Inhaling fumes all day; his poor lungs. No, no chance of a place on the van; that's a closed shop. Doesn't drive anyway. What they have to cover: 280 miles of road and highway, a 28-mile coastline, 800 litter bins, 400 adopted alleyways. The early start and only one day off a week; no double-time Sundays and bank holidays like everybody thinks; the abysmal pay. Tells her how much he takes home a week, to the penny. She's genuinely shocked.

'How do you *manage*?'

'Sure, it's rough. Anything I get goes straight out again.'

'How mean. Don't you get exhausted?'

'All the time.' His bare drawl is convincing.

'So you're being shamefully exploited.'

'Yeah. I know.'

An odd kind of subdued dutifulness to him; and he must answer truthfully. It's the wife, the nurse, who's the earner. Otherwise he could barely afford to work. There's a silence while he thinks about this.

'So don't you draw now?'

'Draw?'

'Scenic pictures of the cliffs, the beach...'

'Oh, that's freestyle,' dismissive.

'So you don't spend your free time doing nice little sketches for the local art shops?'

This time his look is really old-fashioned. 'D'you think I'd be doing this job if I could?'

*

All the things he can't tell her. A father in the army, an engineer, who took none too kindly to him and his dreamy ways, his glances into eternity. The school reports that said: *Dominic lives in a world of his own.* The paternal discipline that somehow failed to reach all of him. His odd, savant talents, for instant observation and recall; for maths, for drawing buildings and machines, for detail, for detachment. The myriad of things he had wrong with him, his heart, his kidneys, his respiratory system, his sickness and dizziness, his neurons, his brain, his giddy, unreliable brain. His tendency to daydream, when he didn't seem to hear what was said even when it was shouted and thumped into him. His sensory overload manifested as an exquisite sensitivity to music, which after just one hearing replayed itself in his brain in perfect cadences; cadence from *cadentia*, a falling; he could hear music, he cried, just before he fell. The endless doctors' appointments; the endless waste of time. Waiting rooms, corridors. The neurological institute, the old Neuro, like some medieval walled village spreadeagled against the hill. He, glued to the football on at the stadium outside until they dragged him in and, if you were lucky, you still got glimpses of them through the windows above, playing below, their shouts drifting up tough and free, while they wired him up again, investigating his dreamy state. Splintering him into a thousand pieces again. All a waste of time, his father said; obstinate as they make them and the only problem with him is he can't bear reality. He was brought up to ignore his condition, to be sturdy and strong, never to miss a day's work. Naturally Bonnie doesn't get a word out of him about all that. Tells her instead about his old-fashioned English mum, from Hastings, although he's never been there as a matter of fact; who made roast and proper custard on Sundays and insisted that he say grace and put his knife and fork together at the end.

Though that's not where he got his tidiness from; that's innate. So what vices does he have? None, surely, with his adorable Anglican air, his combed hair, that's soon taken apart by the sea wind, and surely not sideburns, surely she hasn't fallen for someone with sideburns. Just turning pepper and salt.

*

The conversations continue. Says he loves music, would love to hear her play. When's her next concert? He'll be there. He'll be at them all. Why not? Why doesn't she play any more? Did do until her son was born? No point going into all that. But he gets it all out of her, that whole broken story, fragment by fragment, because, just as he doesn't lie, so he's the sort it's impossible to lie to; everything must be transparent.

'Oh, how interesting! So: that's a real shame, that you don't do concerts any more. Would you never go back to it?'

'It's very competitive.'

'It is?' smiling; it's meaningless to him, who doesn't understand competition.

'Takes a lot of practice. I should be at it now, really.'

'Yeah,' he says. 'You should. No more doing two hours then running down to the prom.'

He's uneasy at that still. But he wants to know. How much money does she make from music lessons? From playing? That much, eh? Accompanying? Favourite music? Does she get much work, and where, here or London? Was she born in London? Parents? Ah, that's a shame, a real shame. Brothers or sisters? And what's her position in the family? What the fuck does he want to know that for? He's got an endless list of questions, his curiosity boundless as the sea, detailed as grains of salt; she sees him ticketing away the answers somewhere, one by one. Somehow she knows he's the type that, once he has the information stored, he'll never forget.

He's got plenty of time to think. Doesn't understand how every five minutes count, how Austin's waiting for her, fretting, waiting to 'set her up', as he puts it, before going off to London for the day. That freelance life is a tyranny; there's no proper segregation of husband and wife. Any second now he's going to be down the prom himself, looking for her, his red head flaring above the bushes. And there's Dominic in his high-visibility vest. Litter-picking on a leisurely spring morning as if there were nothing else to do in the world. She inches into the maze, after him, as if after safety itself.

*

The dreamy state is a giant fist squeezing you. Yawning all the time for breath. Wanting to cringe down in bed again to see if it will go away; no idea how to get through the next ten minutes, never mind the day. Strange epigastric sensations; churning stomach; sweating; food some dry crumbly substance. Sleep, the same figure kneels by the bed and shakes you awake all night long. Cerebral disruption; no two thoughts staying together for a moment. Flashes of the future like half-heard tunes. Heart thudding and skimping beats. Tingling and aching all over, hurting right through the body. Feeling sick; feeling something coming towards you, unstoppable.

*

'We never found our wedding ring.'

They've reached the centre of the maze, out of sight of the early morning dog walkers, postmen on bikes, and Austin striding angrily along. People don't come here too much because it smells a bit, in that UK way, and because by day it's acknowledged to be the province of children; by night, that of lovers. It winds inwards in a spiral, vertigo in dream motion. Spinning them so slow, to the centre. It's a folly the council are always debating about, whether to uproot it and just have some nice wholesome benches. He, slowly picking up all the bits of themselves that people scatter en route; the desire for speed that leaves souls behind, in the petrol tokens; the cancers that catch up with them, in the cigarette packs. She's followed him all the way in, a bird of prey herself sidling into the snare. The sun is a presence behind the thick, high hedges, accentuating the whiff of urine and semen.

'Didn't, Bonnie? That's a shame.'

'Did you look?'

'I'm always looking.'

'I threw it over the cliff. By accident.'

He looks at her, with old-fashioned scepticism. 'By accident? How do you throw a ring away by accident?'

'I thought it was yours.'

'My ring? You were going to throw my ring away?'

She'd be frightened if she wasn't wearing it. She extends her hand to show him, a cautious, quick fist, out of his reach. He snatches it all the same, unrolls her fingers. The green gleam in his eyes. The golden glint in hers. Again her hair starts to billow, his grasp rippling all up her arm.

'It fits, doesn't it? What do you want to throw it back for, then?'

Doesn't she get it, the chances of him landing that fish again? That once in a lifetime catch? Doesn't she have any idea how long they'd have to wait if she threw it away?

'Why would you want to do that?' he repeats, holding her hand hard.

'But I shouldn't really be wearing it at all, you know that. Why don't you give it to someone else? Wouldn't it be easier?'

'There isn't anyone else. Can't you see? It was meant for you. You came along for it. You were there.'

'So if someone else had come along at the same moment, you'd have given it to her?'

'No, no. You know it isn't like that. It was meant for you. You're the only one in the world who can – you've got to take care of it, that ring.'

'Rubbish.'

What a fool. What an utter idiot. Coming in here with him. At her age. She should have known. She tugs discreetly at her hand, enmeshed in the net of his fingers.

'Didn't you say it yourself, that it might be magic? Promise me you'll keep it on.'

'Yes, all right. I will.'

Anything to get out of this. She should have known he was the type to become a real nuisance. She's caught. This is no artist manqué, no philosopher taking existential time out. Austin was right, as he always is. There's nothing here beyond a striking cognitive deficit. She thought he'd be easy, an interlude. Now she sees it, what Austin has seen, that he's disabled for life in some way, feels it in the immense fragility in which he stands poised. And yet, the way light breaks over his face, the way the sun comes across the sea and goes. His air of total aloneness that she's never seen in any other man. Even now he retains somewhere his fundamental essence of sauntering freedom that she wants to share. His warm, protective grasp she can't pull away from.

'Say it, then. Say "I promise".'

'Promise what?'

'What I just said. That you'll keep it on.'

'I will if you let go my hand.'

'Go on, then. I promise.'

'I promise.'

'For ever.'

'For ever. And now let me go.'

Not a chance. He won't be letting go for a long time. He's not the type. She's caught, a fish seeing the hook for the first time. Stands staring at what's coming towards her, ending up with a severely limited man, exiled from her rightful London world. He's not the type to have an affair, a discreet affair. She'll be lost down here for ever. Always condemned to one note. A terrifying reduction of life to the basics: love, water, light. Trapped in the light in his eyes. Already he's drawing her to him, folding her in, his thumb tracing her lips with infinite, dreamy tenderness. Separated from her son. No music; Christ, what'll happen to the music? No intellectual stimulus, no money, no work. Already he's turning her mouth towards his for the kiss that must come with the ring. Holding her clumsily, almost beside himself, trembling. Already she's kissing him back, in her summer dream, all she wants to dream about, ever. Lost in this regressive state for ever. Time standing still, all her achievements washed away. No London, no concerts. Not while he's running his hand down the fishbone of her back, and she has to hold him gently, to absorb the trembling. Not while her hair's flared against the home that's his shoulder and her arms are a ring round his neck. She got to the heart of him effortlessly, so swiftly, like a bird dropping from the sky. His mouth one warm, vulnerable tremor on hers, the tremor of restraint. He's holding himself back, hard. But there's an ocean of chaos behind. Pressing in on her ever more urgently, as she too pulls him closer, reckless of what she might unleash. His arm quivering round her. No peers; no society; no Austin; she may not love him but he's an integral – at the realisation she pulls away and smashes her hand across the other man's cheek before turning and running off.

There never was anything there; just a little frisson on the prom.

It takes her a few days to realise that Dominic's gone, because she's been avoiding him. He's disappeared, there's a big guy with a mended cleft palate and a hearing aid and a pork pie hat cleaning up on the prom now. She sees him sitting on a bench at lunchtime, smiling, with his flask. It's not such a bad job. They can have their tea and they have their freedom. But Dominic's gone, gone far away, she feels it for the first time, his absence; she's here and he's there, gone in his own dream. She's been like all the others; hit him in the face the moment he started to be himself. Now there's just that promise between them. The kind of promise that doesn't wear out over the years. Neither binding them, nor leaving them free to move on to anyone else. He's not the type to change in any case.

She knows he'll never seek her out, never. Not after she slapped him and then ran away from the terrible pause between them, in which all those other blows woke up and started reverberating over his face and she realised this is someone she shouldn't have struck, not like a normal man, who might quite enjoy it as a courtship gesture. Too aggressive and quick off the draw by half, these Londoners. What's she done to him? She hit him, and he vanished like a dream. To reach him she has to abnegate. Can she join him in that dreamland? Is he only accessible then? Turning away from the fresh blue and white seafront, she must go into the scumbag back streets.

In his dreamy state, in the summer sun, he goes alone down those back streets, silent, vertiginous, grey, winding round and round to each other; rubbish stuck under cars, dust drifted against kerbs, and something waiting for him round the corner. Round and along, between the tight little terraced houses, the only sound the intermittent rumble of the barrow as he moves down another few paces, the swish of the brush, and the held breath of the one who's round the corner. Michael's Road, Royal Road, Mount Royal Avenue, Temkin Road, Penfield Avenue, Barrett Close, a tight circle of streets, and someone waiting for him, back to the wall just out of sight. He's not alone any more, has lost his freedom. But he'll elude it as long as he can. If you want to find me, you've got to come in. Right into these streets. Walk down to the gutter. Take the plunge; go backwards. Come into a tinier, tighter life. Accost me on Royal Road, drop me a red rose in the gutter. Here where there's no place to go but round and round, and you have to come and find me. Come find me. There's no place to run. This is a place of high visibility; you can see me a mile off. And now that the streets are clean, the ugliness too is revealed, clearly visible, the naked, banal hubs of parked car wheels, the tyres crowding along the road. The bare, sheeny windows. The right angles of Victorian walls onto the narrow pavements. He's measured the width of each street wall to wall and there's no more room. Along the way are the gasworks, the tall brick walls topped with barbed wire, the sinister round towers within; opposite, the dog-ridden, druggy park where he'd never let his kids play. In a summer season, he lays the place bare. Come find me.

Bonnie goes searching in the dust of the road. Seething with humiliation at having to search her lover out in this way. She too is trapped in this maze of little streets, she who was born for the big dual carriageways, the grand avenues of London. This hateful, downbeat place. Like a regressive trance. She knows where he is. She's developed her finding skills here. Close your eyes, see with the eyes of the mind; then take your direction. North, south, east, west; on the prom, over at Westmount, by the harbour, outside the library: by the gasworks. That's where he is. She can sense. Why can't he contact her? Why does she have to do all the work? But she can track him through the summer dust. Mid-afternoon through those mean streets, asleep like a mean dream. Over the road from the cut-price supermarket which is an alcoholic's thin nightmare, somewhere you might get trapped in a bottle of cheap sherry and never get out. Past the wall of the gasworks with the barbed wire topping. Along the narrow road of Victorian terraces. Past the shabby, seedy front gardens, the shiny, watchful windows. Past some men mending a van, who look at her suspiciously. Round the corner. Thank God he's on his own, the street empty, no witnesses. But he's always on his own.

'How you doing?'

'Yep. Fine. You?'

'All right.'

'What are you up to?'

She shrugs. 'What do you think?'

He's sweeping steadily down the street, in short little strokes.

'Come to give me another slap? Did you feel you want to try for the other side, even things up?'

'Sorry about that.'

'Any time. Feel free.'

'Did it hurt?'

'It did, as a matter of fact.'

'Do you mind?'

He looks at her with shrewd, canny amusement, continues with his work again, brushing away as if to ward her off.

'Tell your husband?'

'What, that I...'

'That you threw his ring into the sea?'

'No. Did you tell your wife?'

'Did I tell her what?'

'That you go round handing out rings to strange women?'

'What's it to do with her? I already told you, she wouldn't be interested in that kind of ring.'

'Why aren't you on the phone?'

'Can't afford it.'

He's not alone in that; like many of the people here; too poor, the place too small.

Again he pauses, regards her, back in his own private joke. 'Did you try and find my number?'

'Don't you have a mobile?'

'Nope.'

How he'd hate a mobile phone anyway; the end of his freedom. She knows that.

'Email?'

'No...'

'I don't believe you. How do you manage, carrier pigeon?'

'We go round to my mother-in-law's, borrow her phone.'

'In this day and age?'

The summer dust continues to rise steadily above his brush round the street corner. She accompanies him, a hedge brushing her back.

'Why didn't you call me? You've got our number.'

'Exactly.'

'Why did you change your route?'

'*I* didn't change my route,' halting completely, bewildered. Doesn't she know his life is ordained? Laid down by others, to the smallest step? It's all prearranged unalterably; he's predestined. He stares at her, slowly resumes.

'What time do you finish?'

'Any time now.'

'And then you've got to go home. Your wife will have tea ready.'

'As it happens. Who prepares the tea in your house? Shouldn't you be home doing it?'

She smiles. Still stepping alongside him as he works slowly down the street. There's a streak of black dirt on his ear, an aura of dampish exhaustion coming off the back of his shirt.

His ears are ugly, rather large.

'Have you had a hard day?'

Her voice trails out, deliberate. He straightens up again, hand on broom, poised, looking at her over his shoulder. She's cool in blue and white stripes, her summer dress, her gold-painted toes. Her face as steady as his. Her own delicate ivory cochlea, unadorned.

'What – while you've been on the beach?'

'You poor thing. Don't you ever want to go down there, too?'

'What, now?'

'Well, unfortunately, you've missed the best part of the day. It was so nice earlier.'

'Even nicer to be away from. Trashy families and mess.'

'There was no trash where we were. Just families enjoying sand and sandwiches. Domestic bliss.'

'Rather be out here.'

'But isn't it a shame you have to work so hard while other people are just lounging around?'

'Yeah? Who's going to feed my kids if I don't work, Bonnie?'

That's not where his cognitive impairment lies. He's as pissed off as any other man would be, at the end of a long, hot, frustrating day in the open. His eyes are suffused with a dark, ugly-green light. She circles round him, along the pavement and into the road, an owl spreading its wings, to continue her taunting.

'We've got the whole summer ahead. I'm quite happy to come and visit you every day, tell you what a lovely time I've had on the beach while you've been working.'

'Stuff the beach.' With a clang he retrieves his shovel, turns his back.

'Would you like that? Would it cheer up your day? Bring a smile to your face?'

'You...'

He's crossing the road, to get away from her; she comes, too, a bird of prey leashed to his wrist. It's not a long road, ends in rectangles of garden walls, house walls, windows; a cul-de-sac. Down the road the first schoolchildren can be seen trailing home along the main road, beasts just about contained in uniform. The air of this isle has turned her also savage, this sophisticated Londoner. Stripped layers from her to the start of a core she didn't know existed. She didn't experience childbirth; she had every girl's dream, being knocked out with general anaesthetic and then handed a baby. The fact that she nearly died – Finbar, too – has never touched her. The one time Austin wept, seeing the birth, the bloody tugging from her innards, all opened up on the operating table, flaps of belly skin folded back over her abdomen. He watched through the glass top of the door they'd forgotten to mask, in the hurry. Now she's living from some place she doesn't know or understand.

'I could follow you round. Watch you work.'

He glances round, hunted. He's always had the streets to himself. Recovers some of his habitual irony.

'Think how bored you'd get, Bonnie.'

'I wouldn't.'

'You'd get a thrill out of following me around?'

'I'm here now, aren't I?'

'Follow me all you like, then. Makes no difference to me.'

How does she know that's his nightmare? She's uncanny, her

eyes blazing into him, into the heart of that reckless defiance which they share. Her owl emptiness, a deprived bird, her golden raptor eyes on him. For the first time, he's met someone as defiant as he. His wife's not that way, she's steely, trustworthy. His air of sauntering freedom, her cool urban sophistication, gone; they stand blazing into each other's defiance.

'And then, every time you look up, I'd be there.'

He steps backwards, into the gutter. By his sharp intake of breath, lowered eyes, breathless silence, she's got him back again.

'Isn't there laws against stalking?'

'I will. I will do.'

'Is that a promise?'

'Yes.'

He lifts a finger.

'You want to be careful, what you promise. That's the second promise. Mind, now. You be careful. I'm warning you. They hold you, you know, promises. Turn on you when you least expect it.'

'I don't care.'

'Go on, then. Promise. If you dare.'

'I do dare. And I do promise.'

Both as defiant as each other.

'For ever?'

'Sure. For ever. I'll always be there.'

What difference does it make? She's already breached the psychic barrier, coming to find him in this way, against her will.

There are three small piles of refuse all along the pavement, neatly amassed from earlier. He goes along scooping his shovel awkwardly beneath each one, his back to her. She slips between the parked cars after him, touches the back of his neck, an owl's wing. He rears round to face her again, defeated. The shovel lands with a clang, the rubbish spills between them. His back is to the wall, one of those dirty brick houses. She's pushed him to the limits of his prison. They're in a cul-de-sac; nowhere to run.

'I could follow you round all day.'

'You already do...'

How else explain the presence that haunts down these dusty afternoon streets that's waiting for him round the corner, stepping out from doorways? The one that he turns round suddenly to get a glimpse of, that he can never quite catch in the act. The one who's always coming to find him, the one who dominates the dream. How else to explain those days when entire afternoons feel like a held breath? When he knows she's there, just out of sight round the corner, waiting. Every move she makes is etched on his brain. Just as she sees the slightest flicker of movement her prey makes. No way he can explain, of course. But she's pleased enough.

'You should be combing the streets for me, not me for you.'

'I've been looking out for you.'

She doesn't realise what that entails, with him, how much commitment. How thoroughly he'd look. What he might find.

'Looking out for me? What's the good of that?'

He was quite happy, throwing his life away, until she came along. But he smiles. They've made it up like this before; that familiar feeling.

'Where do you put your barrow away, the multi-storey car park?'

'Uh-huh.'

She's seen them coming and going there with their dust carts; they have some kind of depot tucked away in the basement there. He stands looking down at her, as if protective.

'Come and see the view up top. It's quite something. All over the harbour and out to sea. No one ever goes up there. I'm about through here, don't have any more on the itinerary.'

'I have to go to the bank.'

He nods; she retreats, half-soothed, monumentally angry.

*

Reminiscence. There's something coming to meet him along this little street. Coming up from behind; he startles round to see. There's something tracking him ahead, some presence emerging from the side street, heading him off from in front, coming to meet him from behind. Sweat breaks out on his forehead; he steps into the road, clutching and startling on his broom; rears up wide-eyed, looking all around. From behind, ahead, around, above; the quick steps of pursuit spanking between the house walls on these narrow streets. Come and find me. I'm waiting.

What does the dreamy state feel like? It feels like a sunny corner of the car park rooftop, the hot ground soaking into your back; bays are marked out but with five storeys below and the place's reputation, no cars ever come up here. It feels like a long kiss at the end of a long day. It's when you start to reminisce about what you only remember in that state; when all those long-lost memories come visiting and you know you'll never forget them again. Homecoming, when you run your hands up her sides at last. In a summer season, when the sun is soft, it feels like you've always known this, long feather grasses blowing along the wayside, pink roses blooming, this voluminous, all-knowing state. It goes back forty years and more, deep, deep into time, so many summers ago. You hold your breath for that second which cuts through all those years into eternity. In the dreamy state, you die if you don't have the one you love. If she doesn't pull out your shirt and untongue your scar along your forearm up to the brown wrinkles in the crook of your elbow, if your mouth isn't tangling the down of her neck, making her dandelion hair stand on end, if you don't knee her apart, if she doesn't bite the street dirt off your ear, if you don't shove her hard into the grit of the ground and clutch the sunlight out of her thick flaring hair. And more endless seconds into eternity.

MR FOX

Foxes. Foxes in the garden, sleekly colonising the place. Whicker and cough of fox at night, just outside. Their breath almost coming through the doors. The child sees them first, of course; spends hours staring out of the conservatory. Doesn't want to go to the beach any more. Sometimes Bonnie feels he's becoming the son of a fox himself, a gingery mite with a strange little snout always pressed to the window; should never have brought him down here.

Foxes rearing and stretching themselves all over the grass, the awkward dandle of back legs as they circle. Their spindly behinds, thin black legs, black stockings pulled to the thighs. The dusty soft-black noses of the cubs, their black line of smile. The wind lifting their fur. Their utter, calm unconcern. No consciousness at all of the humans watching them.

'They're truly wild, aren't they,' says Austin, coming to look also, laying an arm across Bonnie's shoulders.

She shudders. 'They are, truly. A bit too close to home.'

'Something about them, isn't there. How are we going to get rid of them?'

They have their hide beneath the skinny elderberry at the bottom of the garden; dislodged from next door when the old man died, and his son cemented up their hole and all the surrounding tree-roots. Stupid bugger, says Austin, typical of this place.

Shame the foxes didn't burrow out the other side of the cliff and into the sea, he adds, transmuting into sea-foxes as they fell. For they're hard to dislodge, once they've taken up residence.

'There's four of them,' roars Finbar. 'One Mummy and three babies. Where's the Dad?'

He's in the house, his arm heavy across Bonnie's shoulders, his high forehead forbidding across the garden. Nose lifted to the future, which isn't here, he stares out at the other family, an autocratic rufus. Mr Fox: silver-tongued, ambitious and able to read her every thought. She liked him best out of all her many suitors. Destined for her almost from the cradle, almost an arranged marriage, the fond wish of both their mothers. Brought to fulfilment by her parents' early deaths and Sally's guardianship; though all agreed it would have happened anyway; it was preordained, destined. And you can't change destiny.

They all stand looking from the conservatory as the animals go picking their way up and down the lawn. The severe sea-light of that isle falls, chilling the foxes to thin ginger-brown, not the lustrous burnish of rural foxes inland. Bonnie thinks that her husband and son too look pinched, bleached of their natural rich colour. Nothing can quell Austin, of course. But his natural redhead pallor looks white, grey beneath the eyes. And the child, the child in that light looks almost fey. Her own eyes spacey, looking outwards in all directions to what's not there, yet inwards as well, contained. The musical discipline that hasn't been eroded yet.

'It means we can't use the garden.'

'Why not? Of course we can.'

'With the child? He mustn't go out there. Don't take him out there until I get this sorted out. I'll ring the council. They've got humane ways of disposing of them.'

'Don't be ridiculous. We can still go out. Just avoid where they are.'

'Are you daft, Bonnie? Have you never heard of hygiene?'

'But...'

'It's not exactly exile from the Garden of Eden, is it? That scrubland. You can take Finbar down to the beach. Or the park.'

'They're not much cleaner, according to you.'

'Mount Royal Park? It's delightful. I thought you liked being out and about round here. You can talk to your friends in the street. Discuss just how clean the place really is.'

She pushes at his arm, wriggles away. 'Don't start all that again.'

'What, when we've got our very own environmental consultant to hand? Yes, we'll call Dominic in. I'm sure he'd be only too delighted.'

It's been a couple of weeks. Eternity on the roof of the car park: did that happen or was it an epileptic fugue of the mind, sparking and leaping into fantasy? Afterwards, returning to time, he, damp and shaky, kissing her face all over as if to imprint it on his brain; she kissing his as if she too never wants to forget. They fall asleep together for ten minutes. If they don't sleep together, they'll die; the need is overwhelming. Bigger than either of them and beyond all common sense. Faces drenched in sleep turned up to each other. Their breathing like waves breaking on some far-off shore. Wake together, the sun still coming down, her back numb and prinked all over from the grit, he rubbing it, saying what lovers say at such times, very little.

And then it's gone, completely forgotten. They pass each other on the street a few times, giving barely a nod; she isn't even sure it's him, he's so withdrawn, faceless. Another cleaner who looks a bit the same, same height and build, half-hidden under a cap. The poker back, the mask of a face, wrapped within himself. The only distinguishing mark the scar along his forearm; that does jolt her to the core.

How does Austin know, when it may never even have happened, when it may only have been the fantasy of a dreamy summer day? But he's wily, cunning, can sense enemies from afar, in that Reynard way; how otherwise would he have got to where he is now, in that cut-throat profession? In his world, it's death to go beyond the clan. So, with his Scottish farsightedness, his London sharpness, he's given her a bad time without being able to accuse her of anything definite. For Christ's sake, Bonnie! The chap is simple, plain to see, wanting; sorry: cognitively challenged. The way he stares at you. It's not even the ultimate cliché, the Lady Chatterley syndrome, the ultimate middle-class love story, destiny wouldn't allow them to love each other, he swept her dreams away, ha ha;

but at least she's got his ring, a souvenir of her little fling with *nostalgie de la boue*. *Le boueur, le balayer de la rue*, that was Baudelaire, wasn't it? The rag-picker, sifting through all that the city rejects, *sentiments des ruines*. No: how disgraceful is that, inflicting her housewifely fantasies on a vulnerable man. Poor chap. Borderline intellectual functioning, isn't that the correct phrase? Able to hold down a simple job, manage the rudiments of running a household? Couldn't she at least have picked someone normal, a navvy from the harbour if she wanted a bit of rough, a nice Polish lorry driver or something?

'Actually,' she says, 'I think he's as all there as you or me.'

'Oh really? There's nothing wrong with him, then?'

'No. There's nothing wrong with him.'

'Intellectually, in fact, he's on your level. That's it, is it?'

Mr Fox, who knows how the mind of man and of woman works. His insouciant elusiveness first attracted her. The silence behind the volubility, in which he now regards the foxes, like a voyeur regarding his own kind, commanding them from another element, a silent contact through man-made glass and God's air. He always seemed to have some secret place all of his own, like she did. He keeps still his own counsel, guarding his canny clairvoyance along with his acute, private diablerie with words. A magus, rolling his silver sorceries across the page. One who comes of a long line of seers and visionaries. Like her, burdened by his gift, and like her, safe and happy if he can only harness it. In fact, he harnessed it easily, editorships and columns pouring in. The poetry ever brewing in the background. So maybe he's not burdened. But while he shares his opinions round freely enough, the centre, the place of his vision, remains private, all for himself; no shared lands here. On the contrary, he depends on remaining uncaught, like the wild fox. It takes her years to realise that maybe the elusiveness is more interesting than the man, that what he spins out from his secret core can never be the core itself, that he will keep resolutely to himself, until death. But talks on meanwhile, his soft Scottish voice so unlike Dominic's and his trader's transatlantic bark.

The son of two drinkers, Austin learnt self-containment early. Lolling on Bonnie's bed, chatting, telling her how he was going to be a poet, his eyes dark as Guinness, watching, watching all the time, right through her teenage years, from his own secret heartland. She married him to find out what it was. But he spares her that.

No, he spares her, as he always has done. Austin the farsighted, the channel, the plain speaker, who allowed himself to be lured down here for her sake; now wonders if he did it against his better judgement. Friends in the street, and now vermin in the garden, the last straw. Should have rented for a time instead. Take the creeper away and how nice a house has it ever been, really? Its lines are severe, forbidding. So exposed here at the top of Mount Royal. How come they didn't see that? Not like their London cottage, nestling down into the street. Uncosy. Cold. He's not fanciful, but this house is full of someone else's memories, someone who can't forget. Look at the motto on the front door – *Je me souviens* – too right. Is that the curse of the house? Rimbaud, right? *Jadis, si je me souviens bien, ma vie était un festin* – Once, if I remember correctly, my life was a feast – *Une Saison en Enfer* – perfect way to describe living here.

But this is the only house she's ever seen where she feels she can make a home. Surely he feels the same. Can't they sell London instead, put down roots here? —Sell London? No way! Because then in a couple of years he'll be dead and she'll want something else; because she doesn't know what she wants. Her spiritual foundation is on the move, agile and light on its feet. One foot walks in the world of music above, the other on the earthly foundation below. He hopes.

'What's that you've got on? Tchaikovsky?'

He looks at her oddly. 'It's the Brahms.'

'Turn it off.' Unaware of the enormity of her mistake, little as she cares for Tchaikovsky. To her, all music's still the same: noise.

'Will I put on some nice Philip Glass for you?' – sly, that's his preference, not hers. 'A bit of Tavener? Or the Vespers? the greatest job application in the world... You always said there was life before Monteverdi, and life after Monteverdi...'

She wants to listen to something else; the sea, perhaps. Opens a window. Some other rhythm has caught her ear. If she doesn't hurry, if she isn't interrupted, she might catch it properly. A wind rushing down from the sky to seize her back up, into her element. But only at the piano is she in time, listening for the rhythm, waiting until she catches it, the audience hushed; at which she nods, picks it up; plays it. The cosmic footsteps beating on. She hangs out of the window, listening. Listening for that steady tread, coming ever closer. She leans out, further.

'I can hear it. It's like a heartbeat. Or someone walking. If I could only get the beat...'

'Oh come on, Bonnie, stop talking rubbish and shut the window. It's bloody freezing. Haven't you had enough sea air? Or are you determined to get a cold on top of everything else?'

Austin, her minder. Always on her case. Austin's guardianship, rather than Sally's. Austin choosing her clothes as well as her repertoire, picking out her trademark black suit and red shoes for recitals, ensuring even that her hair remained the perfect blonde bob. He took over early from Sally, who did her best; the Royal College of Music, the best Russian teachers, storming up and down the practice rooms, shouting and shoving her off the piano stool, there, now you do it, do it just like that but more, more and more! Play, maestra, play! Play until your fingers bleed! And then play some more! Austin as likely as not sitting in the corner, reading or jotting, his own stuff, notes for her. Austin directing her repertoire, Austin walking her over to the college those days she truanted, saying it was too stuffy and old-fashioned. He saying her problem was she couldn't bear reality. Austin bringing her the exam results she hated to access herself; well, no need to worry, you got a distinction again; his academic results, a year ahead, invariably far better than hers. His suppressed glow of exultation when, after telling her, he'd modestly reveal his own. Like her, always a worker. Always a star.

She'd never have done it without him. Austin setting the timer, the click of resignation as he places it on top of the piano, keeps her at it, the old practice; *con brio*, Bonnie. Accompanying her to concerts to ensure she doesn't go walkabout en route; waiting for her afterwards, with growing patience. The clever post-mortems, awarding her her marks: well done on the *sostenuto*. A first-class interpretation. Massaging her shoulders dutifully when they get home, always at her request; the hearty ringing round of his thumbs, that always just miss the spot. Why does he never offer, when he knows how much it means to her? All she wants is someone to make her a cup of tea after a performance and sit with her, be with her, not saying a word. He adores her, the way he adores himself, she's part of him, his twin. She adores him back; her rock, her muse. And she can do anything she wants in the whole world except that one thing: be herself, open a window onto the outside world. And up until now she's been perfectly happy with that. The dream couple: hardworking, handsome, in demand at parties; living each other's lives.

Yet there's always been this chastity to their relationship, a kind of mutual sibling physical distaste. Right from the first time they made love, in the practice room after a recital, at her instigation, she so needed someone to bring her back, beneath the row of coat hooks, the empty-eyed London mirrors, the spotlights they had to turn off; his fraternal white skin; the wet crackle of his tongue round her ear, squeamish about the intrusion. They remained shy. Never in the Chelsea flat; too incestuous. Or maybe it's the shade of his actual twin, Finuola, who didn't make it, that gets between them.

Why doesn't he want to touch her after a performance? He has this way of gazing at the ceiling instead, arms folded, steeling himself for her account of how it went. For how much she needs to be held as she returns from that other world, to be retrieved physically, to sleep snuggled up against him, which he endures until she's safely gone, when he can go into the spare room and relax. His elusive Celtic soul won't mingle. Leaves her to startle awake alone at 2am. Here that he can take his pick of so many other bedrooms, where is he, when she wakes, in that big dark house? And she's always being judged, not by his standard of course but by hers, whether she comes up to her expectations of herself, her high potential. The fundamental flaw is that he's jealous of where she goes when she plays. With constant conscious nobility he overcomes his jealousy, time and again; but it's always there, a red streak in him. That's why he's so conscientious in his encouragement. Sometimes she isn't even sure how much he really likes her. Whether he can bear anything less than the perfect doll, whether the rasp of her underarms when she hasn't shaved, her blood and fur aren't too much for him. But that's okay, because she doesn't really care for his writing either. He's so right all the time. Whom can she tell, that she hasn't got anyone to sleep with, that she gets into bed every night with the void and has to hang there all night along its edge? That she doesn't like her husband's gingery, peppery, foxy smell, that his yapping drowns out the music in her head, that he was educated by the English and prefers talking to touching, drinking to feeling, that all he wants to do is fuck like a fox?

She can tell the house, who already loves her like a mother. Who watches her with the covert, eager curiosity some crones show for younger versions of themselves. Midnight separations, slammed doors and footsteps, form a patois that Concordia understands. Two languages spoken under one roof, two solitudes. Nights clasping pillows, that longing for a cuddle from the infinite, are formed by a temperament a lonely house shares. She can tell the house. How she now wants a man from another land, who smells of home; who can only speak a pidgin language of the heart and can't translate everything into words, is bewildered by explanations. Who'd sit with her on the sofa for an entire evening with barely a sentence exchanged. Walks hand in hand along the seafront, the only voice that of the waves. A complete sentimentality of silence. The house will listen as she plays softly to it, how alone she is. She can ask the house to send her another lover, pluck one off the street for her, some kind passer-by with a face as weathered and remote as Canada, who's got a bit of time for her. Her fingers on the keyboard conjure the type she wants. Broken tunes, scales that hang unfinished like stairways in the air; it's music to the ears.

*

There's no furniture in the conservatory beyond a rickety cane bookcase and an empty, ornate birdcage hanging from the ceiling; they hadn't got round to buying it and now won't, now Austin wants to put the house back on the market. They had planned a riot of wicker and cushions and trailing green, a canary filling Sunday mornings with song. Instead, they're going to buy a new ring, a delicate gold filigree. It's been chosen. But Austin won't buy it while they're down here; truly, he's taken against the place. It will be a celebration for their return to London.

'I can't wait to go. Get you out of here. Thank God you seem more yourself, Bonnie.'

Although there are still times, like just now in the conservatory, when there's no one there; she's off elsewhere, not with them. That open front door in the mornings that's stood open since before daybreak sometimes.

Now she stands, face lifted to the sea beyond the garden's end, the glow of her hair also subdued in the steely light. Lips and blonde facial hairs etched. Eyes scanning the cliff-line. The straddle of her legs in the short skirt shows how she wants more. How what's in the conservatory, the house, isn't enough for her. Austin next to her is equally outlined in that hard light, his hair definite. The aggressive middle classes, come to a halt on the cliff-top. But Austin drops a quick, hard kiss on her ear that echoes round it, a sea-kiss echoing round a shell murmuring of the ocean.

'That's enough British seaside.'

Meanwhile, they continue to look at the foxes, who pose a new problem to the sale of the house. Mother fox is grooming one of the cubs, her snout extended to its ear as if whispering to it. The kit's face is slanted upwards, eyes closed against the thin island sun. In the house, Mr Fox has slunk back up to Bonnie and has his arm round her again. Her shoulders are a bit stiff, but what's that to Mr Fox? Another maiden to subdue, all in the day's work.

'Three babies,' continues Finbar. 'Why?'

'Why what?'

'Why three? Why not only one?'

'Well,' says Austin, drawing breath, stroking the back of Bonnie's neck, smoothing down her hair. 'That's just the way foxes are.'

The boy pouts out of the window, thinking about it. Two of the cubs are tumbling about as if they own the place, open jaws gently locked on each other. Both parents watch the child's face, knowing what's coming next. It's all concentrated in his snub little *museau*.

'Could we have three?'

'Well, three's a bit...'

'We'll look into it, Finbar,' says Austin, his thumb on the tender spot between Bonnie's shoulder blades, pressing for the wilt.

The child's gaze subsides back to the window. Mr Fox is looking at his fair maiden, who glances back, a vixen's glint in her eye. What he wants to do is take her hair in his jaw and drag her off somewhere, away from his current offspring. Set his teeth on her neck, in a gentle bite. Mark her, his territory.

'I want another boy,' into the window glass, his breath misting it, rubbing it away. 'Is it going to be a boy?'

What, just cut another one out of the universal dough, another gingerbread man? There are worse ways to have a child. But, as Bonnie tells Finbar, we can't always have what we want in this life. Like the fleeing pancake fairy tale, where found items roll away, the heart's desire does not stand still to be caught. Just as well, probably; doesn't the gingerbread man end up getting eaten by the fox?

'Don't worry, Finbar,' says Austin. 'It will all be all right once we get back to London.'

There's nothing like the aching loneliness of a family thrown back upon itself. It fills the conservatory, the whole of that high-ceilinged house, which Austin has renamed the doctor's surgery. Full of spooky waiting rooms. All it needs is a dragon receptionist, says Austin, and some bleak alcoholic GP behind the desk in the study. All that wonderful original cornicing, original brass stair rods, original stained glass in the front door. The cold wood stairs where the ghosts hang out. The sudden little whirlwinds in the hallways. The huge bathroom with the iron bath and claw feet, the run marks on the old enamel, the cracked dark green window, the wind whistling through the overflow hole. The stuttering creak of the door that's always springing slowly open, showering the bather with cold air. It is indeed a place for waiting, this house; has chosen her, Bonnie, dreaming out of the window, not him. Wouldn't mind Austin out of the way. But it can wait. Waiting is what Waste Island's all about.

Finbar's gone, the cold clairvoyant cub, dashed upstairs on some urgent childish errand; or chased away by his father's vulpine desire for his mother, his long white fingers between her shoulders.

'It doesn't come to order, Austin. I'm sorry.'

'I'm sorry, too, Bonnie. The last thing I want to do is pressurise you, especially after all our recent – but do you realise you've been saying that for close on three years? Like I said, Finbar will be four this July, you know. And – can I be blunt? It doesn't help that... I mean, you haven't exactly been accommodating lately.'

'Really? Do you really think that?'

When she's been making a special effort? She might as well have said it aloud; even men like Austin can't bear to have an effort made for them.

'Don't you think it's time to get it looked at? There are some good clinics in London; they'd treat you sensitively.'

'And you.'

Mr Fox is handsome and Mr Fox is fertile, springing a kit on every vixen in the land. But he waves his hand, impatient.

'I mean, I do understand how bloody lucky we were with Finbar; and with you, of course. I do understand a certain amount of psychological reluctance, after that birth, but lately... I thought you'd got over all that. Sometimes I wonder how much you even want another child.'

She stands whitened even beyond the cruel sea light.

'It was the loss of blood.'

Her fear of their blood mixing again. A near-fatal incompatibility. Maybe it was all just too incestuous.

'Yes. I know. I was there.'

It was Austin went and got the doctor, hauled him over to the bed after twenty minutes had gone by and it was still pouring out of her, the red blood of an abrupted birth. How near a thing it had been, when Austin had finally broken through the indulgent contempt for the panicky young father and got the medico to saunter up to take a look.

'How much you even love Finbar, after that birth...'

It's true that sometimes she looks at them both, her redheads, and sees their heads tinged by blood. A long line of Celts, birthed in blood.

'But – of course I do. All that was ages ago.'

'You can be so remote sometimes. And I don't think this place has had a good effect on you.'

'You wanted to buy the house, too.'

'We made a mistake, Bonnie. That's all there is to it. It's like leaving a marriage that hasn't worked. You just walk away.'

'I think you're crazy, selling again so quickly.'

'That may be. All I can tell you is, this house gives me the creeps.'

'Couldn't we at least keep it as a weekend or holiday place? Rent it out some of the time, to make it pay? It was cheap enough. I can't bear to think of it being all London again – that thick air...'

'Nothing on earth would induce me to spend another weekend here, once we get out. I've told you. It's... it's east of the sun and west of the moon. The land of midnight trolls. You know what I mean. You can't be yourself down here. All the things you've been educated for cut no ice here. Trolls don't appreciate fine piano playing, as little as subtleties of thought. It's a place for people who've failed their great task.'

She falters. Her husband, and his prescience, his prophecies.

'What do you mean?'

'Or who don't have one. Like your friend. He has no task. You do. That's the difference between you, the deep divide.'

'He might have. What do you know?'

'His task is to sweep the street. Nothing more. Flirt with the ladies a bit, when he's in the mood. That's it. There's nothing else there. You have your music – or should have. And the ridiculous spectacle of you trying to make a silk purse out of a sow's ear – I mean, he's a fine-looking chap when he's actually awake, your paramour. Decent, respectable working class, I'm sure. But what do you do when you want to talk?'

'For God's sake. We pass the time of day when we meet.'

'I bet you do. You don't want to get stuck down here, Bonnie.'

She's silent.

'When did you last practise? Properly, I mean.'

He takes her hands, bending her fingers straight. Long and firm, with their subtle muscles, capable of summoning other worlds. They're losing their pampered town whiteness, becoming tanned, harder. Surreptitiously she flexes them, pulls away, back to the window and the occupied territory outside.

'Can you not at least take off that gypsy ring? It drives me mad to see it. In fact, I can't understand your insensitivity, keeping it on.'

'It's really stuck.'

He's looking at her, hard. It's as she feared: he's between her and the door. Alone with him in this light, the foxes gambolling in the garden. Any second he's going to sidle up to her again in that foxy way, put his arm round her, proprietorial, his hard fingers sliding onto her nipple, which hardens in response. Indeed, he's got her, her back pulled to his front, his other hand on her other breast, pinning her against him. Above her head he looks out of the window again at the foxes, stark and ruddy against the green grass, his eyes visionary, like a man looking at his destiny.

'Bonnie. Tell me what really happened.'

'What with?'

'Our ring. Tell me. Don't be afraid. I just want to know.'

'Can't you see I don't know myself?'

'Don't lie to me.'

His fingers probing her beating heart.

'I'm not.'

'How did it come to be off your finger in the first place?'

'But I told you.'

'I mean, it's not as if it could have just slipped off.'

'I lost it, I told you. One minute it was there, and the next...'

'It was so precious. I can't comprehend... and I know, I just know it's at the bottom of the sea.'

In London you never have to talk like this. In London, you get on with it, don't let the years slip away in the blue haze of this weird island down here.

'We'll take action once we're back. With this baby thing.'

He's sinking his mouth softly against the back of her neck, deep, deep, making her shudder. Strong and white his teeth against her peach down, bruising, not breaking the skin. Not drawing blood yet. Held in the sharp yap of his jaw, she can't move. His auburn head sunk over her neck. They stand, immobile; if he shakes her, she'll break. His breath comes hard and warm on her, hardening her all over.

'What about now?'

'Finbar.'

'He's upstairs. Come into the cellar with me. We can lock the door.'

Why not? Why not give in to this hard London sex, this lust of dominion and ownership? You won't get a shred of tenderness, but who cares? The guilty are not free. Why not go with Mr Fox into the bloody chamber, lest he take his sword and hack your hand off to get the ring? What beautiful young lady doesn't get a thrill out of being dragged along by her hair to her ultimate fulfilment? Who doesn't fancy Mr Fox, really? It won't take long. To have him say afterwards, 'That was wonderful, Bonnie. Top marks. Well done.' You too can be exultant, can go off about your business again with the foxy shine in your eyes. He'd leave her alone after that, for a while.

And it's dreadful. Every fuck might be the one that brings another child, and his dark-auburn head and his cold ear, straining at her. They lie on some old day bed left there by the old witch, the mattress all cat; already her back is crawling. How on earth could they have missed this one, on all those trips to the dump? The walls are crumbling, with damp, shedding small yellow piles of brick dust. A tiny bit of daylight comes from the coal hatch and it's dark, just enough to see the pallid glimmer of his face; and musty, in this cave beneath the sea. The killing cellar, where the witch dispatched her victims. And then: men who talk; men who ask.

'You know, Bonnie, if you want a bit of rough... I can be rough, too, if you like.'

'Don't embarrass us both, Austin.'

'If you want a really good seeing-to...'

'For fuck's sake.'

Just get on with it. She feels herself blushing in the dark for him. He'd force himself into her fantasy, re-enact whatever has or hasn't happened. What turns you on about him? What does it feel like when he kisses you? What do you do next? Where does he touch you, and how? Does he keep his clothes on, take yours off? What do you do to him, and how? At what point does it take over, become uncontrollable? Did you know that one kiss can blow the sexual act away?

Still, if sex is all that's on offer, why not take it. Why not give in to Mr Fox, the way maidens do. Young, strong and urban. He's determined enough. Not vulnerable. Why not let him break you down into sexual actuality? Forget fantasies. Give in; be bold. Slinky Mr Fox knows just how to cut the fairest maiden to pieces: his revenge for the rings, the one that's for ever lost, but especially the one she can't take off. And once he's cut her down, cut her resistance away, he'll come slinking into her as he always has; he's always known how to get her, get round her. Be bold, be bold. In the underground chamber, in the dark where only the house can see, Mr Fox makes her share his secret: it's the same man, doing the same things. That's the secret of life: the man is the same as any other man.

The man you love doesn't exist. The cellar presses on them heavy and inert, thick with brick dust, coal dust, damp. Filled with the bodies and skeletons of beautiful young ladies, all stained with blood. Be bold, be bold, but not too bold, lest that your heart's blood should run cold.

'I'd better shower.'

'Can you bear to lie there a bit longer? Put your feet up? You know, like they recommend, leave the shower for a bit, give things a chance to... I know it's disgusting down here... do you want me to bring you a coffee? I'll look after Finbar. God. Is that the time? I'd better get moving. Will you be all right for the next few days?'

'Yes, I'll get on and do a bit of practice.'

'Good to see you getting on with it again.'

'Don't be so bloody patronising.'

MAGICIAN

The sound of the piano ripples out, echoing up to all the ceilings of that unfriendly house, down to the chalk caves beneath, bubbling like blood out of the sands to the sea. She's the magician, playing other worlds into being. Her fingers a *totentanz* along the keys, daring to go there, careless of the consequences. On her face the same look of thoughtful, dangerous, daredevil irony as on Dominic's on a Monday morning, engaged in reminiscences of the weekend all along the street. Her back too engaged in manual labour. Her leg muscles working also in her short skirt, the pedals bending and bowing to the tread of her red toes, her performing shoes. Her piano is a percussion instrument, a vast heart that can be beaten to summon energies, to drum into being a dream almost as vivid as reality. Who will listen to her? Who answer her call? The house, who knows she doesn't want a male muse? Her magic fingers are cracking on this skeleton that she brings to life, makes dance, her privileged whorls bleeding onto the keys. The closed-faced people walking by outside don't falter, because they can't hear it, even though the rickety wood window frames are vibrating. Austin can't hear it because he's on his way to London, laptop and mobile in full swing on the train, back to the real world for a spell of work. Finbar's asleep after a bad night, riddled with dreams. Only one person can hear it, and he's at the far end of the bay, drinking in every note.

The wide pathway arching between the rocks; where does it go? Onto the cliff-top? But no, it winds downwards. Dominic pushes the barrow on, cautious of making too much noise against the drift of notes he can hear so clearly. Quite deserted as if no one had been there since last summer, dead leaves, dead crisp packets, tissues washed by the rain and dried by the wind and now bunched stiff in corners. As in a spell, he reaches for his broom, slow, listening for the tinkle of notes along the air. Yes, he has spells like this, when he slows right down, staring ahead, listening. And Bonnie has only to lift a finger, a magic finger, to send him there. It's where she goes when she plays, the place she thought was uninhabited until she heard his footstep, saw his outline ahead. The path winding silent down, as if to the underworld. Utterly silently deserted, a ghost passage carved through the rock; an archway ahead. Pink flowers sprouting from the rocks. Sense you so rarely get in England of utter, complete privacy; respite. No one round the corner, for once. No one ever comes here. Just a spray of music falling from the sky. The tribal cave painting of teenagers: *Jade loves Wayne*; *Ross is an arsehole*; but they were here long ago. He can tell. Jade has long since realised she has to make do with Ross because Wayne, who's in prison again, doesn't give a fuck, and they're struggling with two small kids on the no-go St Michael estate. He knows, because they're his neighbours. They're all around him on the streets of this town, unless he can escape them in places like these. It's a long passage; the cliff is high, winding on down and around, tall rocks either side. Takes quite a while to work down, and he's slow, slow. And all along the way the music accompanies him, down, down towards the front. She's starting with the scales, of course, the foundation of all divine harmony. Music that's contained enough for him, that he can feel safe with. Up and down, up and down, keeping time with his own slow turns as he sweeps to and fro, to and fro. Up and down, from the base of the spine to his brainstem, the limbic regions, the vagal nerve, the Wanderer. As if in a spell, to and fro, up and down, held in the rhythm of the scales. Then, when he feels safe enough, rocked enough, starts widening out almost imperceptibly. Spinning slowly out into an impromptu; still floating him on the golden balance. Like a couple dancing, dancing all the way down, clasping each other, spinning slowly round together down this secret passage to the sea. The music always accompanying, winding down all the bends. Then it ripples out right across the bay.

The wide esplanade, and the bay beyond, a half-moon fallen to earth and filled with sludgy green. It's at the extremest edge of the island, just before it swings round, the coastline of the mainland visible across the water; England, stretching off into the filmy meeting of greys that is the horizon. The music reaches that far and further. England, crouched low across the water, home to a thousand nations. The grey, milky limits of his exile stretch into the distance. On the furthermost shore, the dim outlines of a factory, spread out along the shoreline like a town, and the three towers of a power station. The music spinning out that far. England today, no vistas, fouling her own waters. In front of him, one man searching the rocks, with a blue bucket; three youths at the far end of the wide sea wall, sorting fishing tackle. Just company enough. The bare beige vaginas of rocks, trailed with fronds of black seaweed and spread to the dull-black water half a mile or so off. It's one of those monumental English summer days spread out before you, dull, grey, soothing. Nothing moves, barely the flap of a seagull's wing. Hand on broom, he looks out. The water is wide. One of love's impossible tasks, to clean this isle.

Here's the furthest extent of his open prison. But he's too spellbound to take a step further, to cross the water.

It's time for his break so he stops, sits on the sea wall above the rocks, listening to Bonnie. She's always lived on an enchanted island, called music. Too good for this world, always wanting melodies which the world can't play, which no one but he can hear. She plays on; she's not good enough any more to perform solo, but she's good enough for him; they're in harmony. She carries the piano on the downy arch of her neck, that sways delicate over it. And he lives in a world all of his own. No music can free him. But he listens, transported.

She plays on, the ivories staining. She's the magician, the sleight of hand artist, who pays for her art with red fingers. Practitioner of stage magic, *le bateleur*, one hand in the world of music above, one trailing the dregs below. Who plays from a cone of blood deep within her. Her drenched, red cuticles half-moons, mementoes of that other place. It's where they meet best, she and Dominic, where he can kiss her like a sea wind. She's invested him with magic, the house with life. With a maternal solicitude it doesn't really possess. Waters them both with her creative blood. She's pulling it out of herself, in two red handfuls, from the place where she plays. Creating her own alternative world, playing it into blood-streaked numinosity along the keyboard. The piano has to be tinged with blood if it isn't to be too white, one of her Russian teachers told her. So that it acquires that life-stained tone, pain seeping into the music. A white piano means you haven't played with your heart's blood. Whose heart is she reaching? Who will obey the summons? The spirit of the house rises up in response, starts off slowly down the stairs. The door of the piano room starts ajar, the air's a cold touch on the back of her neck. Footsteps as of black, brittle, shiny, high-heeled shoes, shoes her future self might wear, haunting the house. For she hears the steps clearly, leading ahead, into the future. You'll never live anywhere else, says the house, like the hiss of foam along a winter shore. No more cosy London flats, no more London cottages. You'll stay down here with me for ever. You've left it too long, Bonnie, the music, you'll never get it back. No more red shoes. Your discipline's gone, maybe your magic never existed. You'll never have another child, not with all that blood seeping into the music. You betrayed your muse, Austin, with his Greek god profile, his lifelong investment in you. Play, Bonnie, play with your heart's blood.

She plays on, drowning the whispers out. Playing Dominic into existence. The atmosphere of this house would be different if he were here. Spreadeagled in an armchair at the end of the day, looking up with that shine in his eyes to welcome her. She always had imaginary friends as a small, imperious child, Indians and Eskimos who emerged at her bidding from corners of the room. Skins cured and cracked by the wind and stinking of rancid oil and fish. Eyes gleaming green as Arctic lights, full of intent. And when they'd played to the point they were going to take her away, back with them, she'd scream for someone to come rescue her from herself.

Now nostalgia for the ordinary torments her. She's vulgar and sentimental enough to want actuality, what everyone else seems to have. A kind of tea and biscuits in bed normality, together to start the day; a sloppiness Austin's always despised, too grand and hurried for such dallying; but Dominic would accommodate it, for sure. Dominic has time. And at day's end, he waiting to meet her at that big barn of a station when she returns late from a concert in London, the ticket offices locked up, the dark echoing up to the roof. She has this fantasy that she'll be wandering the streets and he'll find her and take her home with him, that he'll be home. As if Austin would let her walk home alone from any station at night. But she lost her home at thirteen, has been playing alone since she was seven. Her fingers pause in their utter, weary ache for it all to be over, if only it were all over; to be free of this jealous house so heavily sunken into rock and sand. And she can just hear Austin: Wish what was all over? And even Dominic the literal: But you've already got a home.

To be released, to be spinning down that secret passage to the sea, going to a home as light as air, secure, free.

The house, Dominic. Her two lovers. Her jealous brother Austin doesn't even get a look in.

She plays on, only half in touch with her powers. Like a girl poised at first menarche, still at the mercy of other entities, unaware of what's about to flood out of her. Then falters, feeling a presence; turns and there's a fox, come right up to the piano; staring, immobile. For all his talk, Austin has left the doors open on his way out; gone and left her open to the wild. And the house has colluded; not protected her. A fox in the house, two feet away. Its stare is dim and bright, as if it doesn't see her; seems crouched over some intent of its own. She leaps up in terror, closing the piano lid: it's Austin, come back to keep an eye on her; again. Just when she was utterly lost and gone in the music, gone she doesn't even know where. The utter intrusion yet again, just when she was lost in her own secret self. She stands hand to thudding heart, almost overwhelmed, caught in the animal's eyeshine. Can it see her or not? The dip of its back, sinister; the hunch of its buttocks. What was she doing just now? Whatever it was, it saw her; it knows, it's got her secret; she's guilty; how long has it been there, watching? If only she hadn't given in to Mr Fox earlier. Now she's guilty. Mr Fox, she's played into his hands; and now he has dominion over her, the power to send his own kind to her. Fool that she was not to shower, to listen to Austin, not to take her life into her own hands. Now she's exposed, his odour still on her; it's that which attracted this animal into the house. Be bold, Bonnie, be bold!

'Get out! Go on, scat!'

But it's too late. When you play yourself into an altered state of consciousness, more can arrive than you conjured for. It's as if the shock has nicked her heart, the soft and furry heart between her legs, making her spill blood. She feels the bulge between the net of hairs and then her heart bursts, blood shooting out down and through. Spilling out of the place from which she plays, like the ghost of the house stepping out of its place, free to roam. Her heart escaping from its box, to be carried on a platter before her with a dagger through it, like Spenser's Amoret. She's the red magician, full of magic blood, that summons familiars and lovers to her from afar.

'Out, I said!'

She stamps her foot. The blood bulging faster, two long trickles down her inner thighs and right down to her shoes, her flat shoes of soft Spanish leather. She hopes they won't fill, two little sinking red boats, her creativity drenching her body. The fox just shifts its head, glancing over its shoulder. Surely not more red tails whisking up the stairs, scattering through the open bedroom doors. It surely hasn't brought the whole family, dispersing themselves about the house, to go slinking about in the silent watches of the night, a brush against the legs on the 2am visit to the loo. It surely wouldn't come and lay its head on her thighs, as Austin did earlier. It's between her and the door, of course; yet maybe it can't even see her. Foxes don't see well, she knows that. It's the dog fox all right; bigger than the others, calmly curious, proprietorial. The soft fuzz of its ginger museau. The dream of a tail, tipped with white. Its silence. Its intent.

What does a woman do, confronted by a fox the second time in one day? Betrayed by her body, her shoes reddening again? She can scream. Call on her brothers for help, to come and cut the fox to pieces with their swords. She can indulge in a fantasy of rescue: her lover storming in to kill it with his shovel and then taking her upstairs to shower them both down. Or she can handle it herself. Not give in again. Learn. Do it differently the second time round.

Bonnie's brother is far away, on a train just snaking into the London terminal. Her lover's down the seafront and might not want to get involved anyway. She doesn't yet know him well enough to say. She snatches at her scattered thoughts. She was only playing the piano. She was there, on the piano stool. Not spinning across dead leaves and rain-bleached litter, down to the sea. She stamps her foot again, where the harsh ankle skin is crinkling red.

'Fuck it! Go on! Fuck off!'

She sees the quiver of the foxy sides as it breathes, the lush snowy underbelly, the knowing mask of the face too close to hers. Flings suddenly a music book at it, and another, both slipping in her blood-slippery grasp. A cushion. Advances on the animal. Which just grins.

But he heard her, the way he always will. Wondered why she'd stopped playing, and came to see. There's that shadow at the front door again, showing through the stained glass, the crack widening. Footsteps in the hall, shoes reinforced with metal at the toes, a whiff of salt and eau de cologne on the air. A person with a purposeful, responsible aura, in contrast to the urban frivolity of the fox. A glimpse of the fluorescent vest and the ballistic trousers, protective enough for animal teeth, in contrast to her own scatty, bare, reddening legs in the summer skirt. A hand coming round the living room door, his fisherman's big black signet ring, the bold wedding band. The thumb ring a coiled gold snake.

'Everything okay in here?'

Gazes at her, spellbound. His enchantress, swamped by her art. Sees her with red hands and red feet. Red veins of anger trickling down her legs. The red dog ready to lick them off. But some things he's not afraid of. Not when he's charmed like this.

'Want him got rid of?'

'Oh, please! Would you? He won't go! What if he gets Finbar?'

What if he were to go into her son's room when no one was looking, at night, when all was quiet? His foul breath and yellow teeth on his white little neck? What if he then came and lay alongside her? And it's a brute more powerful than she is; won't be shooed away. She's as frightened as if she'd come up against a part of herself, impossible to dislodge. There's only one solution to a beast so persistent, so insidious, so hard to deter.

'Oh, please get rid of him!'

'Okay, honey...'

Here's a task he can do. Shakes his head at the dog fox, who stares back, blatant and unabashed. Goes back out, to the barrow by the front gate, returns with his shovel, stands, hesitating with it the length of his leg.

'Don't want to make a mess of your floor.'

They both look at the old wood boards in some disdain, that no one got round to sanding in the end. The fox lifts its head, sniffing the air as if scenting too late some call from the wild. Bonnie stands, hands raised, wrinkled to the knuckles with blood, legs apart and streaming; the red mage, against whom even the St Christopher medallion he wears doesn't protect him. He stares at her. She has only to lift a finger.

'Go ahead.'

'Stand back, then.'

And in a flash it's over. He brings his arms up above his head and whacks the shovel down hard, once, twice, three times. The scar along his arm bulging and whitening. A few grunts of terror, a yarp of agony, spill of fox urine and blood on old wood, a red dog with a mashed-red cheek for a face. The top of its head sliced off, brain matter spilling onto the wood boards.

'And that's the end of Mr Fox.'

Drag the body up by the hind legs, the bush bouncing behind, erect and dead, slap it into a heavy-duty bin bag which Bonnie holds open, stuff it into the barrow. He's not one of those road sweepers who prays for the insects he destroys as he digs at the weeds in the pavements. Brings in the cloth and the spray, cleans the floor, thoroughly, thoroughly. While she watches, standing erect, applying thick camomile ointment to her fingers with their many cracks.

'Now, what about the others?'

He has his own way of tracking them. Walks the length of the house from room to room, measuring the walls, the way he measures out the streets. From room to room, measuring the house out from end to end, sniffing in disapproval at the tumble of her clothes in the bedroom, at the towels dumped on the bathroom floor, that Austin left a mess. The red water in the sink that appears as she quickly washes. But a house with foxes in it is bound to be untidy. Scenting the vixen and cubs out, picking each one up from under beds, from cupboards, walking down the nervy, angsty feel of a fox-ridden house, from room to room, dutiful, stalwart, collecting them all, contemptuous of all the shadows that skitter wildly from wall to wall; comes down the stairs with his heaving armful, finally turns to her.

'You shouldn't be living with foxes, you know that. Shouldn't have anything to do with 'em. Why, the place is infested!'

He makes it plain that, whoever owns this house, it's not them, Bonnie and Austin.

'Well, we're going,' she flashes at him, defiant in her red-patterned skirt, her bare, reddened legs, her summer hair all out, then goes to the garden door, calls out, to any remaining foxes, to the cliff-top.

'Don't worry. We're going!'

Her voice echoes round the dead garden, returns from the chalk cliffs beyond. He looks at her, sober and sceptical. Arms full of wriggling foxes, his red gloves gripped round their tails, biting jaws under his arms.

'Open the garden shed for me.'

Arms full, he goes cautiously, impossibly, down the spiral staircase to the back garden and flings the armload into the shed. Shuts the door. Walks back to get his shovel, left at the front door. Stands a moment, looking slowly round the kitchen, the mauve roses, soft and blurred at the edges, in a vase on the table, one or two also pinned to either end of the mantelpiece with its welter of ornaments, above the black, broken-down range, so ostentatiously left in for ornament more than use. The table that's untidy with half-cut bread, crumbs and ragged crusts hardening, butter softening in the open wrapping, a fly buzzing at the jam, the coffee jar left open, newspapers, magazines, music, letters, all pushed up against another jumble of ornaments. Very different from his own clinical kitchen, the pristine surfaces and floor, the shiny table and tucked-in chairs, the two geraniums on the window sill, the neat pictures either side of the sink, the round pink kettle on the sideboard, the white fridge humming cleanly and covered with cheery magnets of the sort Bonnie would instantly throw out. With a little shake, goes on, past the open door of the living room, the sheeny chestnut brown of the piano, silently waiting. Pauses with beating heart to look at it; so shiny, so imposing. So evidently the real thing. No ornaments here; the clean, uncluttered lines, high and definite as a hearse. A silent site of hauntings. A magic musical box, holding the spirits of composers, to be released with care. His face takes on a haggard look, as of fear. He lives disconnected, floating from one moment to the next, a bright string of seconds interlinking to make up his day. Could he ever see himself living here? The temerity: in this house that repudiates him at every turn? How dare he kill foxes on the premises? He doesn't even dare go lift the piano cover, in case the keys should smell of blood.

His ringed hand pauses on the shovel handle. Turns back, meeting Finbar in his pyjamas coming down the stairs, who accepts him as another of the strange figures that haunt this place. Besides, they're friends now. They see enough of each other, all those hellos on the prom.

'Hello, son.'

'I had a dream about foxes,' Finbar tells him.

'It wasn't a dream. But if I were you I'd grab some breakfast and get back up to bed while we deal with them.'

Finbar doesn't need telling twice. He's seen the set look on the man's face, and his blood-stained shovel, and the spare pair of gloves which he somehow knows are for his mother. He's gone, a silent little ginger streak through hall and stairs.

Dominic pushes the shed door closed. Regards the foxes like a weather-seamed fur trader, acute, assessing, a voyageur set on skins in some little hut in the middle of the wilderness. Bonnie glowing, exposed and bleeding beside him, a newly washed raptor waiting for the kill. Already scenting more blood.

'Get them into the bin.'

They gather up the kits, leaping and circling round the hut; huddling and whimpering up to the mother, with their weird seagull chittering, nosing the door. Pick them up one by one, tip them into the wheelie bin and leave it rattling. Manoeuvre the vixen up between them, two legs each, and fling her in too; she's dense and wiry, heaving and stinky with a lactating roll to her belly and Bonnie has this odd, irrational fear that her legs are going to come out of joint at the sockets.

They start with the cubs as being more manageable, who go quiet at the last moment, hauled one by one out of the softly juddering bin. Stare up to the roof of the hut, that stillness to their eyes, the white and ginger fluff flaring round their snouts. The stillness of the wild when it gives up. They seem to acquiesce, staring into some sideways place, almost waiting for the blow. Bonnie holds them down one at a time, her hair falling over her face, her breathing harsh. Her hands in Dominic's big red gloves cover each kit's eyes for a moment before turning it front down, again holding the rear legs so the man can get a clear blow to the head with its soft ginger sheen. Three months of play, terminated here. The twist of his shoulders as he brings the shovel up, then straight down again, hard. A soft thud, and another. Muffled crunch of tender bones. The smell of blood and hot fur fills the hut.

'It's got to be done, Bonnie,' he tells her, blue eyes sober. 'They're vermin. The only way to get rid of them, or they keep coming back. You agree, don't you?'

She agrees. And it's a relatively swift way to go, being clubbed to death. Like being in love. Again she places her gloved hands over a kit's legs, the wayward open jaw, the snitching teeth biting on the air, turns her head away.

'And now,' says Dominic, breathing.

The vixen. She's lurking in the depths of the bin, which they tilt heavily down. Green eyes staring at them. Dominic tips the bin right over and she comes skeetering and sliding out, paws braced. She's not as dumb or arrogant as the dog, by no means as pliable as the cubs, for which she searches, circling and circling, while Bonnie stands guard before the soft, dead pile, kicking at her if she comes too close. Which she does, teeth bared. This one wants to survive.

With difficulty, Bonnie holds the animal down for him, sitting on her, balancing on this billowing of knobbly fur and small bones, holding the rear legs, while he places his foot on the twisting neck; aiming carefully to avoid Bonnie's hands, her much-insured, prize-winning hands. One of them round his knee, steadying herself, after each blow. His own hand briefly on Bonnie's head, his touch reassuring. The animal's foul breath on her wrists, seems to have grown almost as big as Bonnie, a woman in fur writhing beneath her. She doesn't die easily, the vixen, squeals and mud-faeces erupting, stiffening and shuddering, seizing again and again in an arc of outrage, fur and blood legs jerking and jerking, until his shoe, too, is red, filled, soaking and slipping as she convulses away from him. Dominic's face also convulsed in a rictus of intent. Bonnie pale as death, her eyes two round pools, hands already thrown off the vixen and clutched to herself in protection. The shovel blade coming down again and again on the vagina dentata of the mouth, full of red teeth. Plunging into the heart of the blood, her jaw a vulva biting blood, red wetting the hairs all round the muzzle, the shovel knocking against the teeth. Knocking the teeth out again and again, breaking them out of her open jaw, until he's made her into a mouth that's slippery with the supreme lubricant of blood, smooth and slithery as a fish. Until she rolls over in her final spasm away from him, her supreme protest; Bonnie also recoiled to the wall of the hut, spattered with blood.

'All done.'

All obstacles to love now battered down. The rival dog, the importunate cubs, the castrating bitch. Now Dominic can claim his bloodied bride, take her bloodied hand in his. Bonnie up to her elbows in blood, blood on his trousers, his socks and shoes soaked. Her head leant back against his thighs, her eyes closed, wan. His hand resting on her head while he rests, catching his breath. Returning, face pale. Both of them facing the small mound of cooling fur, extending its sleeping snouts. Blood spattered on her bare legs, on her skirt from where she sat on the dying vixen. Her own blood soaking through again to meet it, obeying the irresistible call of blood. Dead cubs hunched on their sides, like Finbar lying foetally asleep earlier. The fine line of the jaws stiff. The jackal legs curled slightly;

teeth parted in a baby dream of killing. A heavy pulpy mass of reddish fur she doesn't look at, not wanting to see fleas, flies already buzzing round the wounds. Eyes glazed, half-open. One of the kits with a clean blow slicing the back of the head round the back of the ears, its smile long, almost sleazy, a drunken glint to the half-closed eye.

'I'll get some bin bags. We'd better get rid of them quickly.'

Before anyone else can see, before Austin can return in any shape or form and start calling people, authorities. She doesn't want more of the council's environmental services round.

Bonnie tears off another bag, and another. Holds them open one by one for him to dangle and drop the bodies into, with their acute pong of fox, the tumble of their paws, their matted fur and incisions, their not-quite closed eyes; turning her face away again at each one, looking through the shed window.

'What's that?'

'What?' He turns round, too.

'The top of the steps, by the conservatory.'

'There's nothing there.'

He feared it was the kid again; she saw herself. Older, dressed in black, looking down into the garden, at the shed, remembering what was about to take place there.

'You're just wound up, Bonnie. Give me another bag and we're through.'

He ties the tops of the bags firmly; a job well done. Responsible, neat, contained, he looks, stacking each yielding bag by the door, beside her unkempt appearance, her hair out and matted into wisps at the front, her short skirt rucked, the untidy blood. Face a pallid glimmer of sweat, grey beneath her eyes. But he's got beneath her skin, entered her blood. He'll never get rid of her now.

'You look a mess.'

Vulnerable, open and red. Unlike his wife, who barely bleeds. Always so contained, hair wound and pinned back in the flat, careful chignon for the surgery. He'd never admit to Bonnie how he loves to untangle it, end of the day. Bonnie smiles, too.

'Yeah, and you're a control freak. Look, you've tidied up the whole hut as well.'

'It needed it.'

'I can't believe I've fallen for a tidy man.'

'Even tidy men have feelings.'

'Do they?'

'Sure. They just don't throw them around like rubbish, for other people to deal with.'

'Will I ever get the smell of fox off me.'

'Oh, you will. Don't worry. I've had to wash off worse.'

He gestures at the grey wall outside, overlooking the hut.

'Would you leave this house and live with me?'

She too looks up, through the cobweb black fur of the windows along the top of the hut, realises the house has seen everything.

'Oh, yes.'

'What, leave the piano and all?'

Sceptical, but more about his ability. He's got no home to offer her; that belongs more to the wife and mother-in-law, who put money into it; has saved nothing, can earn nothing. Doesn't even have enough money for a ticket home. His stepfather won't let his mother help him out, beyond the odd twenty dollars she sends the kids. He's chronically sick, disabled. Without prospects. And the wife would never let him go.

'Yes.'

'No room for the piano in my house, you know that. Couldn't even fit it through the door. Still would?'

'Yes. Anyway, I – I want to get away from this house.'

But the house would never let her go.

'Why? It's a good, big place. Bigger than my house, by far.'

'It frightens me.'

'Frightens you? It's just a house,' with male contempt and tolerance. Though it's true, it's not a place to make love, up there, with those walls watching.

'But I'd never – in there, you know—' with sudden heat. 'I tell you now.'

Not on Mr Fox's territory. Not in Mr Fox's bed.

'So you can put that out of your head. But apart from all that – there'll never be anyone else.'

'Promise?'

'Promise. That's my third promise, Dominic.'

'I know. You've had your lot now, can't make any more.'

'And you? Would you look after me? If I look after you?'

'Oh, yeah. The same for me, absolutely. I can promise you that. You're the only one in the world; there never could be anyone else.'

That utter tenderness. One smile linking them like a gentle beatification.

'Now you've got to keep them, those promises. So, remember. You've got to follow me, like you said. I'll be waiting.'

'To the ends of the earth.'

She half-turns to the softly bulging bags. Face glowing with the radiance of a woman who's made her choice. He, softly smiling, the green light tender in his eyes.

'Bin day tomorrow. I can keep them in the shed until then so the seagulls won't rip the bags apart.'

'Don't worry, I said, sweetheart. I'll get 'em taken to the dump. Put them out on the corner for the van.'

'Come in for a wash.'

'Uh-huh.'

'You could have a cup of tea as well.'

Just another day on this enchanted isle, that they created between them. Lost in two worlds of their own. With glowing hearts they turn to each other and start taking off their gloves.

'And after this,' he says, 'I want to hear you play.'

THE ENCHANTED ISLE

The Plains of Waterloo. Quebec Avenue, Meeting Street, Paragon. Geshwind Avenue, Michael's Road, Sea Street, Vincent Street, King Street, Lennox Street, Gastaut Road, Albion. Ville-Marie. The St Christopher Way. Barrett Close, Fagg Close, Concession Road, Prospect Terrace, Paradise. Glen Yards. Mount Royal.

They all link up in a magic network, spin out into the back streets and alleys, to the flat patchwork of fields that make up this isle shaped like a brain. Criss-crossing it like inter-chattering neurons, the old dual carriageway running into it like a brainstem from the outside world. Where no sheep graze, no owls call.

Cut off at the neck. A brain enclosed, that talks to itself and nobody else. No contact, the outside world too far away to touch here. Waste Island. Bobbing in the ocean in the middle of nowhere. Convinced that its own neuronal solipsism is reality. Where relationships can never progress but circle endlessly, messages rampaging the neural circuits, round and round; only exist there, nowhere else, a memory endlessly replaying itself. All those under its enchantment for ever held to their promises, never able to cross the river, back to the mainland and real city.

Waste Island, with its flat marshes, cabbage fields, salt winds, dog-blasted beaches, its natives who stare instead of saying good morning. The kind of place where no matter how long you stay, you're homesick. No trees beyond a few spindly trunks on the cliff-top, whose tops also are shaped like brains, like newborns' heads through the birth canal, elongated by the wind. A few sad sycamores in the town centre. Otherwise, just stunted, slanted bushes on the sand, twigs, seaweed and shale that make up the fringe of this island. Where the wild goose makes the minimum stopover en route for the Arctic tundra. And the sea shushes out all bird noises except for the cry of seagulls that was made to pierce through it.

The place where time stops still, where summers replay themselves. Where that capitalist illusion – progress – that keeps London beating doesn't exist; where you don't have to face pain with two hands held open because pain, which comes from thwarted desires and ambitions, doesn't exist here. No progress, no striving, no memory, no pain. Dominic can never feel any pain. His only signs of ageing will be from exposure. Wind and cold, sun and the sea air will form the great lines that pull his eyes down in years to come.

*

Find me; come find me. I'm waiting. I'm on the corner of King Street, I'm walking the esplanade. I'm following tide out by the harbour, collecting you shells and memories, I'm picking up love in the street. Meet me on Mount Royal; let's rescue each other from Waste Island. Drop me treasures to find on pavements, silver fishes and rings. Leave me messages in the gutter, throw your heart away for me to pick up and keep. Meeting Street was named after us. Write me in the dust of the road, let the rain come and wash it away. Sonnets on the sands for the tides to read, foot by rolling foot, as the sea gains dominion over the land. Leave me a rose on Royal Road, where we settled our differences, write me into a book of love that'll last for evermore.

Where are you?

Start with the island's heart, the multi-storey car park, that grand summer palace where the street cleaners have their residence. Open to all the airs of this isle and the scurries of sand from the harbour opposite. At night it resounds to the boom of the sea, to the memory of a town's summer quarrels, echoes of car doors slamming, the wind whining down the lift shaft. The ghosts of rejected lovers walk the floors, looking for the way out, for a glimpse of the moon out to sea. Generations of babies conceived on the roof by the town's teenagers. Come find me in the aching summer dawns that arrive hours before the street cleaners do, the litter slowly tumbling over the spaces like wounded seagulls. Sea-mist rising clammy through the levels; stairwells filled with the thick glue of urine. Trailings of seaweed on the entry; maybe seal-women visited during the night, lolling up the ramp with the tide, looking for human males. Siren songs, whistle of the wind. Find me.

But Dominic's still hunched, yawning over his hash browns and bacon, in his little house on the St Michael estate, nodding to the wife for more coffee, while she's buzzing around filling his lunch box. Keep the king of the road happy. The nurse. She does things for him Bonnie would hardly do; Bonnie would hardly make him as comfortable. The youngest child clambers onto his lap, damp and sweet with night, mouth open for morsels which he feeds her assiduously, sleepily. And Bonnie's gone, along the seafront where the waves roll orange metal beneath the rising sun. The piano calling her with every beat; every step taking her further and further away. They hurt in the same secret place, she and Dominic; but the difference is that she's free to roam. Could even go to the island's strip of runway where the little planes take off for the mainland, bobbing wings and noses spinning across the sea. Whereas Dominic's even now heaving up his garage door to get his bike, to make the same ride to work, taking the same five or six minutes, to relive the same day along the same streets. Bonnie can have a different day every day if she wants.

They arrive. There are seven of them. Seven angels to guard Waste Island and pick it clean of human trash. Bonnie can tick them off as they come lurching and limping in, watching, arms folded, from a corner of the car park. They're all people to her now, the habitants of her half-world: Percy the shambling alcoholic, who was a solicitor in this town for thirty years; Graham, serene in his pork pie hat, his deaf aid, his mended cleft palate; Simon with his gargoyle leer and wandering eye, head nodding and nodding, dragging his club foot; Wayne, just out of prison and still grinning defiance; Nathan, who goes round plugged into his headphones learning Mandarin Chinese and doesn't speak to the public; Jack, the builder who fell on hard times after his daughter went over the cliff and the wife went to pieces; Dominic, fallen from the skies, swinging off his bike at the entry. The poor, the halt, the maimed. Go out quickly into the streets and lanes of the city. The ground floor, dappled with early sunlight, echoes to their shouted badinage; magical beings who pass through doors no one else knows exist, the grey battered doors of the lift, the doors marked Emergency Exit Only, along the corridor of congealing pee to the unmarked door of the break room. That haven of male camaraderie, a conglomeration of broken-down armchairs, the torn posters of females in awkward positions, and on the table at the side, all the odd things they've picked up in the street. They fling the doors open; the smell of coffee drifts into the morning. Dominic's out at once, his swinging stride.

Enchantment, like the snap of an owl's beak. Like the sting of a needle. Rectal Valium. Shoved up you to st-st-stop st-st-status epi-epi-epilepticus. That brown twilight where the seizures won't stop, dull-eyed flickers across the neurons hour after hour, or full violent paroxysms with universal convulsions and coma. A memento of love on a hospital bed, curtains drawn. His wife's cool hand administering. That's what brought them together, in the A&E no holiday should be without. Enchanted at having escaped the real world, he played around with the drugs just a little too long; pretended he was normal, that he could do without them. This would be the year he'd be able to give them up; it'd all be different here, away from the mainland and all its procedures. Too defiant by half. Then he opened his eyes to see her at his bedside, a chill blonde angel. She smelt like all the nurses that had ever haunted his childhood and her hand was on him.

Seagulls floating, white knots in a crying, billowing net way above his head. The loveliest skies in Europe. The wide, empty esplanade, swept clear of all people. Sea roses blowing along the cliff-top, washed of colour by the breeze. The ghost ferry, a square box drifting in to this strange planet spinning off the coast of England.

Permanent holiday. His wife buggering him with the diazepam syringe; the ecstasy of her taking all the responsibility; her gloved fingers, sachet of lubricant jelly. Shove it up me hard, honey. With his wife he felt something he never felt before: safe. He came over to this island once on holiday and was told he need never go back to the real world again.

*

On his trail, following the route he's walked. Looking for pavements brushed clean and combed, their partings neat in the middle. Counting dead bodies of bin bags slumped on street corners; for the scatter of trash that warns of his approach. A red rosebud in the gutter, to show he passed this way. Hearts chalked on pavements. A pink arrow atop a black bin, waft of salt on the breeze, luring her on. Mornings opening out. His shirt softening across his back. Works on, at his slow best. Eyes turned down, or looking over the shoulders of the crowd, self-enwrapped, remote; sees and hears everything. Every flicker of every passer-by. Every move she makes. He never whistled for anyone. Who's following him, like a woman possessed?

An enchanted isle is the only place to hide. It sinks away out of sight every night at sunset, rising again in a golden morning mist.

On Boundary Road they vow undying love, on London Road take it back; swear that neither time nor tide will separate them on Sea Street; divide for ever on South Shore Road. Ignore each other on the high street, stick to opposite ends of the prom. Agree to migrate to the mainland on Quebec Avenue; get as far as the beach. He's walking the tideline like a fisherman, looking out to sea for the catch that darkens the waves. A strange marine sea, not England; at his side, some mermaid he landed, her tail between his legs, tripping him. He falls, entwined, to the sand. A great fall to another land, as from the Sea King helicopter hovering low and yellow out to sea; dizzying down not to land or sea but to sand, insides churning. He spreads her, trembling like a fisherman's net, his thumb's spreading her open, she's hooked like the fish on his thumb, his slightest movement enough to make her bend and move. He has her impaled on his thumb, has only to jerk it for her to jerk and die like the fish. Faces pallid, beading sea water. Helpless murmur of endearments, like the enlapping wavelets. The susurrus of the surreal waves, an intensity of aqua tipped with white at their feet. She convulses against him, he stiffens and quivers like the fish. But he never goes to the beach.

The enchanted island, where a man's footsteps keep time with his soul.

Find me. We can walk the same streets, watch the same skies bunching out to sea, slate-grey etched against clarity. I know that wherever I go I tread in your footsteps, that you've passed this way a hundred times. No passage you haven't travelled, in this small town, no shop window that hasn't taken your reflection. You've got a map of love in your head: Quebec Avenue, Mount Royal Avenue, Penfield Avenue, Mountain Street, McGill Street. From street to street, from the river to the ends of the earth.

Across the road his eyes light up green as sun on waves and his smile is like the changes of the moon, uncanny. Bonnie doesn't know how changeable he is. She swears she'll track him for as long as he draws her, he vows to call her until the stars fall into the sea. He holds up a hand to stop the traffic for her, she divides the waters to let him pass. She vows to follow him barefoot with the tides, back and forth until time runs dry; he swears he'll stop time itself for her. He has the power; didn't he do just that when they made love on the roof of the carpark, didn't he silence her, by taking her to the country of no time; doesn't he do it for himself a few sacred seconds so many times a day? That sacred feeling stealing up his arm, numbing his mouth; he looks upwards, as if summing up, blinking, chewing hard and rhythmic; neck arrested, staring at the sky. And he's gone, off into eternity again. Shrugs his shoulders, hand groped at his front. No longer sees her next to him, no longer feels her touch on his arm. Half those summer days she's pursuing someone who isn't there.

*

Epilepsy is an enchanted island. But only solitary voyagers can travel there. By special dispensation, by enchantment, by a great fall in a dream. Bonnie, who fell in love with his distance, doesn't know that he's always visiting his own private isle, alone. For a few seconds, for a minute or two, what does time matter, in that absence? He has no real time for her, always departing as she arrives. She doesn't know she can charm him there; that the drugs are powerless against her, that love sends him out of time and out of control.

So bland-faced, just that quiver at the mouth and hand, from invisible currents in his brain, movement snaking over it like the waves of the sea. That ocean of chaos held back in constant check by the drugs; seizures like wavelets flickering and retreating, dipping him in and out of consciousness. Bonnie doesn't know that love is like a tidal wave. That by pursuing him she is becoming his epilepsy, his true stalker.

Find me, follow me, if you dare. I'm waiting.

Looking out. He's always looking. For Bonnie, who knows the hairs on his head are all numbered, all the cells of his brain ticketed. For his wife, who knew she'd always have to compete with his condition. For the aggressive public, who can land you in hospital with a broken jaw faster than you know it. For the mother-in-law, who saw him talking to Bonnie. For the recording angel, who's keeping note of all this for judgement day. He's out all day, visible in all weathers. Vulnerable to attack. Played with his control and paid for it; is still paying for it.

He never knows when he's going to see her next, what street she's suddenly going to appear on. She comes along and starts another conversation and there's the sound of destiny falling into place. She doesn't seem to have a routine, or ties. Her music, her child, seem like things she can pick up and drop at will. The child has a place at nursery mornings; but then she appears afternoons, without him, her eyebrows a question mark. Says the father's looking after him, that aggressive redhead; or that he's with his grandmother for a few days. Says she's off to give a lesson. To give a small lunchtime concert, to a likely audience of seven; would he care to attend? When does she practise? Shop? Do her housework? A bright bird of prey, shimmering in the distance; he can see her from one end of the harbour to the other. There's no hiding her. She's always round the next corner, coming up from behind; he startles round to see. She's not under control. Her footsteps coming towards him. From behind, ahead, around, above. She sees him tremble on Sea Street and think it's with desire, on Glen Yards feels him shake. She knows he's sweating wherever he goes. Waits until she feels the longing coming from him, then drifts out, to meet it.

She never knows what he's going to remember. He's disconcerting. Remembers that bit different from everyone else. How many hours it is since they first met; how long they might have left. He remembers everything she's told him. How could it be otherwise, when entire conversations replay themselves in his head? With the weight of so many behind him, he can never have just one. You can see that in the flicker of his eyes sometimes. Each new encounter becomes more difficult. But how is he going to get through his life without her? He begins well. But he has to keep beginning because he's always being interrupted; his day is a series of beginnings. He doesn't know how he's going to get through his life, because every day his life begins a hundred times.

He never knows where he's going to have her next, in what enchanted nook or cranny: down some cellar doorway, along the corridor by the seafront casino, in flagrante in the street. The public conveniences on the prom where a notice warns that a male cleaner is in attendance: on Bonnie, on the floor of the tiny office with the frosted glass and the crooning radio, her hand on his neck. Towers of loo rolls teetering all around them. Round the back of the La Métropole hotel, on Foy Beach in a hurry against the incoming tide, against the gloom of the car park wall. By the lift he tumbles forwards into the void, the closing doors swallow him up, he spins into infinity down the shaft. Her back arched over the prom railings, she goes falling down the endless chalk, her cry floating back up, the cry of all girls who go over the cliff. She won't make arrangements; says she'll find him. How does she do that? He walks seven miles a day. Yet her homing instinct is infallible. From coast to coast, from end to end of this isle, she can sense the slightest movement he makes; closes in on him remorselessly.

Who's watching him? His supervisor, grey and lean and keen-eyed, cruising by in the van. One or two of the others, when their paths cross, like solitary explorers in Labrador. The grand twenty-six tonne garbage truck itself, far beyond him, the guys seated up there three abreast like the triple eye of God. The people of this town, who pay his wages. His wife. Those early mornings she's summoned from her bed to go down the town and pick him up because he's had one of his turns in the car park depot, just before they all go off on their rounds for the day. His colleagues standing round in silent sympathy, he coming round slowly, face in hands, slumped on a chair: Please don't call an ambulance. Please don't call an ambulance. They know not to do that; the wife came down and spoke to them special: On no account call an ambulance. Her headlights in the dark of the multi-storey, the slam of the door, the quick patter of her footsteps, her unbrushed hair a halo round her angel's head. Come on, sunshine, let's get you home. Get you cleaned up.

Bonnie couldn't cope with that. He already has the perfect wife. And he's pretty perfect, too; keeps house and garden neat, can cook anything he wants to, darns his own socks and is ready with his rough comfort when his wife comes home weary from her evening shift; such a darling. And so dedicated to his work; you could set your watch by him. Bonnie doesn't get it at all. Why does he work so hard? Is he in love with a tidy town or what? She's free; a ship adrift. Call her the *Perseverance*. Can't he cut loose, as she's done? But it's his third job on Waste Island, and he's got as many kids; and he needs the drug of manual labour as much as the money; turns his back, walks off.

He looks so free. Whereas he's thoroughly institutionalised, in his open prison, this town which counts every one of his footsteps.

She solicits him along Concession Road, lurks just out of conversation range on Vincent Street; lounges opposite on Laval Lawn, watching him sweep; smiles at his irritated glances. Ambushes him on the prom, waylays him on Westmount. Taunts him again on Paragon, disappears; but he knows she's just out of sight, waiting, and it ruins his day.

Where he can catch her finally at the harbour bus stop, his aggressor, pin her against the quivering glass pane, because the people here, dumpily waiting with their dumpy shopping, dumping their litter, are blind to love. Where there's no one else there, just the wind, blowing sparse sand into the shelter, the sea untidily rolling on the other side. His hand on her belly, its faint, silvery striae and mauve pulls, its slight lingering softness from childbirth. Just them and the island.

'Town bad this morning?'

'Oh, it's a mess. —So were you out last night, throwing rubbish about?'

'I was out, but I behaved myself.'

'What: like you're doing now?'

Summer sweat pouring from her armpit onto his shoulder as she strives to contain him. She's released a ball of electric energy she can't control, it's rolling her all over the shelter. He's shuddering and slumping heavy down her, she has to hold him up. Afterwards, limp, sprawled against her.

'Why don't you like him, then, your husband?'

'He doesn't need tenderness.'

'But he comes from a rich family.'

'Can you see it?'

'See it coming right off him.'

Kissing his bitten mouth, sponging it better with her tongue. Convulsion is always a shock to witness; the pallor, the cyanosis, the uncontrollable movements of the limbs, the unearthly cry which signals it all off. His cry as he falls can be heard all over town. But she doesn't notice. She thinks it's just love.

Enchantment like a lover's bite, almost through the lip. His silences. His absences. Those days when he nods in passing from that great distance, or looks over her head as he walks on by. When he stops for his coffee at 9.30am, on the pavement outside the bakery, and stares across the road at her before turning back to his colleagues for some exclusive male banter; the mothers' meeting, she calls it. When she rages at him. He's coarse, vulgar, married; the way his jaw hangs, coarse. Those afternoons when she dawdles after him down the alleys, laying down a psychogeography they'll be condemned to tread and retread, day in, day out, for years to come. Where the hollyhocks harden and the loudest sound is the seethe of his breath as he turns and sees her there, again. Then he stabs between the nettles with the litter grab, hard-mouthed; pushes his dustcart on. And still she follows. Her back against the wall of an overgrown garden, love demanded and seized with both hands in garden sheds. Hearing the faint chatter and shriek from the beach; the occasional drone of the helicopter going out to look for someone the lifeboat can't locate. His broad fingers, with their chipped nails, tangled in her hair; himself tangled in the roots of her throat. Bitch, he says, you cock-sucking bitch, swallow me, go on, swallow me, darling come find me, find me please come find me and never let me go again. His eyes close, he disappears, into that void. But it's of his wife he thinks when he makes love to Bonnie.

At the top of Mount Royal she gives him her book of love to keep for ever; he throws it back, says he can't take it, that there's nothing between them. They separate on the hill, stalk down on opposite sides; reunite by the supermarket at the bottom, which floods every time it rains. Walk down King Street together, walking swiftly together, stride for stride. She begs him to come away with her, not to spend his life here on this nowhere job, endlessly walking the streets of this nowhere town, to come to London.

'I probably will,' he says, smiling at her kindly, with all the creases of his eyes, and she knows it's hopeless.

She takes her book of love and rips it apart. Sets it free, sets it loose. Scatters the pages one windy night when stars are blowing all through the streets and out to sea. The thick pages disperse in chunks, whipped into separateness by the wind. Already as she leaves she sees a passer-by pick one of them up and look at it, curious, as it buffets against her ankle. The papers blow up into the wind. More work for him tomorrow. That night she dreams he's the hook and she's the fish; wakes with a metallic taste in her mouth that's somehow familiar. From when she was first pregnant with Finbar.

*

The blessed isle, where Austin lost a wife. Saw her spinning off into the sea winds, blonde hair haloed out. Find me find me find me...

SAFE HOUSE

The house saw everything, watched everything they did in the hut together. Perched atop the cliff-top, Concordia used to look out for ships in distress on the treacherous sands seven miles out, and the view extends right round, all over town, into every derelict garage and hidden doorway, down every weed-sprayed pathway and secret passage, beneath the littered arch of the railway bridge, the beach shelter that didn't shelter Bonnie and Dominic, with the grey benches that splintered further beneath them. Nothing escapes its surveillance. Watches them both down every last street and alley. Right down Harbour Street and the esplanade to the end of Glen Yards which gives out onto mud flats, sunken boats, half-swallowed buoys. While she was stalking Dominic, the house was stalking her. It heard their every whisper of love, weighed every drop of sweat, measured every kiss; recorded it all, their shattered words becoming part of its fabric.

A house that absorbs memories is a dangerous place to be. When Bonnie returns from tormenting Dominic, at dusty 4pm, it's to have her own torturer close in around her. Concordia's a lover that knows how to make her writhe, embraces her in that special way as she steps in, with the pinch of reminiscence. *Je me souviens.* Starts replaying her day as she comes through the huge front hall with its remnants of red carpet, the two antique gilded mirrors reflecting the crystal chandelier and each other to infinity. Reflecting Bonnie, a whirl of disintegration penetrating deep on each side, sunburnt, hair blonded again and salt-stiffened, the street glare in her eyes. Welcome home. To the faint, lingering smell of cat pee, that other indefinable dankness that fills the nostrils; to a house that won't be tidied, stacked with the crates they never unpacked, full of possessions they no longer own, the moving carrier bags en route to the charity shop, migrating up and down the stairs and all over the house without ever departing. That small upstairs bedroom full of junk that Bonnie dare not explore, let alone throw out; all the witch's other leavings that keep turning up from attic to cellar: burnt saucepans, fur stoles, candles and candelabra, sprays of fake Madonna lily. *Je me souviens.* A house that never escapes its boundaries, like some vast province far away. So big you don't know if anyone else is in or not.

Such houses are sites of tenure, possessed places where thought, emotion, spirit, may have manifestations other than bricks and mortar. May have spaces that are precarious, standing structures that announce its dissolution. This house of rooms that are there one day and not the next, stairwells that give out after a few twists, doors that open onto the void. The birds flying in the wall, shapes bulging outwards all up the stairs. Why does Bonnie run up to her own attic every afternoon with her hard-earned cup of tea, freezing the roof's constant shuffle? What music does the house play in return to freeze her blood?

Concordia is one of those crossover points where the potential of architecture and poetry meet. A space for possibilities, for entities to be more than themselves, mediating between abstraction and fragmentation. It's haunted, by unfulfilled potential. It was built for watching, not living. For waiting for the next wreck to come along. Bonnie shouldn't be in such a house, but in the air, free as a bird. But she runs upstairs to the attic as if running for safety.

Just as Dominic's tumbling off his bike at the end of his cul-de-sac, the blast of exhaustion coming off his face, to go and lie full length in his secluded garden that runs parallel to the railway line just beyond the high steel fence. Shirt off now he's private, showing the flying goose tattoo on the small of his back and Bonnie's love bites puffed on his shoulder, that he begged her not to inflict, which the wife touches reminiscently. Mosquitoes? An allergic reaction? Smear of cold antiseptic cream, and that's the summer day wiped out. Flung onto the sunbed as onto a lifesaving raft; it's shipwreck without Bonnie, shipwreck with her. He's asleep beneath the breathing pines before the wife can bring out his own hard-earned red-and-white mug; she places it down quietly and stands looking at his back.

His garden is his space for possibilities, with its sideways strip of lawn and flower banks, sea pinks, blue cornflowers delicately pricked up; not the clean blonde house that barricades it. A sensible choice, not overlooked, at the end of this little street with its hard, dry, working-class frontages. The garden's a clean, well-tended place, slap bang up against the railway where the trains roll their last into the terminal, brakes wheezing and fluting. Trains almost going over his toes as he stretches his legs, just beyond the garden fence. But they made it nice. Bushes to screen the railway line, paths where the pebbles look as if they'd just rolled out of the waves, sea-cleaned. An urban garden, for show, full of little patches, a flowerbed here, a plant in a tub there, all under control. A neat pile of gardening tools, solid, clean plastic watering cans; the right tool for every job. They're all hot to the touch, with a warm, plastic smell, the garden a golden strip, sun pouring in. The wife arranges the shade at the side of the sunbed. Bonnie'd never take such care of him. She'd let him burn.

Tea's laid on the garden table, solid, good quality wood, that he put together to last a long time, unlike Bonnie and Austin, who make do with cheap metal and plastic fold-up things that rust and break each season, though they decorate them with fancy shades. The two boys are zinging up and down on the trampoline round the side, oblivious, until they see their mother standing there. They climb down at once, sent hot and scuffling to wash their hands, sit at table, kicking each other in a wordless dialogue. The family eat quietly, even father-in-law, sidling off soon to his internet dating site at the public library, even the toddler queen, small mouth pursed thoughtful round her food, eyes on the recumbent figure on the sunbed. He wakes a few minutes before the wife leaves for work at the evening surgery, face marked in two strips from the plastic cushion, sits in silence to the cold chips and congealed pork chop. No one ventures to ask if he wants them heated in the microwave. The three kids retreat into the garden hut, where their toys are kept. His wife, neat and blue in her uniform, puts a fresh lot of salad in front of him, pins on her watch, and runs.

In the summer evenings, Bonnie has the house to herself, all three floors and basement, all listening out for the shuffling in the attic to restart. Long beams of golden dust rising from the streets. Maybe the ghost of a cat behind the quivering curtains on the second-floor landing, basking in those last rays. The golden notes floating and dancing slowly up and down the stairs. Here she's safe. Until the phone calls begin, strange manifestations from another world; Austin hard and clipped, a warrior ghost striding through the mists of time, Finbar quavering and whispering like a little shade from Hades. Bonnie herself a spirit summoned grudging down to take the call in the huge front bedroom overlooking the harbour. The room's full of memories of the living, with its unmade ornate iron double bed, covers heaped almost ceiling high. But Bonnie's moved into the attic, with a single mattress and a dormer window open to the sky.

'Bonnie?'

His voice is sharp, with that edge of exultation she knows so well from his student days.

'Yes.'

Who else could it be, of the multitudinous possibilities swarming in this house? But her voice sounds strange.

'Are you all right? Sure? I do wish you'd keep your mobile switched on; I've been trying to get you all day. I've had a really good offer. Look, could you handle it down there if I went to America for a couple of weeks?'

'I should think so.'

'You know, get some people down to stay. Sally can bring Finbar back any time, stay with you a day or two. Or you pop up and collect him. I mean, you're coming up sometime soon anyway, aren't you? It's lovely up here, we've just taken Finbar over the bridge to Battersea Park. Gorgeous light on the river. Copper gold.'

And if she listens, she can hear that this river has already left her behind. Then the jubilation can't be kept out of his voice any longer: but a really good offer, some conference they want covered. Impossibly palmy, a fantastic job, the type you just don't get any longer, in these austere days.

'What about your passport?'

'I've got it.'

'So you knew this was going to happen.'

'I had an inkling, yes.'

'Don't tell us or anything.'

But she doesn't care. His secrecy is her freedom, absolving her.

'Ah well, it was more likely not to materialise.'

'So you've escaped Waste Island.'

'Sorry about that, Bonnie.'

It was bound to be some time. Oh, and it'll mean postponing the move back to London, of course. Not that they could do it much earlier unless she wanted to stay with Sally, of course. He's given the tenants notice and the lease'll be up on Hammersmith the third week in August. Just time to move back in and get Finbar off to school, even if they are just camping for the first few weeks. Can she bear it, being stuck on Waste Island for a few weeks longer?

'Oh,' – just before he rings off – 'and how are the foxes?'

'The foxes? The council sent someone round. You rang them, obviously.'

'No, not yet. So word gets round effectively enough on the enchanted island, does it?'

'Well, they've gone.'

Dominic saw them off the premises, bags gathered in one hand, pausing while she stood to reach up to give him one last kiss.

'Already? I thought they were well-nigh impossible to get rid of. What did they do, the council?'

'Battered them to death.'

'Oh – jolly good.'

It's the only thing that gives him pause in the entire conversation. She slams the phone down. And in a frenzy puts everything to wash: all Austin's clothes, gathering them up by her fingertips from bathroom and bedroom, all the sheets, stripping that high bed, all the towels, every one of which still seems infiltrated with a foxy smell.

*

'Bonnie. It's Sally.'

'I know.'

'I wasn't sure it was you. How's things? How're you getting on in the land of garden gnomes? And apparently they've all escaped the factory and are walking the streets, right? On the prowl, looking for a good time. Hey, could you fancy an ornamental concrete man? Austin sure did make me laugh, I never knew there were factories actually made concrete gnomes. I always thought they reproduced the way the rest of us do, when no one was looking.'

'Some of us could use a little IVF.'

'Oh, Christ! I'm sorry, Bonnie. So things are still…'

'Yes, if that's what you're ringing up to find out. Won't he tell you? Austin and I do fuck, but nothing comes of it.'

Bonnie is Bonnie still, hard and cutting as ice, unmanageable. What's possessed her to speak to her darling Sally in that way? Just when she needs a confidant, too.

'Sorry. Really sorry.'

'Well – we all fuck. And I understand it's a sensitive subject… Listen, honey. The boys want to stay a little longer. Well – you heard about Austin's trip. My God, he's thrilled. He reckons it's not worth coming back down there just for a day or two. He can take what he needs from here, clothes and things. Yeah, he's still got so much stuff stored here.'

Just like a first wife talking to a second wife.

'Sorry? Bonnie?'

'Nothing.'

'So he won't be back before he leaves. Okay with you? Not going to join us yourself, see him off? Well, every woman needs solitude, tell me about it. Getting plenty of practice in?'

'Yes.'

'What's the matter with Finbar?'

He's been trailed around like a mascot, that's what. A little totemic creature. Wherever Austin wants to take him. His very own toy fox cub.

'What do you mean?'

'He's kind of quiet. Isn't saying too much. Has he been sick?'

'No. Not that I know of.'

'I mean, he's fine. Just a bit clingy. Quiet. Might be going down with something.'

'Yes.'

'Are you on your own, Bonnie? Or do you have company? I can ring back.'

She has company all right, glances round the huge room that used to be the watch-house's main office, with its four windows loped with velvet curtains, two onto the harbour, two onto the open sea. The triple-mirror mahogany dresser piled with trinkets, antiques, ornaments, her various hand creams, the most expensive of which she used up on Dominic this afternoon in a phone box. The photo of Austin, looking out like a wizard. Their wedding photo, Austin in his kilt, Bonnie in her knee-length ivory silk ruffles. Books spewed over the table, newspapers, half-empty bottles of wine and unfashionable vermouth, stained crystal glasses, Austin's collection of antique daggers, boxes overflowing with strings of pearls. A sea-chest spilling over with evening dresses, shawls, scarves. Well-worn teddies and dolls with staring china faces and yellowed lace piled pell-mell with velvet cushions in a huge armchair. A self-conscious Remington typewriter on a school desk in the corner, a pile of typescript in small, black, dogged type. The heap of her soiled underwear and summer-stained skirts, blouses and dresses which she couldn't bring herself to put in the washing machine alongside Austin's clothes. Dominic still refuses to come to the house, but she'd never invite him up here anyway, his gasp of horror at the mess; his fingers would be itching to tidy it all up. She can just see him, turning to her at the end of two hours' hard work, every pillow corner in place, beaming: There. Now that's better, darling, eh?

'So maybe he's just missing you. Sure you don't want to come up?'

'I can't, Sally. I'm on a roll.'

'With the music? Well, that's good news. Austin said how you'd been giving a few local concerts.'

Bonnie puts the phone down on the bed, leaving the tentative voice quacking away to the summer evening, strolls out to the landing where the window overlooks the back garden. Down there are the ribs of the sixteen foot foy boat that used to venture out to rescue stranded sailors. Sailors facing death neither on land nor at sea but in sand. The tunnel through the cliff down to Foy Beach said still to exist, its opening beneath the garden shed. The boat landlocked, weeds growing through the grey spars. Who'll foy Bonnie? Not Austin; he's gone home now, to a river gleaming with the last of the evening sun. Who rescue her, stuck on her sands? No shadow at the front door, come visiting the summer evenings; that shadow's reclined on the cream faux-leather sofa before the glass coffee table and huge flat screen TV, whose switched-off screen reflects the summer clouds. The living room's basic neatness pulsating through the abandoned toys on the shiny teak floor and oatmeal pile rug. Black and white prints of ships, insistently smart and stylish. His sketches, pastels and charcoals, the skyline of some city far away, ethereal, gaunt: glass skyscrapers, high-rise offices, pavilions, stadium, dome, cruciform office tower, basilicas, oratory, queen of the world cathedral. The family photos, of any man's children and any man's wife, blonde and considering, a kind of lingering, speculative simplicity, chin tilted; by her look, he's taking the photo. French doors open to the garden bounded by the railway line and the high fence. The wife herself guarding the front door, his lemonade in one hand, sandwich plate in the other. Kids ring-fenced all over the house; can see through walls even when most deeply absorbed in games – where you going, Dad? The ghetto street outside, populated by local characters, who'd all clock him leaving, too; she never lets him out in the evenings, not unaccompanied. Father-in-law: popping out for a swift one, mate? can I come? The mother-in-law, never too far off, would see the slit in the door widening before he ever got a chance to step through.

She caught him just as he fell, his wife, stepping back through the front door in her uniform, back from the evening surgery; always just in time. He was about to leave. Had just opened the door; she thought it was to look out for her, coming down the street. She saw him, looking fixedly along. And then he fell, backwards into the hall, arms flung out in repudiation, a great fall into another land. She was just in time. Always catching him as he falls, as Austin used to catch Bonnie when she flung herself backwards, wilful child and artist, over the void. Like the child's game of trust, where you fling yourself backwards into waiting arms. Half-fell with him, the weight of him, her bag scattered down the hall, laying him front down on the clean corridor of this house where he can safely fall.

Where did Foy Beach get its name? The locals talk of foying, the practice of rowing out to rescue those in peril on the sea. Austin might quote Spenser, who used foy to mean allegiance, from the French *foi*, faith. In Scottish dialect, a foy was what Sally gave Austin and Bonnie at their wedding, a farewell salute or gift given to a person departing on a journey. They had bagpipers. Foy comes from the Dutch dialectal *fooi*, from Middle Dutch *foye*, journey, from Old French *voie*, way, voyage, from Latin *via*, road. It all goes back to the road. There are no new metaphors. Life is a journey, the way a road. What do you give someone who's always departing round street corners? All a man needs to be on the road all day is a map in his head. A mug of water. Solitude.

Bonnie replaces the phone on the hook, because left off it emits a piercing whine after five minutes, and she can't find a way of turning the old-fashioned appliance off, or even down, while the plug seems to be buried in the wainscot. It's a beast of a phone, a squat black devil with a circular dial. Its ring shrilling all over the house. So maybe she could sleep in the garden shed, to get away from it. But you can hear it ringing even at the end of the garden.

'Bonnie. Hello darling.'
    'Where are you calling from?'

Silence. She doesn't ask who it is although it's not Sally, nor her own mother, nor any of her women friends, nor, she would imagine, Dominic's wife, though the two of them would dearly love a chat sometime. But that might go better face to face.

'Why didn't you answer the phone before?'

'I've been running for the phone all evening. It hasn't stopped.'

'I've been calling all evening, love.'

The voice has the coo of real concern. Like the maternal presence of the house. The rate at which she's living, Bonnie's going to need some kind of mother, and she's just cut Sally off. She's sure of one thing. It's a London voice. A kind of East End gurgle, a faint sultry roll. Her one fear; that it's coming from the roof right above her head. But Bonnie's cool. She might really be talking to her own mother.

'Couldn't you get through?'

'Where have you been, Bonnie? You haven't been here all this time, have you?'

'I – I went for a walk.'

'You should take your mobile. Where did you go?'

'Down the harbour.'

'I know where you've been. You don't need to tell me...'

A streetwalker by the blowing shadows of the port, past the sails and poles clanking, past the cafés with their flapping awnings, down to the *quartier dangereux*. So who would watch her stroll down?

'...Me, of all people. You've been out walking again.'

'I just said I went for a walk.'

'No, you've been walking. I saw you.'

Walking, walking; a ghost, a streetwalker, walking

herself into an altered state of consciousness, walking herself into that other place.

'You thought Austin would save you, didn't you? Stop you gadding about? You won't find it on the streets, I tell you. Go and look at the wallpaper on the stairs here. I'll tell you a secret: those geese used to be real. Alive and flying. Seeing sunrise over the ocean. Why did you go out walking again?'

The voice sad, loving, reproachful.

'I wanted to get out.'

'You've been out all day. Did you see him?'

'No. He wasn't there, he's never there. He doesn't even exist, he's just a figment of my imagination. But where are you calling from? It's the attic, isn't it? I know it is!'

She drops the phone, runs up to the boxes and shadows, her solitary mattress, the shuffling wind.

That's none of it true. She never went near the harbour, scenic and blue. She went inland, towards the station, that huge, barnlike terminal at the end of the line. She was circling his house, in an acute agony of longing that the ordinary little place was powerless to address. Desolate and drawn out against her will in the summer evening, down those used-up little streets on the St Michael estate; the stalker is as much a victim as the one pursued. Past the women in doorways, the men in the street outside the pubs, the teenagers gathering on corners. Drawn up right outside the house, tucked away behind two or three ugly trimmed shrubs and a tiny bleak lawn, just maintained, the net curtains thick and clean. The name in curly white lettering on the front door, *Montcalm*. Not the sort of place you'd imagine Bonnie, that spoilt Londoner, ever living.

Empty and shut up, the wife gone to work, father-in-law on the rocks with his line, Dominic on the field with the kids. Why is she hurting, when he loves her and she has power over him? She goes round the side but can see little through the big fence; climbs onto a pile of dry grass cuttings and tree prunings, stands hand clutched to the fence, looking in. Sees it all. The order, the neatness, such as she'll never have. It's definitely not the sort of place to burst into and announce a broken heart. He's married. Safe here. His garrison, a secluded place for exile, beneath the nodding pines. Completely detached, not overlooked at all, a province unto itself, at the end of this rough little street. She sees it all. The house airy with light and cleanliness; the squeaky-clean washing up; his folded shirts, the street rinsed from them. The bath bleached white, piles of fluffy white towels in the airing cupboard. The medication ready in the locked bathroom cupboard. The fairy wife, with whom he spun this garden into being. The loving day by day care that built a substantial home here, tucked away from the world. The years of anniversaries honoured and birthdays remembered. Her own emotional greed.

But it's too late; he's there, summoned by her longing, a bolt from the blue, larger than life zooming round the corner and there; halted, gazing at her, breathing. He came back to get a bottle of water for the kids. Feet sinking into the dried grass and pine cuttings, which give off still their faint, pleasant smell, she stands paralysed, hand on the warm, thin wood of the fence. He gazes at her, speechless, suspended in disbelief. She's not real. She's just a manifestation of his poor, ravaged brain. And she's not totally hardened yet, caught giving herself away like this. She's ready to sink into the grass and die.

After all they've been through together, such an encounter surely shouldn't upset them that much. Didn't he walk into her house unannounced not so long ago? But she's got her hand on his fence, about to invade. His Quebec, his fortress. She's got her hand on his fence, when she's never been to his house before; when he knows she shouldn't be there. At this hour of the timetable she should be home. She's not real. She's just a golden aura come sliding down one of those last sunbeams. But she drops something, a bag of cherries she was bringing him, to leave at his front door. The brown bag tumbles down the mound of cuttings, scattering three or four cherries, and he steps forwards and picks them up automatically. Warm, red and ripe. Edible proof of her actuality. So this streetwalker's stepped off her beat. She's taken that step outside their established playground, the streets.

They both know what'll happen next. The inevitable next step. Some other fine afternoon, she'll be back. She'll breach that last barrier. Climb over that high fence, from the pile of dried grass cuttings, leap lightly down on the other side. Grasp his back door handle. She's living it now, as she stands, clutching his fence, looking down at him, the late afternoon sunlight shading her face. Knowing she's out of control. The back door's unlocked, gives easily and silently and inside it's all just as she imagined; she needn't have bothered coming. Kitchen clean as a new pin, tea towel draped over shiny taps; a glimpse of the wife's back, knelt to the fridge, hair already done up in the blonde bun for the evening surgery.

A lettuce on the kitchen table. So this is Montcalm. From upstairs comes the sound of the children, bursting out of a bedroom; Bonnie withdraws into the downstairs bathroom as they come pounding down and out into the garden. Lily of the valley disinfectant, old-fashioned and domestic, slightly depressing, like the confines of childhood. Then along the shiny corridor, past the living room with its parquet floor and cream lookalike leather, up the stairs light and two at a time with their good, well-trodden, well-hoovered blue carpet and straight into their bedroom. She could be anywhere, with the low white bed and big white and blue cushions. The windows onto the railway line and a distant confusion of roofs, two or three long sheds; the station. The slight vibration as a train rocks by, chocking slowly on the rails. She folds his wife's dainty blue summer pyjamas, left strewn on the pillow, slips them underneath, feeling until her fingers find his navy cotton; sighs like a child. Undresses. Folds her own clothes neatly, puts them under the bed. Then gets in, drawing the duvet up to her bare shoulders, and waits; 3.30pm. He's a man who's never going to be late home. She hears the door open downstairs, his call as he goes down the corridor, the clamour of the kids. He'll be up once they've eaten, for his shower, will be in after that to get changed, the white towel round his middle, his shoulders beaded with water. Meanwhile, the chink of plates and snatches of conversation floating up to the bedroom window, the bright coastal patter of the wife, his hard gutturals. Faint shouts from the playing field adjacent, the background gunfire of the kids. She listens idly, snuggled into the duvet. It smells zingy clean; how do some women get their washing to smell so fresh?

And that's the end of his life, when he opens his bedroom door and walks in. No drug's as powerful as that kind of love, greedy and grabby, that seizes what it wants and won't let go. It would send him threshing right across the bed, swallow him up altogether.

Again the phone. An insistent shrilling from the other side. By the way it rings and rings, starting again after every ten rings, refusing not to be answered, she knows it's Austin; a paranormal caller, who won't be denied beyond the grave.

'How dare you put the phone down on my mother? She's in tears. You cold, cutting bitch, Bonnie.'

'Well, why don't you both stop ringing up, then?'

'Are you drunk?'

Some women turn rabid in the first days of pregnancy, blood drumming in temper at neck and cheeks, pounding round the abdomen, tantrum hormones washing round like a savage sea. Her appalling brattishness is as good as a pharmacy test. So are her breasts, two white globes pulsing with blue veins and still shivering from the rasp of Dominic's chin four hours ago. The slight drawmarks and sag from breastfeeding Finbar gone as if they'd never been. It can only be a couple of weeks or so. But she's exquisitely sensitive. It's no phantom pregnancy. She can't tell Austin, how this time it'll all be different, pregnant by another man; different blood. How already she knows it's a girl. Besides, he won't let her get a word in edgeways.

How dare she, treating Sally like that; her own true mother. Who's so upset that she can't even be fucking bothered to come and see him off at the airport. And what about Finbar this fine summer evening? The child's fallen out of her life as easy as falling off a log. If she isn't careful she'll end up alone. Or maybe that's what she'd like. Riddled with romantic and sexual immaturity and addiction; childish fantasies, destructive relationships. A woman who won't keep her mobile switched on, who's cut herself off.

'How many times do I have to tell you. I may need to get through to you quickly.'

'But there's no signal here, you know that!'

So maybe she's happier if he can't get through to her at all any longer, she who only connects with ghosts and derelicts now. And if you don't settle down a bit we may have to consider whether you're really the best person to look after Finbar, if he should even come back to you. Because, get this: he doesn't actually want to come back down there. He doesn't like it there either. He's much happier up here. Only failures are happy down there. Place is tailor-made for them. Waste Island: a shoreline littered with burnt boats. Believe me. You're just a casualty, Bonnie.

*

She can continue where Austin finally left off: In a state of possession. Emotions at gutter level, the rag and bone shop of the heart. Cut off from those who love her best. But open to being terrorised by whatever entity chooses to come along.

The silver ring on her finger already sinking slightly deeper into the skin; already she's spread out slightly into her new state. Letting go her first child and her art, and a husband made of gold. Pursuing a man she knows would much rather be left alone.

She flings the receiver against the wall and stands above it, waiting for silence. Which eventually comes, along with Finbar to say goodnight.

'Goodnight, darling. Be good for Sally.'

'I am good.'

'I know. You're always good, aren't you.'

'Yes.'

'Mummy will see you soon.'

'Yes.'

'Have you had a nice day?'

'Um... yes.'

'What have you been doing?'

'We went for a walk. Went to the park. Mummy?'

'Yes.'

'I went on the big slide.'

'Did you, darling? What's that? Speak up, sweetie. No need to whisper with Mummy. Are you all right?'

She can't hear what he mumbles before the phone goes dead at last this haunted summer evening.

*

Only the ocean would swallow this town more effectively than sand. Clutching the phone, Bonnie looks out of the window to the harbour, at the green shifting sandbanks way out. The sand is said to be moving towards the town, which would leave it stranded several miles inland. In time, just its roofs and chimney pots showing. Maybe there are worse fates than being lost at sea. From her music room on the third floor the view is even better, over those deceptive, sand-soft green waves, and the footsteps start up again overhead in the attic. Who observes Bonnie and Dominic embracing the length of the summer streets, watches down stairwell and hill their tender goodbyes? The spirit of the house, the shadow that breathes down from the attic to meet her; her future self, already an established inhabitant of that place. The caller on the other end of the line, who won't say where she's calling from. What does she say to Bonnie the summer evenings to cause her unbearable anguish? That she's made a bad mistake, should kiss Dominic goodbye, return to London, practise twelve hours a day? But there's no one left to be tough with Bonnie, now that Austin's letting her go and Sally's scared of her. There's only the house. This entity isn't interested in her psychic well-being. It tells her what she wants to hear: that Dominic isn't imaginary but real. She used him instead of her art like a drug to create her own alternative reality, and now he's real. Not a trophy bit of rough to boast about to her middle-class friends in London, not a lover from a foreign land, but ordinary, limited, frightened. Frightened of her most of all. Of himself, more. An imagination as narrow as the streets he works down, a pillar of the community. He appeared at her bidding, powerless to disobey, even outside his own house. Even though she couldn't make him speak, he appeared and stood there, staring at her. Like one of Sally's concrete men, like one of the imaginary friends of her childhood, he came to life, by a mysterious, magical process known as love. And now she's stuck with him.

Whatever inhabits that attic believes in her alternative reality too, and encourages her in it. No one left to pull her back, to catch her as she falls. She's the victim of her own powers, that got loose like a sail in a storm. No longer contained by her art. In this space, Austin disappears of his own accord and Finbar lives in suspended animation, cared for by someone else. Concordia plays its own music that drowns out hers. That house is a liar. Got a lot of patience, too. Plenty of practice in spinning fairy tales. Ones that tell you to wait. To sleep, sleep for a hundred years. Luring her to a sleeping beauty syndrome.

No wonder Dominic won't visit the house. He has enough alternative reality of his own. In any case, he doesn't really believe in Bonnie any more either; that's why he ignores her half the time; or as much as he can. Thinks she's just a figment of his automatic imagination, produced by electrical activity of the brain; a golden aura fraught with broken music. Besides, how could he explain to Bonnie that he only feels safe in the streets, validated by the presence of the public, the outside world. He hates houses; been unemployed too many times to relish four walls. Or maybe he's guilty, too. Maybe in another life he drew the plans for the house that Bonnie's living in now, and he too finds his own creation scary. Maybe the real reason why he won't visit; because he's afraid that once in, he'll never get out again, or just because he knows there are too many rooms, too many caverns of the psyche there. Or maybe he's coming up the stairs now, gleaming with intent. To take her away with him, to his unknown land. Everywhere and nowhere, like the spirit of the house. Like the geese fluttering in the wallpaper up the stairs, their wings ever more frantic.

Night comes and, between phone calls, she can hear music.

'Bonnie, love.'

But Bonnie's lying asleep in the attic, worn out with the day and early pregnancy, dreaming that she and Dominic are two halves of one whole. It's a long, complicated dream, to do with the infinitely complex forming of the embryo within her. She can't take another call. Besides, it's 1am.

'Austin's left you.'

Half turns over, mumbles that she doesn't care.

'You do know that, don't you, darling? I have to tell you. He's left you for success. For silver streaming Thames.'

'Oh, okay...'

'Your fingers are cold, Bonnie. Better go and warm them up on Dominic. Do a few exercises.'

'Oh, fuck off!'

'Listen, Bonnie. If you don't get up and practise, your fingers will turn to stone. And Dominic will turn into a concrete man. You've got to keep him alive.'

She's awake all right, propped on one elbow, listening carefully in the moonshadows.

'Only constant practice will save him from petrifying. Keep the faith, Bonnie love. Keep your fingers supple.'

'It's too lonely.'

'That's right, Bonnie. Sit up. Good girl. Talk to me.'

She sits up and talks, the moonlight streaming through the attic window, her profile soft with sleep. She was pushed out onto stage at age seven, alone, a little princess with fingers of pearl, into an immense cavern behind the stage lights, a Fingal's cave of shadows and eerie echoes, the piano a far-off rock. Almost needed a rope to haul herself onto the stool. But scrambled up. All she had to do was hang on.

The music played itself. Her first prize, a box of chocolates; the forfeit, relationships. And, like other talented children, swallowed the deal in one gulp.

From then on her parents were shadows either side of the stage; she inhabited a centre where adults were long legs moving in spotlight towards her, voices into microphones way above her head. Staring dazed out into darkness at other voices. Her audiences murmuring on the fringes of her consciousness like the sea. The piano became the box in which she lived, the barque in which she sailed.

'Austin put you out to work, too, didn't he? He was none too happy at your malingering. But that's all in the past now, darling. I need you to understand that. I want you to know it's safe for you here.'

Bonnie sits up straight, the better to hear, not the speaker, but the music, beginning to circle the house again. Memories of other tunes, other times. She can identify any composer in a flash, from a few notes. So she should surely recognise this. A bagatelle falling down the stairwell like autumn leaves. But the voice continues, distracting, that East End ring so familiar that she can almost identify the speaker.

'You do know that, Bonnie darling, don't you? It's safe here. Besides, you haven't got anywhere else to go. Have you?'

*

It's high summer but already splashed with endings, the rain and wind a duet at the attic window. They're Bonnie's friends, she should listen to them, should listen to time passing, get a move on. Shut the attic window, pack, get on the next train for London. Sally's the one she should talk to. Always on the end of the line, waiting for her call. Sally would identify, feel her pain for her; no one's been through as much as Sally. One husband she drank to death, glass for glass, the second lives in Scotland; the third she fought cancer for and lost, the fourth did battle with her and finally pulled out a real knife. Now behind bars for life and still says it's preferable to life with her. Sally knows all right, what life and love are all about. She should talk to her brother, Austin, he's a good man. Maybe tougher and more generous than she gives him credit for. Got a haunted imagination, too. She ought to be careful, whom she confides in. But Bonnie talks to the house.

*

It's deep night, and Bonnie's that manifestation in Dominic's house she hoped she'd never be. Come in across the silent glinting lines of the railway and the black pines, a shadow full of desire at his bedroom window, heart leaping and bounding, a revenant far more scared than those she comes to visit. She's done it, as they knew she would, done the unthinkable. Walked or floated in on someone's life, while he was there living it, with his wife. She knows full well she shouldn't be here, in this tidy modern bedroom, his uniform for the next day laid out on a chair, the breakfast table laid downstairs. The neat clutter of cosmetics and little shellbox of jewellery, the furry bear clutching a red heart sitting beside them, his Valentine's gift. The radio on his side of the bed, the nursing journals and chick-lit on hers, on matching glass and steel bedside tables.

The faint *sifflement* from father-in-law downstairs in what used to be the dining room, dreaming of that big fish. Outside, the trains all asleep in sheds at the end of the line, the silver glint of a fox in moonlight padding along the track. His house is a protective shell, its job to keep Bonnie out. Even to think herself here an intrusion. She knows full well she's going to get caught. Trespassing in the unknown, beyond the pale. Not put off by his hand splayed on his wife's blonde curls, his deep, peaceful breathing. The low, modern bed, clean sheets and plastic sheet beneath. But she's more fearless than the angels, rushing into the innermost privacies of the brain, the deepest folds of the soul. Comes slipping into his bed on the other side, takes him in his sleep, irresistible. Such a violation of privacy. Tearing off the domestic navy pyjamas to get to the essential man beneath. Making him stiffen and jerk in the night. Forcing what she needs out of him; making him into her kind of lover. When all he wants is to be left alone.

The phone rings again in the dead of night even though the line's pulled out and the instrument at the bottom of the sea. This time it's her dead mother on the other end, but the only noise that comes out is a bat's squeak.

Wake up, Bonnie, and practise.

'Austin. Austin, are you there? It's Bonnie.'

It's his intake of breath and his voice all right, but his shadow, the answerphone. Full of the complacency of the living. Rattling off their assurances. That they'll return your call, as if the barriers between the living and the dead could be breached that easily. It's her last call to him, to save her from herself. To save her from the music pervading the house, the rushing of goose wings up the stairs, from her own predatory intents. From the realisation that she herself is the resident ghost, a woman haunted by music she couldn't play. But she leaves no message. She pulls the line out of the crumbly old wainscot and runs out of the house into the streets whose silence is still the plunging of the sea at their ends.

A HALF-READING

You'd think people would steer well clear of him, in this geranium town where all the houses are made of chalk. What he thinks about is so complicated. He's got every meeting on every street stored up in his brain, with all the dates and times. Scary. But everyone loves him. They can't see inside his brain. That familiar figure in his yellow waistcoat, his leisurely barrow. He's an ambulant therapist for the broken, whose wounds match his. Ever being stopped for chats and confidences. Hears heartbreak with equanimity. He knows what damage is, and they know it. Swarm to him like bees. He's spoilt by tea-ladies, free cuppas and chips at any of the cafés in return for listening to the story of their half-lived lives; welcomed by the old codgers walking their poodles, who find his politics sound. All those people who sit out on benches, they see him coming, and they all look on him as their friend. He's so socially adept, can relate to them all on their own level, his gentle 'I know' slid under their disclosures. But they don't know what they're doing to him, adding to his store of memories.

Summer in full swing, they're all out, on the streets, and they all want to talk. The public. They tell him everything. How they're marine engineers who are going to build an underwater art gallery offshore to attract the Londoners. How they're deep sea divers going to dive for the wreck of the *Christopher*, lost off this coast in 1857 en route from London to Montreal on the old Allan Line, and find the gold bullion in the watery sands. How they're international meat traders going to fly sides of beef into town by helicopter. Why? What for? Who knows? He's gotten to the stage where he doesn't believe anything anyone tells him any more, though I hope you believe me! says Bonnie. Oh, I believe you all right.

He's a peripatetic fortune teller who knows them all from summer to summer, hears much more extravagant fortunes than he could ever foretell. They're going to occupy the cliff tunnels in a secret military operation against the arrival of a fleet of UFOs from across the sea. They're going to raise a new kind of cattle on just seawater. To auction the mummified extremities of the town artist, cut off in a fit of madness one day in 1876 and just discovered in a trunk, with a £1 million minimum bid. Start a wind farm that'll blow this island away to the other side of the world. Turn the public conveniences into works of art for the Tate Modern by the simple expedient of leaving them unflushed. Build a new shopping centre on the Goodwin Sands. They carry the ashes of the dead round with them in urns, under their arms, to display to anyone who's interested. They're going to turn back time and make those ashes walk the streets, they're going to resurrect lovers long gone with just one kiss. They're going to live to a hundred and see Arthur wake from his long sleep beneath this fortunate isle. Aren't they, Dominic? Please tell me it's possible. Isn't this Avalon, where dreams come true?

They all want him to predict a dream future for them. Gloved hand on broom, he stands listening patiently. Ventures a few kind hints in line with each querent's personality, the way fortune tellers do, not untinged with mockery. Well, seems like you're the lucky one, eh, planning that. Sure: you're gonna make a fortune with that one. So why don't you do just what you said, then; sounds like the right future for you. Ten years? I'm sure you'll have it finished long before that. Rich and famous, that'll be you – eh? Street readings. The road sweeper's reassurance. With as much value as the litter he picks up. His mainland accent lends him glamour, he's still the stranger, the newcomer, the one who might foresee things differently, breaking into this island stasis of 2,000-plus years. He knows, none better, how this isle is made up of a vast pile of garbage, plastic debris bobbing along, a trash vortex you can walk on round the circumference of the world. Where people voyage into the nonhuman zone in boats made of plastic bottles. Every one of them worth an annual half tonne of waste, 541kg. A hundred million tonnes of flotsam swirling round, lost. His job to find and rescue what he can. On a good day, he likes it when people talk to him, feels he's doing a useful job, cultivating his special humility along the filthy centre streets. Picking up all those half-readings tumbling along the gutters in the wind. Half-lived lives, half-told fortunes. This summer, though, it's different. Listening, repeating what people have just said, that's about all he's fit for right now.

His wife, the nurse, informed by mother-in-law and alarmed at the return of his nocturnal jerks and morning falls, got the doctor to up his drugs and now he can barely think. That keeps him under control. She makes sure he takes the stuff, too. Meets him at lunchtime sometimes to supervise the midday dose. Did you swallow, Dominic? Same question he's always been asked. Brings the youngest child with her, the longed-for daughter, two and a half. Tell Daddy to swallow. Thus we indoctrinate, from generation to generation. Swallow, Daddy! Show me your tongue. Her he can't refuse. Yes, darling; yes, sweetheart. His wife sits back on the bench, satisfied. All he's got to hold over her is his special threat, of the status quo breaking down; if you don't treat me right I might seize... Might not stop. You know what stress does to me. Who else could he play those games with, except his mother? She wasn't tough enough for him either; not like his wife. Scruffy and docile, he kisses them goodbye after the picnic, automatons along the streets. Yellowed, distant. He's learnt to cultivate his street face, keeping off all comers. Looks through people. Some are devastated at his unfriendliness. What's happened to Dominic? He looks dreadful. He goes along with a certain steady, settled bleakness of motion; you can tell he's not passing through. The town centre is hell. It's a relief when the professional travellers arrive in town to set up the summer fair and he's put on cliff-top duty again.

Up on the cliff-top the air is clear and he remembers some kind of story someone once told him about a fish and a ring.

*

There's a little fair called Dreamland, tattered across the cliff-top beneath the scudding summer clouds, overlooking the English Channel. Swingboats, roundabouts, shooting galleries, all peopled by giant soft toys, ghost heads of candyfloss and everywhere the nut-hard people hauling on ropes and gigantic switches. They're a different race with their ponytails, gleaming brown backs; mature at nine, old at twenty-five, toothless at forty.

Sunday, after a storm. The lightning slit the night, writhing out into its own wild electroencephalography, tracings racing right off the brown sky. Abnormal signalling in the heavens, explosions of electrical activity firing at 500 times a second, the heavens one mad constant flicker. Dendrites flickering and flaring out in hundreds of branches, beads of neurons firing. Irregular discharges of electrical activity, a status epilepticus of storm, endless convulsions of thunder, rolling the body of the sky over and over. Not until dawn did it pass into universal deep coma, last jerkings of thunder passing off into the distance, silence and rest.

The innocent unworldliness of it all, raindrops glittering on the grass. The heat gathering again for another day; thunderclouds gathering also, bunching along the horizon. The timeless roundabout rides of childhood, the way one ride can last an afternoon. The hard bronzed youths lifting the children on and off the swingboats, casual about time, letting the five minutes turn to ten, fifteen. As in a dream, Bonnie watches Finbar having his turn. He's down for a precious few weeks, like love itself, evanescent and fleeting. Austin and Sally let him return, reluctantly.

Austin has acted, not just given their London tenants notice, but got the future planned; has told Bonnie that whatever happens, come autumn Finbar will be taking his place in the Hammersmith school they've had his name down for these last few years. Yep, so she'll be one of those skinny mums at the school gates, all swapping tips about diet and allergies and meeting up in their trainers for a run after the morning drop-off. So she can scrub Finbar off the list for whatever local sin bin she had in mind down there, where the mothers are young thugs with blonde ponytails and heavy blue tattoos, smoking just outside the school premises only because the law forbids them to smoke inside. She'll be back to that slight aura of artistic glamour, of someone who's becoming famous, someone to watch, Finbar'll be back to his native roots, they'll all be grounded again. And if Bonnie doesn't like it, tough. Because that's what's going to happen. Meanwhile, it suited Austin and Sally for Finbar to have some sea air; full-on summer holiday's a bit much for them both. The busy middle classes. Sally's got her recovery meetings to attend – the fashionable ones, in Chelsea – against that fatal first drink. The fellowship, the programme; demands a lot of commitment, to avoid the ever-prowling danger of relapse, stay sober. And Austin's got work to do. For he's more successful than ever. In demand, went off on that press trip, and then more work came in, the way it does. So, with the opportunism of their kind, why not take advantage of a seaside house for the summer; yes, on balance, the advantages of leaving his son with Bonnie for a few weeks outweigh the disadvantages after all, fey though she's undoubtedly been since the move down there. Probably better for her stability too that she stay where she's happy, for now. They'll tolerate her wanting to spend a last few weeks down there, refusing to come up to London. Doesn't Bonnie have any say in the matter? Where she wants to live, where she wants her son to be brought up? But she's the latest in several generations of unmothered mothers, what does she know? Wouldn't recognise an abandoned child if he were sitting on her lap.

But she's glad to have him. Slightly taller, with a new, adult shadow in his eyes. Glad to be back with her, too, but wary. Attending to the swingboat business just a little too assiduously. It takes time to coax his spirit back from the urban hinterlands where it fled.

*

'Want a reading, love? Want a reading, I say?'

He emerges from the scruffy little Tarot tent, spotting a seeker on the instant. In spite of the warmth of the day he wears thick corduroy trousers and a cloth cap; heavy, limp shirt and jumper; a weird bird, all right.

'Only five pounds, love; or three pounds for a half-reading.'

Bonnie laughs.

'Which half do you read first? Supposing it's the wrong half?'

He looks her up and down as if this were a delightful meeting, his eyes reading, reading as he speaks, she too interesting to pass by; the flattery of one who depends on first impressions to make his living.

The path to psychic disintegration is littered with such people. But we all need candyfloss sometimes. When faith, hope and charity are just too hard. We all need that bought hug from an indifferent stranger. The one who can read our wishes and relay them back to us with sufficient accuracy to content the ache of the heart, for a while. Just for a day or two. Yes, the love is reciprocal. Yes, you will have what your heart longs for, when the time is right. Then we can let the cold harsh truth come creeping back in, a bit at a time. Let no one despise the fortune teller, paid to dispense denial. To allow sufficient room for our fantasies. False comfort. It's a psychic soother of the first value.

'Oh, I always read the important half first.'

Only here would it matter, the saving of two pounds.

'Go on, then. Let's have the full works. You're Lavengro, I take it?'

His name is pinned up above the garish decorations on the tent.

'That's me. Lavengro, do you know what that means, love? It's Romany, means word master. I inherited it.'

Been doing this for twenty years, since he was fourteen. His face retains an unlived-in quality. Bright and pallid. Feather-brown hair, alert, bird-brown eyes. A deep, round smooth hollow at the larynx, pulled into whitish wrinkles, suggestive of a burn, of ghastly initiation rites. His remnants of voice wispy. His accent is northern English; she can't place it, of course, in her parochial London way. Just north of Watford somewhere.

'Got into it naturally really, never knew I was different... thought everyone had this intuition... could get into white witchcraft if I wanted, but I wouldn't touch it with a bargepole... I'd say you're very intuitive yourself, sweetie, very intuitive indeed... In fact, you should have your guard up a lot more... Isn't it the same for me? Oh, it is, it is. Thank you for noticing. There you are, you see: you've got the third eye, like I have. I'd say you'd done some reading yourself. No? You surprise me. Well, one way to test out your psychic powers is to read me. Go on, have a try. No?'

He flows on, traditional ingratiating tones mingled with chatty northern bluntness. Yes, she's different herself, indefinably so in her mud-green T-shirt, her fashionable black shorts whose top button she has to leave undone now, her gladiator sandals, her ponytail and cap, that any girl might wear. It's like – the nearest he can get to it is a kind of battle dress, absurd though he knows that sounds. She's dressed for duty in some way, got a job to do. Is he right? A warrior princess, with her stray, foreign little son by an invading chieftain. That is her son over there, isn't it, on the swingboats, the one she's watching so intently? Thought so. There's a spiritual likeness there he can pick up, a kind of moral likeness to their auras, if that makes sense.

'Hello, Sidney.'

It's the young men of the roundabout and swingboats, a huddle of youths over the way there.

'Hello, Sidney,' comes the call again, mocking.

'Hello,' he replies, coldly.

'How you doing, Sidney?'

'Doing all right there, are you, Sidney?'

Surely not his relations, with their hard tans and ponytails, next to his tall indoor pallor, his dried-up laryngectomy. But Bonnie recognises the tone of family, family dragging down the black sheep who's tried to better himself; pretentiously to change his name; the ex-swingboat hand with aspirations. Sidney turns his back on them.

'They're so crude. And all because I foretold an early death for one of them, Levi. I was right about Declan as well, the police did come for him. Now he's away for a long, long time. You've got to be so careful, in this calling. People don't like it, hearing the truth.'

'Well, no.'

'You know, I always say to people, if what I say doesn't come true, come back to me and you can have your money back. No one's come back yet.'

'I suppose there's no point doing it unless you do tell the truth.'

'Exactly! Exactly! I had a fight about that last year with another Tarot guy, Ronnie, you may have come across him. He said, you're just a fairground reader, people don't want to hear about that kind of stuff, they're here on holiday, just want a bit of light entertainment. Don't tell all you see, he said. I say he's wrong. Don't you agree? I was thinking about it all again last night, you know, wasn't that a dreadful storm? Couldn't sleep, thunder always gets me. Electrical activity in the air. Still hovering, can you feel it? Anyway. Sorry about all that. That young man upset me.'

'What, them?' Again Bonnie glances at the group of fairhands.

'No, no... my last reading, just now... You may have seen him going, just before you turned up, did you? Him and his mother… He was dying. Don't think I've ever done a reading for someone it's so close to. On his heels, love, stepping out of the tent after him, did you see? You probably saw all three of them, knowing you. Travelling together. The third one on their tail the whole time. Consulted people all over the world, he told me. Told me I was one of the best, that's something, I suppose. What could I tell him? Sometimes I wonder if I've bitten off more than I can chew. All my querents, it's always the same… and people want to know everything, everything…'

'Go on, then,' says Bonnie, to console him. 'Let's have that reading.'

'Sure, love? You're not just saying that because you're a nice person, are you? No, I can see you need to hear something. Does your little boy like biscuits? Do you like Jammy Dodgers, young man?' complacently leading the way to the tent as Finbar runs up after his ride, handing the packet. 'There's always someone—'

But he jumps up, beating at the tent flaps where other children are listening, giggling. Certainly he doesn't seem used to the pressure.

'Look, buzz off. How can I concentrate if a querent comes along? This is a calling, not a game. Why don't you put your little one in the playhouse there, love, Old Mother Hubbard's. They won't mind, they know me. He may not need to hear what I'm going to say. Look, I'm still a bit rattled. Out of kilter. Mind if I just have a fag?'

She and Finbar wander over to the play tent, hand in hand, dubious. Ahead over the sea, the dark roll of thunder is travelling inland, a heavy press of clouds, charged. Below lies the port's back yard, a sprawl of quays and walkways, the faint prattle of a loudspeaker. There's a defunct lift, battered turquoise with faded red lettering, graffiti, the windows boarded up. Along the coast the three towers of the power station smoke gently, witches on huge hips, biding their time. A far-off glimmer of steel pipes and chimneys from the factory beyond. If only Austin would return and save her from this flat, barely developed island that still remembers the arrival of the Vikings.

'When is Dad coming back?'

Who needs psychics? He's just like his father, this little intuitive.

'Tomorrow.'

'He's been gone for weeks and weeks. Three months.'

'Three weeks and two nights, actually.'

He sure spun it out, that press trip. Found other things to do.

'Will he remember me?'

'Course he will! He's dying to see you!'

Returning, she waits for Sidney in the stuffy little tent, the three hopeful empty chairs ranged outside; his coat, with its thick unwashed smell, hangs over the back of her chair so she doesn't know where to lean. Watching the drift of smoke from between his fingers as he stands outside, she can read him easily enough, this sexless nomad, abandoned early by his parents, one of nature's weirdlings, who compensate by gaining power over their fellows, yet are still dependent on their interest. He's branded his karma on the notice outside the tent: 'Sympathetic', and this is indeed his curse, for ever condemned to instant sympathy with whoever he meets.

'A brother is concerned about you. You'll be hearing from him in the next six weeks.'

'I don't have a brother.'

She's forgotten Austin already. He looks at her in dismay.

'Could be a psychic brother. Hang onto him anyway. You're going to need him.'

That's that one out of the way; the joker. She's responded rightly; challenged him. Proved her intent. Now he must gather himself for what he can't help doing over and over again, for what is destroying him. For what he must enter again now, any second. An uncoupling of consciousness. A regression; a dissolution. A return to more primitive ways of seeing. A state where the usual mental tools don't work, where signs and symbols are your only hope. His waxy face glimmers; he pulls at his dead shirt, fingers the laryngeal scar as if that's the eye, wrinkled closed, from which he does his seeing. Bonnie looks out of the tent door, to check Mother Hubbard's still there, holding Finbar safe, hasn't blown off the cliff-top in the sudden breeze that's set the tent ropes quivering. It's a welcome breath of fresh air in the closeness. She sees, with repulsion, how it lifts the feather hair off the seer's gleaming forehead, dispels the moist nicotine breath coming across the table.

'Shuffle the cards.'

Her fine fingers are clumsy on the big, greasy cards, which her own sympathetic intuition pictures as muzzed with use and with human greed; the greed to know, to be sure.

'Concentrate on what you want to ask. Work, money, relationships? It's relationships, isn't it?'

It's always relationships, they both know that. Who in their right mind would ask him about money? He takes a deep breath, as if summoning air from the intense closeness, poised between vacuum and thunder.

'Cut the cards.'

She does so, hands them back. The insides of the tent seem to be beading with sweat.

'What have we cut on?' displaying the chunky pack back to her.

'The Fool. The unnumbered one. Freedom. Vagabondage. See how he's tripping along cliff-tops, about to step over. Like I said: maybe you should be a bit careful here, love.'

He looks at her, waiting for her to ask. But she says nothing. Again the wind picks up, rattles the tent poles. From afar comes a remote crack, a single streak of electricity across the sky, barely audible in the hubbub of the fair.

'I lay the cards down.'

They come down in curt slaps, like the wind smacking again at the canvas. Glancing out again, Bonnie sees the people etched with a dark grey-silver light, the storm rushing up the grass behind their feet. She should stop this; looks at the unsavoury seer. What is he summoning?

'Now, excuse me, I have to look in your eyes... Yes... I'd say you're a warm person, sweetie, but you don't always see clear. You tend to rush. To rush in... It hasn't always been an easy life. You don't know where home is. But you're learning that home is where the heart is, aren't you, love? Your parents... they went away long ago, left you to bring yourself up, didn't they?'

'Well – yes.' Like other people, she's not prepared for the truth.

He nods. His lonely, untutored gift has him in its grasp. 'Relationships.'

He looks at the spread. There's a lull, the air thick around them. His bird eyes are remote. His eyebrows flicker, rise, as if he's seen something he doesn't want to approach; not quite able to handle his gift, its difficulties. Bonnie, watching as keenly as Austin himself might do, without mercy, is yet surprised again.

'This is complicated.'

'What is it?'

'The Mother and Son card. Did you ever want a daughter?'

'Maybe.'

He leans forwards, staring into her eyes again as if into her ovaries themselves. She meets his stare staunchly, can't help flinching away from the dank shirt and scraggy jumper. Again there's that sickening split in the sky, felt rather than seen or heard.

'I don't think you can, can you?'

She's truly startled, affronted. 'Well – I don't know.'

'That's the Mother and Son card, you see... no... you won't have any more children with your current partner. Maybe with someone else...'

Again he pores over the cards; looks up, meets her eyes.

'Never mind. You've a lovely relationship with your little boy, I can see that.'

She's not sure she forgives him. But Sidney's brooding over the spread again.

'Who's the guy with red hair around you? Domineering, arrogant... thinks a lot of himself...'

'My husband...'

Typical of Austin to persist when he's not wanted, to continue his psychic spying on her. To load her with guilt from afar.

'Ooh, he wouldn't like you being here, though.'

How little he'd like it shoots through Bonnie; a pang of degradation. Putting the child in a gypsy play area, sitting listening to this insinuating scruff. Breaching another psychic barrier, the most subtly destructive of them all: to know what's ahead; and no going back afterwards.

'Discord, disagreement... You treated something he valued like rubbish. You didn't mean to, mind, but he'd never accept destiny as an excuse. He makes his own destiny. He's a worker... keen, ambitious...'

He looks up, gains more confidence from her listening eyes.

'Yes, very ambitious... gone on his way without taking too much notice of you... been ignoring you... No, he's a selfish sod.'

Again he glances up, bursts on. 'I feel sorry for you; you married the wrong person. Have I upset you?'

'No, it's okay.'

What querent hasn't heard all this before? Hasn't come for just this very reading? Oh, the dream of it. The vain dream of it. Like the bluish flickers of lightning now playing down the tent poles, gone just as you see them.

'There's someone else in your life. You've got another man. Much more your kind...'

He's reading on, intent; pulls a face over the central cards.

'It was a half-reading you asked for, love, wasn't it?'

'No. A full one.'

'I'm not sure if I should read this next bit.'

She bites her lip, smiling. He does the patter well, this scruffball. And they've entered the same zone so smoothly together, she barely notices how accurate he is. He's tuned into her all right. Or maybe it's her telling him. On this level of quantum interchange, it doesn't matter.

'Say what you like. I don't mind. I don't mind paying.'

'Ah, it always comes with a payment. You do know that, love, don't you?'

'Yes. I do.'

She'll pay any price; not having thought of time.

'Good girl. Okay. Now listen. He cares. But the path of true love doesn't look that smooth; more like the garden path he's led you up a bit here. Difficulties and disappointments... Not that he's doing it deliberately, to hurt you or anything. He's just weak. He can't help it. God made him like that. He came unfinished from the potter's wheel, if you like.'

She sits still, frightened. 'What do you mean?'

'I don't know. He's got a scar, hasn't he?'

'Yes – on his arm.'

'This one's deeper.'

'Where is it, then?'

'Inside, love. It's from a long time ago.'

'Do you mean a psychological scar?'

'No, a physical one. A wound. A real wound, one he was born with.'

She leans forwards, hearing the ring in his voice. 'But where? What do you mean?'

'That's all I can see, love.'

'How weird.'

'I warned you, didn't I, love? I speak plain. I don't know

what I'm saying, see. I'm just the pipe, the channel. I'd better stop there, hadn't I?'

'No, that's all right. I always knew he was damaged...'

'Damaged, that's the word. You said it yourself. I'm sorry.'

'It doesn't matter. I'm never going to see him again, it was just a summer affair.'

'Was it?'

He takes a deep breath; sweat stands out on his forehead. Less elven now, his weird insinuation of power diminished; just another human being in the grip of what he doesn't understand, as the world outside is now increasingly in the grip of the gathering storm.

'Our last card. The Charioteer, reversed. Oooh, no love, very nasty. A nasty bit of work. The one that's shallow but thinks himself deep. Rides roughshod over others. He'd love you and leave you. He's the type'd get you pregnant and bugger off. Much more aggressive than your husband. No respect. And mood swings; terrible mood swings. Can you accept this?'

'No.'

Sidney shakes his head, helpless to read otherwise.

'That's major arcana, that's very important. But you're just as bad. Excuse me for saying so. The perfect partner. You're with him for life, you know that.'

She jumps up. 'Rubbish. Don't wind me up.'

'Wind you up, love? What would I get out of that? It's all here,' gesturing at the crude cards. 'Nothing to do with me.'

'I don't want to be with him for life. Doesn't anybody understand? It was just a fling.'

'Just watch your step, love, that you don't go out of control here. Cos out of control for you is out of control for him, and there's consequences.'

'Oh yes? The proverbial gypsy's warning?'

She wipes a tear away, angrily. We can only be told a future we already know, a destiny we have already arranged. Doesn't she know it too well already, that she's his misfortune.

A quick, imperative, bossy drumming comes on the tent; the rain at last. The sickening breath of wet on over-dry land rises, dispersing quickly in great breaths of damp. They both look up, see the lightning jumping out in a network of green lines.

'Well, thanks very much,' opening her purse, flinging ten pounds across the table.

'Cut the cards and make a wish,' a final card slapped onto the table even as he, too, rises, shrugging himself into his coat.

'There's the Rest card. There'll be rest for him. Don't know what you wished for, but it ain't to be; not this year, anyway. Five pounds. Thank you, love.'

'Take ten. It was worth it.'

'No, love. Five.'

Sidney's reaching up to the tent zip, to seal the day off with the drumming rain, to seal the whole lot off: his clients, his foresight, his own total want of tact.

'There's your change. Anyway, be careful what you wish for. I'd say, cut your losses and walk away. Don't pursue him, love. Let it be. Try and patch it up with your husband... the cards never lie... there was more but I couldn't see it. Not today. In fact,' digging into the horrible cavern of greasy pocket again, 'call it a half-reading – no, no, love, do take it. Take the two quid back. No, honestly. I'm sorry you were unhappy with the reading, I hate it when that happens but like I said, some people just can't take it... My phone number's on the board there, any time you've got a problem you want to discuss...'

*

The storm gathers force. Harmony in the heavens, all the electrical impulses marching in the same direction. Flashbacks. While Bonnie's having her subconscious probed by Sidney, Dominic's undergoing something more drastic. His wife complained again, how his condition's deteriorated; the medication failing to control him, even at the higher dose. How he's going round in a constant dream. Stupefied in a seizure shadowland, replaying himself like a broken record, between his ongoing aura and the drugs which keep him there. Got him referred, for a complete review. Back in the Neuro, the old neurology hospital. Assess the possibility of surgery again. No real question of on-the-spot operations, of course; you need long and careful neuropsychological tests before that. And in these days of sophisticated keyhole surgery, the barbaric Montreal Procedure, where the bony skull cap is removed while the patient remains conscious and the surgeon probes the exposed brain tissue, would surely hardly be used in fact. That's just Dominic's personal nightmare, to have the top of his head sliced off like an egg, dating from childhood. Maybe some egocentric neurologist did threaten him with it once, in a moment of exasperation, at his uncooperative ways. A difficult patient he always was, dreamy child, self-involved and silent teenager. And these doctors so often think they're God. But the wife pushes for surgery: she wants Bonnie excised from his life, however brutal the means. Eating up space in his head, a ghost making him startle and fit; she's fed up of him talking about Bonnie in his sleep; and he's a man who sleepwalks by day. The surgeon agrees. How many times has he heard the same complaint; the patient suffers love. A difficult to treat syndrome for sure. Symptoms persistent and recurring. Quite unsustainable in everyday life; often intractable. Very sad. Only the most drastic surgery promises a cure; and sometimes not even then. Bring him in; we'll see what we can do.

She goes with Dominic, of course, no way she'd let him go alone. He'd forget his destination, just wouldn't go. Ramble round that vast barn of a station for a while before going for a walk along the line. But now he's in. This is the life of which Bonnie has no inkling, that he'd rather die than reveal to her; this is what he does on his day off. Gowned and mute despite the fact that they've promised him the chance to talk about whatever issues he likes. In his experience, it's the neurologists who do most of the talking. So maybe it's his poor brain misbehaving again. Or perhaps it's just the effects of the pre-op sedative. But this is what he hears the consultant say...

THE MONTREAL PROCEDURE

Good morning, Dominic. I'm Dr Deu, and I've treated you before. Many times. And I seem to remember you can be a little bit stubborn about your turns, as your colleagues call them. Don't always like to admit they're coming on. Would rather go sprawling across the pavement than take shelter in time. You did it again the other day, I hear, sweeping up behind the van first thing in the morning. The others asked you if you were all right; they could see you weren't well. You denied it, of course. Next thing is you cause shock and upheaval to everyone, completely disrupt the morning routine. Apparently you saw someone you knew? What a paltry excuse. People have to be able to walk down the street without you falling down in a heap at the sight of them. The van driver's new, doesn't know the drill; calls an ambulance, reports it to the supervisor. Distress all round. He didn't know you rely on your colleagues' collusion to get through. They're extremely tolerant, aren't they? They never report it. Make a joke of it, as you prefer. And what happens when they're not there? After all, you spend the greater part of the day alone. Didn't someone find you lying outside the gentlemen's toilets, too, recently? And again you said some woman had startled you? Came up from behind and gave you a hug? —Well, really. All this is very hard on your wife, you know. She's told me all about your lack of compliance. You've been cheating on the drugs, cheating on her, too, by the sounds of it. Not good enough, Dominic. Your wife's a bright girl. A specialist epilepsy nurse. Did a paper on Charcot's influence on café life, she tells me, the *gommeuses épileptiques*, the epileptic singers of Belle Époque Paris. Highly commendable. How lucky you are. —What? I'm sorry? You haven't read it? Never heard of Charcot, father of neurology? I see. I venture to suggest that your wife is wasted on you. — Attend to me. You must take medication as prescribed, eat lots of fresh fruit, and lead a healthy, low-stress life. Avoid people who are a vexation to the spirit. Accept you have epilepsy, the falling sickness. It's got a very ancient heritage, you know. If not, Dominic, if you insist on being wilful, human, defiant; if you insist on your right to disobey, if love continues to strike you down like a bolt from the blue, then I've got just the right intervention lined up for someone like you.

It's called the Montreal Procedure, and we might just try it out today. A treatment for intractable seizures. For a brain out of harmony, a life out of key. An infallible cure for the torments of love. We will show you. Love is no more than a tic in the brain, a quiver of diseased grey matter, a mere aberration of tissue. We will operate, take out the scar which causes such harrowing convulsions of desire.

Where is the scar? We will find it. We will cut a little window into your emotional world, and observe your innermost soul. We will have a little glimpse into how dreaming occurs. A small excision in the skull, to expose the brain tissue. You will not feel the skull lid being cut away, nor the electrodes' endfeet sliding over your cranium, like dragonfly legs seeking out sensations; nor the chill of the theatre air on what should never be exposed, nor the physician's intent. Instead, you will feel what the electrodes excite. Fear, evoked by stimulation of the amygdala. A deep, explosive joy. *Déjà vécu*; that familiar feeling that comes when we prod the temporal lobe. You will guide us by telling us what you feel as we probe different parts of the brain, using the electrodes to find seizure source. Your feedback helps us isolate the damaged part of your brain.

Tell us. Tell us what you feel. You're surely not all scar and no heart? Every probe of the electrode will call forth an emotion, a memory, every move gets us closer to the wound, the site of excitation. You will feel the touches not on the brain, but on the bodily areas to which they correspond. Parts of your body may move without your volition. You may hear, smell or see things which are not there. You may remember things that haven't yet happened, hear music that no one has yet played. But you can tell us; you must tell us what you feel.

Here at the Neuro, we rely on your compliance. You must guide us to the source, the scar. Together we build a delicate and intimate trust, closer than that between lovers, closer than that between mother and son. Together we will ask all those questions that have been lost in your brain for so long. Everything you've ever wanted to know about yourself. You have the answers. Tell us, tell us. Here at the Neuro, we depend on your transparency. The more accurately you respond, the closer we can zone in on the wound, the exact location of seizure activity. Those fibrous cells arranged radially about the wound; like the spokes of a wheel with the site of the former stab as the hub. The ones that start spinning with seizure activity, that spin you into that sickening dreamland.

Where is the scar? That cicatrix laid down by a complex process of swelling and fibrositis in microglia cells and astrocytes about the wound, undergoing clasmatodendrosis or fragmentation closest to the area of destruction, just as you, too, splinter closest to your area of destruction. Surgical resection, removal of the brain tissue in this location, will help end the strange daydreaming of which you complain. Those seizures of love, that cause you so much pain. The Procedure itself will do the rest. By the time we've finished with you, you'll never need to dream again.

You don't mind my students attending? For what am I put on this earth if not to instruct? I'm Professor Deu, a global authority in the field. The surgical resection of love my special domain. My shows outshine Charcot's, draw a bigger crowd. Standing room only. The great ringmaster of the Salpêtriére was nothing to me. *Chef de clinique* supreme. Ladies and gentlemen, welcome to my theatre. You are privileged to attend. Everyone scrubbed up? You all scrubbed up there? The patient ready? Head shaved, securely strapped down? Silence, please! Gentlemen, ladies, we will begin.

Sterilise the scalp. —You will remain fully conscious throughout. —A little injection of local anaesthetic. Begin the incisions. A little trepanning, a little cutting away of the protective bone. Turn the bone lid over, like the top of a coconut shell. Some spray to keep the cortex damp. Angle the ultraviolet lamps so they don't shine on the brain matter. Yes. Here at the Neuro we still use the Montreal Procedure. Unexampled accuracy. In this day and age? When we have God helmets, fitted with electromagnetic field-emitting solenoids that pulse out wavelength patterns of a precision that will induce the subject to believe he sees the divinity? When we have stereoelectroencephalography, SEEG, skulls whitened by dollops of electrode cream like seagulls' splats? When fMRI correlates with intracarotid amobarbital procedure or Wada test in around ninety per cent of cases? Yes. Too many variables in fMRI. Remember Bennett's elegant, witty study, which discovered the area responsible for emotion in dead fish? 'Neural correlates of interspecies perspective taking in the post-mortem Atlantic Salmon', making just that point, of the unreliability of fMRI research. We still find the Montreal Procedure, as pre-surgical evaluation, more precise than any other method. We find patients highly responsive when it comes to deep stimulation of the amygdala with the Procedure. It evokes terror like nothing else.

Switch on the current, a frequency of sixty cycles per second. Start with 0.5 volts, progressing swiftly to one volt. Position the electrode so it comes into direct contact with the brain. Into that sheeny seascape. Move into the temporal lobe. Evoke the dreamy state. A return to more primitive ways of remembering. Other years step forwards, dreams, old tunes. Flashbacks. How they return with the touch of the electrodes, replay themselves across the brain; the subject is transported into a hallucinatory reliving. Today I demonstrate how we will make him relive it. I will evoke his scar. Voyageurs and voyeurs of the brain, we will recover for him what lies beneath that gently billowing seascape, mementoes of feelings he could never otherwise articulate.

Navigate the brain folds, using the central sulcus as your prominent landmark, that deep chasm which separates the rolling frontal and parietal lobes. Ride the undulating sea of your dreams as you shape your course across this most complex and uncharted organ. Across Broca's area, Wernicke's area, those vast regions that stretch back so many thousands of years. Come, sail the seas: Come! *Navigare necesse est*. Tenacity of purpose: the great Wilder Penfield's secret. Who crossed the ocean in 1924 from America to Spain seeking the source of the scar, which he knew existed, which he could not prove. Those elusive glial cells which gather round an injury, at once part of the healing process, and the origin of the abnormal electrical activity underlying seizures. They could not be stained by normal methods; would not show up; they were, as he said, no more than ghosts.

The physician belongs to the future. What Penfield said then remains true now: 'How little we know about this brain which made social evolution possible... How little we know of the nature and spirit of man and God.'

We stand now before this inner frontier of ignorance. If we could pass it, we might well discover the meaning of life and understand man's destiny. One day we will be able to stain the soul so that it shows up silver on this strange petri dish of life.

*

Ladies and gentlemen, some patient background. —This subject has well-established cognitive difficulties and memory problems – indeed, they caused him to abandon his career. He was once a promising architectural draftsman. Intelligence normal, even good – but wrecked by abnormal electrical activity in the brain. Had to leave his job as he was accused of zoning out all the time, to quote his own words.

From childhood has experienced staring spells, diagnosed as complex focal or partial seizures. Commencement of excitation in the auditory temporal lobe. Seizures, marked mainly by silent staring, typically begin with an aura of hearing music, and may, indeed, not progress beyond. Progressing on occasion to GTCSs, generalised tonic-clonic seizures, which his medication fails to control. For details, kindly refer to the case notes.

His current occupation, of repetitive and mechanical motion, is ideal for his twilight states, when he is often dominated by ongoing seizure activity, too subtle to be obvious to the bystander, but when his consciousness is most definitely impaired. A kind of somnambulism. At such times, the patient is not in touch with what we call reality. He may continue automatically with routine tasks and movements but is unaware of his surroundings and may have no memory of them later. He is, in effect, absent.

His memory in general unreliable in the extreme; tends to forget conversations and events as soon as they're over. A prime source of frustration for family and friends. The other is his sensitivity. He is unable to bear emotional stress. The control of the emotions is a key factor in his seizure control; but achieved with very variable measures of success.

We consider mood changes to be this patient's chief disability. Irritability rather than frank violence is his hallmark. These variations of mood are due not to personality defects, but to the electrical changes in the brain, and can resemble the mood swings of bipolar disorder. There is, however, one marked distinction. This mood is of sudden onset. By extremes of mood, we do not mean that the patient reacts or overreacts to life events, such as grief at his affliction, or difficulties with relationships. We are saying that the experience of epilepsy demonstrates how unreliable are the emotions as barometers of reality. Feelings cannot be depended on merely as feelings. They cannot be taken at face value. The effects of underlying brain damage have to be taken into account.

Prognosis, poor. Even with surgery, I foresee he will continue to experience the progressive cognitive impairment that is an inherent part of the epileptic process. Even our procedures can only do so much to arrest this.

And now. Charcot, poet of the circus, ever abreast of the fashion, made use in lectures of the very long feathers in women's hats to demonstrate the different types of tremors. The trembling of the feathers enabled him, as he said, to distinguish the individual tremors of various diseases. So let us read the quiverings of this subject's brain tissue as I use the electrode to question him today. Tell me, subject, what do you feel?

'I don't feel anything.'

'How enviable. And if I move the electrode here?'

'Nothing.'

'Nothing? Come, come. *Ex nihilo nihil fit*, you know. We must do better than that. Don't you have any feelings?'

'Well, no, not really.'

'Come, man. Have a heart. For your wife, your children?'

'Oh well, yeah, I mean... That's just normal.'

'Normal? What do you mean by normal, subject? Does a feeling have to be abnormal for you to consider it as such?'

'I don't know what you mean, doctor.'

'Very well. I'm going to move the electrode now, to try another part of the brain. Now, describe what you are experiencing.'

'Why should I?'

'Ah. Ladies and gentlemen, note this first response. A typical reaction of aggression related to the amygdala. Still don't feel anything, subject?'

'Nope. Nothing. Nothing I'm telling you, anyway.'

'I must take you to task, subject. Please be civil.'

'I'm always civil.'

'Really? I'm going to move the electrode on... a quick prod of the ventromedial hypothalamus. Also a prime source for aggression. How about it?'

'Keep trying, doctor. I'm sure you'll get there in the end.'

'Don't be insolent with me, subject. I'll make you talk all right. You won't even know you're doing it.'

'Oh yeah? If epilepsy's taught me nothing else, doctor, it's taught me how to resist. I won't lose control.'

'Oh, indeed? Then brace yourself like a man; I will question you, and you will answer me.'

'Not me, doctor. You'll never break me.'

'No? Do you know who I am?'

'Oh, I know who you are all right. You're God Almighty, unless I've made a big mistake.'

'Yes, ladies and gentlemen, you may well murmur and gasp. My apologies. My patients are not usually so recalcitrant and rude. Do you know who you're talking to, subject?'

'Yeah, like I said. I'm having a conversation with God. Who else? You sure know all about me, don't ya, doc, what's best for me?'

'Be careful, Dominic. I can make you and unmake you, you know, with one flick of my finger. My scalpel is light; but you'll feel it.'

'Go on, then. Do your worst, God. You're the expert in torture.'

'Your vision of the Almighty is somewhat skewed, young man. Very unwise of you to challenge *me*.'

Ladies and gentlemen. As you can see, this subject has no understanding that we are harrowing him for his own good. He falls prey to an interpretation that abuse is being deliberately visited upon him in this theatre. You are familiar with the influence of ictal fear on paranoid ideas as discussed by Gloor, by Hermann and Bear, by Sengoku et al. Indeed, it is more than possible that electrophysiologically, the frequent electrical discharges in the limbic system, especially in the amygdala where affect is centrally localised, would over time lead to a bizarrely emotionalised concept of the world, possibly resulting in psychosis or a paranoid-hallucinatory state. We're not reaching him. I think I will have to be a touch more invasive. How about here?

'Oh...'

'Ah. Ladies and gentlemen, see his expression change. The temporal lobe always yields results. Well, subject?'

'I get a faraway feeling...'

'Better. But not there yet. Here?'

'Here... I'm alone in another world.'

'Describe it.'

'Like a dream... I feel I'm in a dream...'

'And now?'

'I... I'm being watched... being followed... following me, all the time...'

'Who's following you?'

'I don't know...'

'Who is it? I said. Answer me.'

'I told you. A presence. She's there... round the corner... waiting for me. Again, waiting for me again. I've seen her before... No more questions, please. No more, I won't answer any more.'

'You will if we increase the voltage. She's waiting for you, is that it?'

'Yes... she'll do for me, doctor, I know she will. Following me all the time... she'll push me over the edge, she really will...'

'Yes?'

'I'm going. —I can see a long way down... I'm going to fall.'

'Go on.'

'I'm falling, doctor... Free-falling, a long fall... to a strange and fearful world...'

Gentlemen. As you see, the subject experiences delusions of pursuit upon stimulation of the brain, which evokes his aura. Reports the approach of a threatening presence, déjà vu, that typically takes a female form. Feels he's tracked by invisible presences, just out of range. Let's investigate further. —Don't resist, subject. After all, I decide what you feel. —A little more voltage there, will loosen his tongue. —Now then. Who is this woman?

'That's what I want to know! I don't understand it...'

'Don't you love your wife?'

'Well yeah, of course I do.'

'So what are you doing, messing around with this other woman? What do you feel for her? Is it love?'

'It's...'

'Yes? Loosen up, man. I'm going to apply a little more pressure here.'

'Oh... it's a kind of longing.'

'Yes? Just tell.'

'There's nothing more to tell.'

'Just a little more pressure, then. Trust me, Dominic; how rarely we know what's best for us.'

'Oh. That's... it's... unbearable. Why isn't she here? Give me something to take it away, doctor, take her away... I can't bear it, the pain... Why have I got to go through all this? Give me something to keep her away... it'll kill me, kill me... she's not here...'

'But she loves you, by all accounts.'

'That's even worse. Please, stop! My God, it'll kill me.'

'Ah, so that's your malady. You can't bear love.'

'I never had a thought of anything before I met her... I was quite happy with my wife...'

'What, making love once a week on Saturday afternoons while mother-in-law has the kids, once you've put the shopping away?'

'What's wrong with it? With three kids and no time to turn around? Don't see what more there can be.'

'She's shown you, hasn't she? This other woman. She's given you a little glimpse into another world. That's why you can't forgive her. You just want everything to stay the same. It's set in concrete with the wife, isn't it? She absorbs all your time and attention. She completes you. You're one snug unit. But your new woman, she'd make you live outside that – and you can't cope. Can you?'

'I... none of your business!'

'You're not fit. You're not fit for love. Yes, you want to be very careful, Dominic. She's not good for you. Let's see if a little erotic stimulation gets you up to speed.'

'Oh, that's... amazing. Why, she's right beside me. I can see her... right here, she's right here... so beautiful... but I can't touch her... ah, fuck... she's gone... Why do you do that? Why make a fool of me, give me a desire that can't be fulfilled? Show me that she exists, and then deny me?'

'Yes, I'm particularly good at simulating images of the beloved. Quite real, wasn't she, subject?'

'Why put it in my mind, give me the hope of it? Don't give me hope, doctor. That's the cruellest thing of all. Don't give me hope. I was quite happy without hope.'

'Why shouldn't you have hope? Everyone else has always had hope. Why should you be exempt from the pain of visualising what you can't have?'

'But it hurts, it hurts.'

'Love is meant to hurt. You do love her, don't you? Admit it.'

'I won't admit anything.'

'No need. It's plain to see. Laid out here in the grey and white folds of your brain. As Charcot read the feathers, so I read you. Just quivering with the agony of love.'

'I don't want to love, I don't want her, just want to forget her... I forget everything else... what use is my brain to me? It won't let me forget her... it's useless, useless...'

'What can't be cured must be endured. Why are you crying, subject? Other people have suffered love as well as you.'

Brain surgery is a terrible profession.

Loss is something we must all go through. It always makes the patients cry. We're making good progress, ladies and gentlemen. Tears are a good sign that we're approaching the scar. More voltage there. Seek out the area of desolation.

'No, no. It's utter... utter desolation... I know she's not there, when you do that... I can't go on. I can't go on with my life, I'm falling... falling into the void, falling to pieces... No more. You give me visions of love which I know can never be fulfilled. This isn't real. This is just a dream... Why, why give me those longings? She's not here... How am I going to get through the rest of my life? I can't get through the next five minutes, the next minute... It's overwhelming... I didn't know it was possible to have such pain and live. No one has the right to touch me there. Not even God.'

'But God does touch you there. Especially God. Otherwise that spot would not exist.'

What a thing of marvel is the brain. You wouldn't think that even in this simple workman, who can barely speak, there existed such exquisite capacity for suffering. Such depths of sensibility and refinement. Look at him. Floating in a sea of pain, pure pain. Isn't it wonderful how we can arouse such acute, impossible desire in this way? Here, on this spot, is the scar. The source of all his tears, which even now is making him weep. That which we will be resecting today. After that, such feelings will trouble him no more.

This isn't cruel; we are only mimicking real life. Titillating the temporal lobe in this way. We excite you, then tell you the object of your desire doesn't exist. This seems reasonable to us. It's no more than life. Take the jokes of the universe in good part, subject. It doesn't do to be ungracious. Emotional and sexual torture is no more than the normal processes of the imagination, so often self-inflicted. Ah, he's gone. Escaped us again, in his usual way... Lost consciousness. How he has always dealt with life's difficulties.

Thank you, ladies and gentlemen. Your applause is music to my ears. I hope today has demonstrated that the problem of neurology is to understand man himself. I leave it to yourselves to determine how far you identify with the patient.

Well, subject. Back with us? Remember any of that? Or suffering a little postictal amnesia? A touch of confusion after the seizure? With your devastating transparency, you're the ideal candidate for such neuro-teasing: you believed every word, didn't you? That was all a joke, about slicing the top of your skull off like an egg. That was all just a little warm-up, a little tickling of the temporal lobe while the electrodes went in. No harm done. To quote the great Penfield yet again: 'Surgeons can remove areas of brain, physicians can destroy or deaden it with drugs and produce unpredictable fantasies, but they cannot force it to do their bidding.' Today we are using SEEG, intracranial investigation, to locate seizure source. Some fifteen electrodes, implanted within the temporal lobes. You didn't even feel them going in, did you? Still invasive, of course. Still with risks. Now that you've signed the consent form, I can tell you: brain haemorrhage and infection, which can lead to permanent neurological impairment or death. How much difference would it make to you, I wonder. Now that I've known you a while, sometimes I think you're all scar. Never mind. Now for the real thing. Let us commence the session. Tell us, tell us. What do you feel?

PUNCH AND JUDY

'Where's the baby? Wheeeere's the baby, boys and gurrls? Has Mr Punch thrown it down the stairs? Oh it's a prrrrity baby, it's a beautiful baby. Mr Punch, Mr Punch, where's the baby?'

'It's in the coal cellar.'

'In the coal cellar, oh you soppy sausage!'

The baby came in with the sea, a rush of potential. A mélange of salty fluids tinged with foam. Started life as fish. Swims translucent, gills in weird places, and black dots as markers for the future. It's one vast, dark ocean in there. And already it's pleading for more. More water, more food, more rest, more sex. Like us all, it can't get enough, turns its mother sick, starving, and insatiable with its minute flips and dances. Already fish is extending tubby pawlets towards a land life, already grasping.

It's a good crowd for the last show of the summer, watching Mr Punch purring and skedaddling around before the little backdrop marked *Prison*. Behind the little striped theatre box, the Professor's hard at it. Ladies and gentlemen, welcome to the show. A one-man outfit, run by the Professor for many years. The same nasal flatness underlies Judy's ghastly gentility, the tortured epiglottals of Mr Punch, strangled into life by swallowing a whistle in his throat. Sitting with the other kids at the front, Finbar watches in enthralled dismay, his ice lolly melting unheeded down his hand. It's the end of August and the air is changing, the shops full of mothers buying uniforms.

'Brrrrrrrt! Sausages and sand for tea!'

Plodding large and grey over the sand, a woman is taking round a collecting bag, her dress striped like the hangings of the puppet box.

'Remember Mr Punch. He has to pay the council. Please give generously for the last show. A nice send-off for Mr Punch, please, ladies and gentlemen. He has to pay the council. Ladies and gentlemen! Remember Mr Punch...'

Goodbye, Mr Punch. Maybe he can winter in Capri, or emigrate to Canada. He sure isn't wanted here. The notice on the kiosk announces how it's the last show not just of the summer, but for good. The council won't support him any more, with his stick and his odd ways. His attitude to women. His contempt for the offspring he fathers, then denies. His curious changeability, his moods. His helpless irresponsibility. It's a shame because he's such a hit. The woman with the collecting bag has to hassle a crowd of loiterers for their contribution, standing behind the row of triangular union jacks. The adults look and listen as hard as the children, desensitised by television, who are discovering that it's violent enough, even for them.

'What that baby wants is a stick of rock and a gentle tap on the head.'

'Don't hit him, Mr Punch. Put your stick down.'

The baby's obviously dead already, its little black gape of a mouth, its face a stiff white mask of grief, dignified.

Fish spins on its nose, dives into unplumbed depths. Dances with joy in its own ocean. Knows no light but trusts its eyes, round black dits. Drinks seawater with black mouth wide open. Starts thickening into opaqueness. Trusts its two halves, mother and father, which ceased to exist when they merged. That divine hooking into the uterine wall. What finger would unhook that?

'Stupid baby. You shut up.'

'Don't hold 'im upside down, Mr Punch. The blood will rrrrrrun to 'is brains.'

'He hasn't got any.'

'Wa-jer mean, 'e 'asn't got any?'

'What I say. A brainless nincompoop, that's what he is. I'll just test him with my stick, very gently on his head – and a *one* – and a *two* – and a *three* – that's the way to do it!'

'No, no, Mr Punch! You'll scar 'im for life if you do that!'

But it's plainly too late for this baby, with its long pointed eyebrows, its dignified distance, a madonetta of grief.

*

'You're back.'

'Yup.'

He's appeared suddenly right beside her, as if he'd swarmed up through the sand, in sunglasses, litter stick in one hand, plastic sack in the other. She sees him at the very last moment, just as he's taking a lolly wrapper from by her bare feet.

'Where have you been? I've not seen you for weeks.'

'Oh... I've been around.'

She'll never know; not if he can help it. The surgery, harrowing him to the bone; the turgid hospital stay, the long convalescence at home. Has it worked? Has the operation been a success? Can he look her in the eye?

'You've had your head shaved. Very sexy.'

Her fingers go to the bristle of his hairline, at the back of his head beneath his cap. He stiffens; his neck arches, his shoulders ripple to her magic fingers. So maybe he's not totally healed yet.

'You're looking well fit.'

Tanned, lean. The scar on his brown forearm whitish and shiny, with its eternal question mark. The abrasions on his head clean and crusting, and invisible beneath his cap. His expression also hidden by his aviator shades that he doesn't know are fashionable.

'That's not what I came down to talk about.'

'What are you doing down here, then? I thought you hated the beach.'

Just as street cleaners are a few grades down from the bin men on the van, so beach cleaners are the lowest of the low, community service. He'd never descend that far; he is the community as far as he's concerned.

'Been put on beach duty. Too many complaints about litter from the visitors.'

They both know it's not true. He should be up on the prom; he spotted her from above, the way he always does, picked her out unerringly from among the milling crowd.

'Supposing I wanted to add my complaint to theirs?'

He shrugs. 'There's a freephone number.'

'That could be the most interesting call they get all year.'

'I'm sure you'd be very eloquent, Bonnie.'

He came down to tell her it was over; she must leave him alone for good, like the doctor said. Not to mention all the expert advice from his wife. Give him his best chance; he's thought it all out. The surgery's left him able to think more clearly. More aware of what's going on, more aware of what he must avoid. A man who realises his ruin will surely work to avoid that ruin. No, he isn't going to throw it all away, on this castaway.

But he hadn't reckoned on the real, live Bonnie, soft and warm in the summer sun; the tiny hairs above her lips all golden, her soft mouth open in welcome, her motherly cleavage, her faint, happy scent of cherry and holiday. Her general aura of soft, living, breathing gold, her touch. He can't resist a quick kiss. No one's watching; no one except Austin, who's also coming down the prom steps, fresh off the train from London in his white shirt and jeans, swinging his backpack; stops halfway, breathless. It rips open another world, one he never suspected. Not so much the lover; he kind of knew that. He's ripped apart at the tenderness that lingers in the air between them, that he can see from here, like a genie that emerges of its own accord and hangs there, a separate entity over which neither has any control.

'And throw the baby down the stairs! That's the way to do it!'

What happens when fish reaches out towards land? Memory and emotion start casting their long shadow forwards, hippocampus and amygdala forming. The advanced embryo brain is a fine network of veins, speckled with cells of the future. Glia and neurons have begun their dance. The rudiments of systems in place: motor systems, special senses, the emotional motor system: smelling and tasting; seeing; looking and focusing, crying; facial expressions, speaking; hearing; chewing, breathing, gasping, coughing, licking, sucking, expressions of voice. All rhythms of life, unfolding in that vast sea.

On the stage the baby puppet is tossed about like the image of a foetus on a scan. Bonnie turns away.

'Dominic.'

'Eh?'

'You don't like it down here, do you?'

'Can't say as I do, no,' slowly. 'You know that.'

'What do you think of this?'

It's a job application for a draftsman, in an architectural company in London. Stick and gloves tucked under his arm, he takes off his sunglasses, looks through it, breathing, eyes alight.

'In London...'

Now that the surgery's improved his prospects. He could give up his long freedom here, that's no different from prison.

'You could do that. Take it up again. It's surely not too late.'

'What – start life anew, eh?'

She sees him light up with it, absorbed in the possibility. Live their entire future together in five seconds. One of his sudden initial excitements. She too smiling slightly, into his eyes. In her long blue dress she's as full-blown as the summer sea, tide in, her own eyes large and occupied. See yourself, that tiny glint of fish reflected in them. But if he doesn't see, she's not going to tell him; not yet.

'I'm Dr Quack and I cure all manner of diseases:
    Whatever you pleases.
    If you've got the twitches I can chase them out,
    And if you've got the funny fit just give me a shout.
Now, Mr Punch. What's the matter?'

'I'm dead.'

'Oh well, lot of it about this time of year. How long have you been dead?'

'Two weeks.'

'I see, not a bad case. And where are you dead?'

'In the head.'

'Very well, this calls for a spell:
Morbus sacer, morbus dives
Morbus Herculeas, morbus caducas
Morbus comitialis, astralis, demoniacas, lunaticus!
No better? No? Oh dear. This calls for sterner measures. Now boys and gurrls, I'm going to get a liquorice stick to give him, I'll give that man a taste of his own medicine.'

'Oh doctor, doctor, don't beat me, don't beat me, put that stick away, oh I'm falling, doctor, I'm falling...'

'Oh dear, oh dear, then you must have the falling sickness. Pick yourself up, man.'

'Up I come, up I come. Here, doctor, taste my stick now. And a *one* – and a *two* – and a *three*. That's the way to do it. Only when I fall do I get up again – what a pity. Oh, what a pity—'

He's reading on, stabs suddenly at a line, the heart of the application. 'The applicant must be in good health.'

'What – aren't you in good health?'

So tanned as he is, strong. A few heads turn from the Punch and Judy, at her cry of astonishment, at the man drawn back from her, arrested; a better show here? Austin too watches, from the halfway platform of the prom steps. Best view in the house here, and he wouldn't dream of interrupting before the end. No, this isn't the kind of act where you intrude. Dominic hesitates, draws breath again. As if trapped in a corner of that wide beach where the two of them washed up from cities on the opposite sides of the world. Bonnie's flotsam, lost overboard, and he's jetsam, thrown away. Flotsam is what the sea flings around, goods and debris floating on the water from a shipwreck, there by accident; jetsam is cargo or solid trash that's been deliberately thrown overboard to lighten the load in a storm. She looks up at him, hand on his arm, a cork bobbing in the ocean. He looks out to sea, jettisoned.

'I have epilepsy.'

'Oh. So that's it.'

'It's – it's under control.'

So that's it. He already lives in two worlds. Why ask him to do more?

'And?'

He looks at her, then back at the piece of paper.

'That needn't make a difference, surely.'

'So you say.'

'It's a company where... the director's a friend of mine. I could easily take you along, introduce you... if you'd like to do that, any time... We could go to London...'

Again he looks at her, then across the hot, dirty, crowded sand to where the water's striving fruitlessly at the land. Puts the job application carefully away in his pocket; at least he doesn't bin it in front of her. Draws breath again.

'Thanks. I probably will.'

'Mr Punch, what do you want?'

'I want a kiss.'

'What, in front of the boys and gurrls? They'll only laugh.'

'Oh widdy-widdy – give us a kiss, Judy. Just a quick one.'

'Oh dear. Very well then. Make it quick.'

'Brrrrrt! That's the way to do it!'

'Oh, please leave me alone, Mr Punch. Please leave me alone now. I'm never going to do it again, a thousand times no.'

*

She has no idea how little it takes to make him happy, how deep is his acceptance of his life, of safety and repeat prescriptions. Lunchtime picnics with the wife and daughter, sitting on the bench outside the library. Day trips to France on the ferry, just for the ride; they don't get off. Sunday walks down the hill to the old Pleasurama, with fruit slot machines and ride-on toys for the kids. Work. The invariable routine. Notes in his packed lunch box: *love you.* The contented arc of his legs as he cycles slowly home after work, the scruffy red backpack slung across his shoulders. His patience as he waits for the traffic, to cross the final road, lifting a hand to one of his many acquaintances. Then across the grass wasteland and up the alley by the railway line to his house.

Into the tiny storm-porch, crowded with kids' jackets and fishing rods, down the shiny corridor to the garden, stripping off his socks. Flexes his feet, examines his bunions, his nails, wide and short and chipped like those on his fingers. The early days, when he peeled toe skin away with his bloody socks, hands calloused and sore from the broom, back aching. Now his soles are thick and yellowed, impervious, know that the earth is dead beneath his feet. Then tea in the garden, where he can sit with his faint street smell and grumble gently about his day. What need more?

Today will be the same as any other. This afternoon he'll be home, ten minutes after finishing work. The boys scuffling round his neck, his wife bringing him a cup of tea, his daughter clambering onto his lap. How can he find anywhere for Bonnie in all this?

'This has got to stop, Bonnie. It's getting way too much.'
    'Yes. I know.'
    'You're making a fool of yourself, running after me.'
    'Right.'
    'I got no place for you in my life. Nothing to offer you.'
    'I hear everything you're saying, Dominic...'
    'So – you and me...'
    'We can just be friends, eh?'
    He turns away, twitches another piece of litter from the sand.
    'Just acquaintances.'

How could he ever fit this conversation into his life? He hasn't got anywhere to put it, there'll be no place for Bonnie later this afternoon, when he's mock-fighting with his boys and throwing his little girl up to the ceiling? It's like some weird doubling of reality, this other woman, her hand now on his bare arm, when no one's got the right to touch him but his wife. This Bonnie, pleading with him for what he hasn't got to give: his warmth. Him telling her to lay off; it's really getting on top. She's to leave him alone, stay off his beat. Stop haunting him. Does she hear? —Stop following him; stop following him. You couldn't call it stalking exactly, but only just short of. In his opinion. Should go and make it up with her husband, bite the bullet, sell the house, go back to London where she belongs. Stop asking for more. Leave him to work his own life out. If he's happy doing what he's doing, what business is it of hers? He's married: okay? Does she get it? Married. And she's spoilt; wants her own way too much. Her middle-class refusal to consider his job – his lifeline – a job. He wants the pavements back to himself. Those summer afternoons on the deserted back streets, those short roads doubling back on themselves, the long winding avenues, where the work is steady and minimal and you go along with your broom like a thin toy. Baking brown like biscuit in the sun, no one to disturb you. Time to think. His fidelity unblem-ished. All he can say is that he can't take it; just leave him alone. Her life and his, they're separate. Is that plain? He can't put it all into words: that she's decadent, morally irresponsible; too much her own person; too much time at her command. Undisciplined; when she should be at her own work, her art. Her piano, she should be giving her time to. Too free. Her life's beginning to go by her, slowly at first, then faster and faster.

How could he possibly tell his wife what Bonnie's saying in return, which he can barely take in himself, that she's fed up of all this, too. Wants her heart and soul back from him, that he's to hand them over, give them back at once. Him protesting that he hasn't got them; hell, what does she think he is? Her thwarted rage and tears, snaffled and choked by the Punch and Judy, her child's long, uncertain, blue look. How she's insisting he must have picked them up somewhere, spiked them on the litter grab, put them away in one of his bags; maybe even now they're landfill, lost among a million others?

'Rubbish. You're on the streets too much, d'you hear me? Should stay home, like other women do.'

'But I'm not like other women. So you've always said.'

'I'll say! Most women know when enough is enough. Why aren't you home looking after your kid?'

They both look at the small boy, absorbed in the crude, antiquated show above his head.

'In that house?' Its late summer stillness. Its seedy damp. Phantoms and sand on the landings. Inching its way towards the cliff edge.

'And anyway, I might move back to London.'

'With me? You're a fool, Bonnie, if you really think that.'

At the raw jeer in his voice, she sees he won't change back. His set face, the Capricorn tilt to his chin. So he's doing a runner. Maybe he can't stand it, having revealed what he is. As if that made any difference to her. Gives her first smile, a cruel bird. She can change too, just like that. And if he were attending to her, he'd be running for it truly, wading through sand and crowds as fast as he could, back up the cliffs to safety.

'Anyway, what about your piano, eh? What about it?'

'Don't you start, too. I'll take care of that. When I've finished with you.'

'What?'

Frightened for the first time. A man exasperated, thoroughly worn out, at the end of his tether. But with much further to go yet. Recovers himself, in control. Dealing with the public, formal, final.

'We are finished, Bonnie. We never even started. You just didn't notice.'

'Well, you leave me alone, then, too.'

If he were attending to her at all, surely he'd feel sorry for her, despite her new aura of health shimmering round her in the afternoon sun. Her live hair, puffed soft and electric. Her eyes, looking out to the horizon, to the depths of the sea, as if for rest. It's late summer and she's tired. If only he'd leave her alone. Stop summoning her. Stop appearing round street corners every time she thinks of him. When she's so weary of the chase. Like any woman at this stage, just wants to put her feet up and sleep in the afternoon sun. He and his silent peremptory demands, that she visit him the whole time. It's he who forces her into being a predator. Just try telling him that.

'You think about me all the time; I know you do.'

'You've got a problem, Bonnie! You're out of control. I tell you. Don't want anything more to do with you.'

'Where are you going to go? To get away from me?'

He looks out to sea again at that.

'You're trouble! You'll ruin my life!'

'What about me? How can I go back to London after this?'

'Train? You'd be there in two hours. If you hurry, you'll just make the 13.35.'

'You bastard.'

'I'll come help carry your bags to the station. Buy you your ticket, make sure you get on. Tell the ticket inspector to keep an eye on you so's you don't get off too soon, try come back. You're going to lose me my job. The other guys all know and everything. Even the supervisor's got to hear about it.'

They're all tired of hearing about it, in the break room. Did find it funny, but have long since told all their jokes – diverting her attention onto themselves, going round in twos, getting a police escort, etc. – and now listen in silence, fingers shifting round their cups of tea.

'My wife finds it irritating, too.'

'Oh, too bad. The ultimate. I am sorry to hear that, Dominic.'

'So you should be.'

His rough, brutal irony. Only he's completely serious.

'Well, that's a classic. Went running home and told her, did you, when it all got too much? And then come back and tell me?'

'You better not insult my wife.'

His first jolt of panic, as she realises what she might do. Just how she might come between them. Sweat starting out on his forehead. Doesn't she realise? It's no common relationship she's out to disrupt. No one can come between them. His wife, his safety. He chose a wife who wouldn't resound. His wife. She's the only one who can keep him under control.

'Your mother, you mean. Think Mummy's going to protect you from me?'

'You... What a low thing to say. I find it degrading even to be talking to you. I don't want you near me.'

As if he had any choice in the matter. When she's so close to him. Part of himself, you might say. Almost the condition in which he has his being.

'Well, that's tough, because I'm here for the long term.'

Yes, it could be his epilepsy itself talking to him. Insidious, persistent and mean. How come she personifies it so accurately? Exactly what he'd imagine it saying if it could talk. It'd be funny if it wasn't so... Who is she? Stares at her, eyes darkening. She's a jingle in his brain, endlessly replaying herself. Doesn't he have to take medication three times a day as it is, to keep her at bay? To spend his days walking, walking away from her? Those days when he doesn't have epilepsy; it has him; it is him. He has no life of his own, no being of his own. She's everything to him. He brings his hand up to his face, pulls at his ear, quick, agitated. His eyes dark, clouded. Rams his sunglasses back on, turns away.

'Popping up all the time... Why don't you leave me alone?'

Always creeping up on him, like the waves up the beach. If she would only leave him be. But it's not clear whom he's addressing.

She's only too pleased to have got him confused. Moves a little closer to him, puts her hand on his arm, feels him shudder. Puts her fingers to his lips, feels them quiver. He can't help but respond. Like that other inseparable couple, Punch and Judy, at it hammer and tongs, in flight and in pursuit, they're together for life. What Sidney said was true;

she knew it, it chimes with what she herself saw at their first kiss, what she sees and feels now. She smiles again, looking round at the wide, crowded beach, then back at her man. She's made him quake in his boots. That's enough for now.

But it isn't, of course. There's just one more little thing. She has something else to tell him, something private and important, wants him to come round the house later, when he finishes; he refuses. What, with her kid there? Just to talk? No. No way. They have talked. What more can there be to say? He's just made the most intimate of disclosures to her; trusted her here in public, told her what he is; she can do the same – raising his voice and his litter stick. Anything more she can say it here and now, on the beach. But she doesn't; sinks down on the sand. Applause breaks out as he stomps away, back to the steps up to the prom; why, they quite stole the show. The admiring audience turn back reluctantly to the Punch and Judy, now labouring to its well-worn finish. Dominic forges on up, the holidaymakers shrinking from him as he shoulders them out of the way. He doesn't even see Austin, now descending for his entry onto the sandy stage.

Another pause, another crowd drifts away, like the waves of the sea. A couple of youths come over the sand, balancing mugs of tea on a tray. 'Give that to the Professor.' From the back of the booth, a hand reaches out between the stripes.

Finbar detaches himself from the scrambling children, comes rushing up to Bonnie.

'Daddy! It's a surprise! Surprise visit! Daddy's here!'

Austin's right behind him. His eyes meet Bonnie's, steely.

'Yes,' he says. 'I found I could get away for the day. Well. That was a good show. Highly instructive. Shall we go home now?'

*

And by mid-afternoon everyone's gone home; Austin and Finbar to London; Bonnie to her strange spiritual abode in the attic; and Dominic, to his little house as normal, shift done and the rest of the sunny afternoon before him. Tea's nearly over in the garden, his wife raring to go after the day with the kids, already in her uniform for the evening surgery. Now's his time to tell all the anecdotes from his day. How the public entertain him.

Tidings of the strange woman who haunts him slip unheeding out of him; the bewildered light in his eyes; he rubs his head, unable to make it out. Could this be change? He doesn't mean to tell; he just talks about it that bit too much. The wife's blunt, explicit advice. Not her again. What does he think he's just had all that treatment for?

'Your first week back at work and she's already breathing down your neck again?'

'Well – yeah.'

'You're too nice to people.'

'Well now; it's on the job description, you know – you've got to be polite and helpful to the public at all times.'

'When were you ever rude to anyone?'

'I'm always civil...'

'She's just like the rest of them: a nutter. A street crazy. The only difference between her and the bench people is that she's got a home to go to. Just ignore her. Walk on by. Or tell her to...'

'Shh.'

The kids all agog.

'She's out to rescue you, babes. Take you away from your sad life here, off to London. She thinks you're a prince in disguise.'

'It's not that.'

'She's totally barking.'

'I know.'

'I mean, you've made it plain.'

'I've made it plain.'

'How many times have I told you. You shouldn't let her stress you out.'

'I don't.'

'Eat up, anyway.'

Food, rest and sleep; exercise, fresh air. Lots of walking. Just what the doctor ordered. Not too much excitement. Keep the stress down. Regular hours. Bed around 10.30pm, up at the same time each morning: 4.45am. It all helps. You sleep so much better when you've been out in the open all day. No more bad dreams. Regular schedules; knowing which country you're in, hoping to stay there. No sudden emigrations. She watches his plate, anxious, as he picks at the pie, pushes the plate back, with sudden decision.

'Anyway. I did tell her.'

His wife's gathering her bag, her case, pinning up her hair, halts. 'You did?'

'I had a word. Told her to push off, once and for all.'

'How'd she take it?'

'All right.'

She knows what that means, from the edge in his voice. But no time to discuss it now.

'Did you tell her about the op? No, you wouldn't, would you, babes. Rather go through it all again, eh? How's the scar?'

He bends his head to her cool fingers, that softly probe before she drops a kiss on his head.

'Healing nicely. All right, angel. Love you.'

'And you. See you later.'

'See you later.'

This is his world, his boxy house and lifestyle, the shallow topsoil where he's insecurely rooted. He doesn't know that he needs any more. He goes back out, waters the plants, a long, thoughtful job. The kids tumbling about. The little girl brings him his sketch pad, asks him to draw her some pictures; which he does; tall buildings on a hilltop. She snuggled in his lap, watching, thumb in mouth. He's got a shelf full of them, these pads, *art brut*, that no one but the family ever sees, and his closest friends; though who could be closer than his dear friend Bonnie, who'll never see them? Portraits of his mother, his wife, his daughter, and now of Bonnie, as postmodern buildings, functionality inside, embellishment outside. They wouldn't recognise themselves.

After an hour's rest he rises, says it's time for the park, already glad to get out and stretch his legs again. Later, he'll see that they get to bed; puts them down separately; otherwise the boys, they got bunk-beds, you hear all this crashing and banging around... His life is beginning to go past him; it was slow at first but now it's faster and faster and from counting in fives, soon he'll be able to count in tens, even sooner in twenties, his years here. But it's all one long day. He might make a sandwich for the wife when she comes home; go over the road and clean mother-in-law's car. Cut the grass, that always grows back. He has no other aspirations. There are no hidden depths. He's as transparent as he ever was.

JOKER

The pipers are drumming the summer out. Across the cliff-tops. They scatter behind them melted ice creams, phantoms on the prom, forgotten tantrums on the beach. You never sent me a postcard. Their white boots shake the high street, the worn grass on the front. Followed by women and children, a police car crawling in front, blue light flashing, a couple of street cleaners litter-picking slowly behind. The bandstand echoes for the last time this season. The battering of their drums can be heard to Dover, to France. Bonnie's drum locked up and silent in Concordia. You never sent me a postcard. You let the whole summer go without one word.

September days, slants and shadows of sun. Shortenings. Sea breezes, dispersing the summer that still hangs on the beach below. Concordia's leaves turning. A delicate clustering of leaves at the kitchen window, green hardening into dark stems and veins, red creeping in through windows. Up here on the esplanade you can see autumn coming in over the waves, a chill, sheeny light blue. Maybe the shadow from the blackberries beyond the cliff-top railings, that no one will pick. Wallflowers and pink valerian shrivelling in the wind. An endless St Vitus' dance, the masts shivering in the port below. Boats coming in to rest for the season. Dry dock. The cliff arching on endless around the island. The road sweeper always ahead in his high-visibility vest, like some tagged wildlife, to be approached with caution. I didn't know that when I met you, Dominic; asked you the way somewhere as if you'd been anyone.

Dominic. Stop a minute. I've got your ring to give you back. Here, clutched in my palm. Like the summer, I disintegrate as I walk. Here, take it and go free.

He goes down the hill, his loping amble, turns into the multi-storey car park where little can be seen but the shadow of his sullenness. Picking at a tattered sticker on his chariot, waiting for the lift. Battered cap, mud-green short-sleeved shirt, the fluorescent slung over, the signet rings lined up along the barrow handle, all shambled together like any bin man. And underneath, the vast fragility, cracking at the edges; she can almost hear it. Half-turns at her wary approach, a dangerous profile, about to rear; eyes go electrified in contempt.

'Thought I told you to stay away from me.'

'You've got a fucking cheek, Dominic! This is a public car park.'

'Oh, so you didn't just follow me in.'

'Yes. I followed you. All the way along the esplanade. Didn't you feel it?'

So that's what it was. He felt it all right. But at least she's here, in the flesh, where he can see her. In a clinging white dress like a dream of summer, hair drifted on her shoulders. The last glints of summer electricity coming off it, summer storms. The faint drift of the pipes and drums behind her, from way up on the cliff-tops. Holding the ring out to him at a distance.

'I don't want to talk to you. Just take your ring back.'

'That trash? Some crappy bit of metal from the street? I wouldn't even bother to pick it up.'

'It's silver. Real silver.'

'Yeah, what you thought it was valuable? Thought it was worth something, you kept it?'

'I promised, remember. Now release me from that. Take it back, and let me go.'

'Nothing to release you from. That didn't mean anything. That's just a figment of your imagination.'

'But – the way you talked to me – the way you behaved...'

'I talked to you' – he thinks – 'I never said a word. I talked to you – I talked to you like I talk to anyone. Where's your kid?'

'At school, of course.'

'Here?'

'In London.'

How does he know? How does he know that Finbar hasn't been here for weeks? That he left with the summer, and won't be back? Austin packed his bag in silence when they returned to the house after the Punch and Judy, and when Bonnie finally came out of the attic, they'd gone.

'And you're here? Surely you should be up there with him?'

She winces. He knows where to get her, where it hurts. He knows that she's forfeited trust.

'My husband... He and my mother-in-law have him during the week, and I just go up for weekends... They're not keen on me being there. They say I unsettle him.'

Her little fox cub, gone all polite and distant until Sunday afternoons. What's it to Dominic, that she's no longer trustworthy? That Sally and Austin took her son away and kept him? Now dole him out like a precious sweetie, when she's been good, that is, present. When she can tear herself away from the magic isle, can bear to face London.

The lift arrives, doors opening, empty and grey; swings back down again. He's looking at her, intent.

'So you're here on your own?'

'Yes.'

'Getting a divorce, is that it?'

'No. Not yet.'

Austin and Sally don't give up that easy. They'll try any workable arrangement first; workable by their terms, that is. Their terms are, return to London, therapy, and above all, no more seaside life. Resume her career, such as it was. In return, she can have Finbar back, all she wants. They've judged her incompetent. And with such a long history of judgement behind them, their word is law. All those years of intense guardianship aren't that easy to break out of. Meanwhile, they're denying that they might need a real court of law. The only banned word in Sally's vocabulary is 'unmanageable'. And she's not there yet. She still thinks Bonnie's going to come back. Give her space, she says. It's just a fling. She's just acting out. Every woman has a Dominic in their lives at some point. But it's a funny thing; when the great return to Hammersmith took place, Austin forgot to have Bonnie's piano moved back. It's hard to go back to a smaller life, cramming the great white-toothed beast back into that little London cottage, where it took up all the dining room, all the air.

'But how can you do that? A little kid like that?'

'He's at a good school in London.'

'What difference can there be between a good school up there and a school here? None, I'll be bound.'

'What business is it of yours?'

'Why didn't you fight for him? Fight to keep him?'

'It's in his best interests.'

'Best interests? What crap is that? It's not right, him being away from you, his age. My wife'd never do that. Some mother, you...'

'He's better off – with them...'

'And leaves you more free to pick on me, eh? That's it, isn't it?'

'You're not listening, Dominic. The last thing I want is any contact with you. Just take your ring back, okay?'

He is listening, but not to her. The pipes and drums are coming; being drawn after her. Down the hill, coming closer. She would. She's the joker, the odd one in the pack. A characteristic reversal of the Hamelin piper, her leading them all by the nose. Sure enough, there they all are, the pipers, just coming into sight down the shin of the hill.

She steps up to him with the ring, in her white dress, of light, fine wool that clings to the slight rounding of her abdomen. But Dominic sees only her early autumn eyes fixed on him, gold and sheeny-blue; an odd, navy cast over them, a thin veil. This time he looks deep, in the gloom of the car park, sees himself reflected. Hesitates. Who is it? Him, her, or both? Teetering on the verge of betrayal. Wavers into her eyes; pulls back, dragged back by the fear in his.

'That ring, that's just an excuse on your part to contact me. How plain do I have to tell you? When we never even had...'

'How can you say that?'

When it was so electrifying between them.

'There's nothing there, I tell you. Nothing at all.'

The stalker's delusion; that there is a relationship. That they're communicating on some deep, mystic level, beyond that of normal consciousness. The keening of the bagpipes comes nearer and nearer. They've reached the bottom of the hill and are standing there, waiting to cross: *Bonnie Scotland.*

'I never even fancied you. —I don't know you. You're just some-one I see around the town. You're just a member of the public to me.'

'You don't want to know me. You don't want to know me.'

Flings his hand out, more in self-defence than anything, knocks the ring to the ground. She swoops after it like an owl after a mouse; rises, looking at him steadily. Sees a spot of dried dark pickle by his upper lip, a Jacobean love patch. Licks the tip of her forefinger, wipes it off. Sees him flinch, not at her, but at himself.

'What would your husband say if he knew you spent your days following me around?'

'I do not. How dare you.'

'You don't? Seem to be there every time I look up. Want me to tell him?'

'Anyway, I don't even speak to my husband any more, do you realise that? We only ever communicate through email.'

Those curt, clipped, hateful communications, full of contempt. But neither of them can face a solicitor yet.

'Well, that's your problem. Why tell me? I talk to my wife all right. As a matter of fact, I promised her not to talk to you any more...'

For his own good. She knows what's best for him. She made him promise. But some promises you're just plain driven out of. He trails off, eyes agleam. As if listening to something else. The pipers, no doubt, just turning into the car park and still full of themselves.

'Not to talk to me? What are you doing now, then?'

'This isn't talking to you. This is telling you. —On my tail the whole time... stalking me... Think I don't see you?'

'Stalking you?'

'That's what they call it, isn't it? Didn't you realise there's a name for what you do?' – pressing the button for the lift again, and again. The pipers flooding in all around them. His voice raised husky against them. 'I saw you this morning. Dodging round the town centre after me. I saw you, plain as I see you now.'

Or almost. He can't explain, how she never really came into focus; how he knew she was there, a presence amid the crowd. Brings his hand up to his ear and tugs at it agitatedly as the pipers come to a squealing halt all round the car park.

'You've got some front, Dominic. I haven't been near you. I was doing a school visit this morning. A music workshop. Showing the kids how the piano works.'

'Oh yeah?'

'Well – you can ring up the school.'

'Oh, you'd have someone ready to answer the phone for you, tell your tale for you. Someone else you'd fooled.'

'But I can't do any more than I am doing, keeping out of your way. Ask the others. Ask the other road sweepers, Paul and people.'

'I have. They've seen you about all right. The whole town's seen you.'

'Not this morning. I've said. I wasn't there.'

'Don't believe you. I was on the town centre all morning. And you were there, all the time.'

'This is ridiculous. Look' – scrabbling in her bag – 'my bus ticket. See, on the other side of the island. Issued at 7.45am. Why would I pay for that and not use it?'

She's reduced to talking like him, facts, details.

He examines it, doubtful for the first time. Who's her doppelganger, then?

'This yours? You could have picked it up anywhere, this ticket.'

Looks at her, baffled. The whine and sagging moo of the bagpipes all around, the last burr and rattle of the drum vibrating through him, from his mouth all down his shoulder and arm out to his hand, filling the ground floor and dispersing through the upper levels, like consciousness dispersing.

'I wouldn't deign to lie to you, Dominic. I've got better things to do than trail around after you, I assure you. Why, I haven't seen you for weeks.'

The keen of sincerity in her voice seems to reach him. He stands holding her ticket, staring at her.

'Who is it then, follows me round all the time?'

Twigs snapped and shoved into garden gates, to show she passed this way. Feathers drifted onto the pavement, words spelt out in drops of rain. Damsons trodden underfoot, her heart's blood. Lessons hidden in stones, messages scrawled across leaves, that only he can read. Two-hundred-foot trees packed into an acorn rolled across his path, here where there are no oaks. A single red maple leaf left in the middle of the road, so far from home. And she says she isn't around? That she stays away? Why, she's calling him every day this time of year, this windy little isle; how can she deny it? Footsteps just heard in the wind. Figures that vanish when you look round. Blending into the wooing of the telegraph wires, the sounding of the tide ball. A low singing in the prom railings, the ruffling of café canvases, an insistent sibilance from the furled sails and masts below. Her footprints on every step he takes up Mount Royal; that dedicated single trail across the sand at tide out. She's behind the eyes of every woman in this town.

'If it isn't you? Who is it?'

His face is pallid, haggard, his eyes strained dark, as if from the effort of holding them open; staring at her intently; a green gleam in the dusk by the lift.

'Well, I'm sorry, it's not me.'

'Because you're always there...'

Surf thundering up the beach early mornings. The smell of pounded seaweed, foreign, English, like sewage from this little island. Flecks of yellow sea-foam flying up to his lips and cheeks as he works the prom. Graffiti in the car park. Sandbags set out in Harbour Street against the spring tides. A V-line of geese out to sea. The long rattle of the can down the esplanade. The whining of the wind in the lift shaft, the sickening smell of rubbish from the street bins. A sighting of a fox on a street corner the misty mornings, as he cycles to work. The last of the moon keeping him quiet company across the ocean. That neurological haunting that takes a woman's shape. Coming to meet him from the side streets, taking him by the throat. Throttling the consciousness out of him, then letting go. Letting the dark blood rush back to his eyes and head. My partner. I'm waiting, round every corner.

We'll glide along these cracks in the pavement, this neuro fault line together for all time.

'Dominic. I may visit you sometimes. But not all the time.'

'Yes,' he insists. 'Always. You're always there.'

'Do you think it isn't the same for me? Do you think?' her voice breaks. 'Do you think it's any different for me?'

Following afternoon silences down empty alleys, the track of his wheels spinning clues. What did he let fall? Grains of dust in the tidiness, thistledown on the breeze. His absence, down all the streets. His attention is caught. There's a light in his eye. As if her words stirred a memory. His head is half-turned to one side, as if to attend to the unconscious.

'Every time I look up...'

He sounds like a man in a dream.

'But I've just said. I haven't seen you for weeks!'

'Makes no difference.'

'But I've been so careful to keep out of your way! Don't tell me I've lost the freedom to walk down the street.'

'I know what I know. It is you, I know it is. You promised that you'd always be there. And you're the type keeps your promises.'

'Well, free me from that! Free me!'

'Free yourself. You did that. Made that promise of your own free will. Didn't I warn you? —Nothing to do with me.'

He turns aside, as if turning away from his thoughts. She sees clearly she has no chance of reaching him either.

She holds the ring out to him again.

'Can't take it.'

'But what will I do with it?'

'Do what you want with it. Throw it in the sea. And now leave me be.'

'But – it's not like that. You're everywhere, in this small town.'

'You see me, just pass me by. Pass me by, pass me by. — Like you're doing now,' with coarse, desperate humour. 'I tell you, my job's on the line. The supervisor, he's warned me.'

Was sorry to do so, after five impeccable years; their best worker, conscientious, punctual to the minute, personable and polite. But it's not the job for those kinds of visitations.

She's fed up of him. Slowly and deliberately puts the ring back on. As if charging herself with power. Like a white dream, static coming off her. Her live hair. Steps up to him, into his zone. Sees the lights change in his eyes; the ugly, uncanny flash of fear.

'Fuck you, Dominic. I'll walk where I like. And I'll follow where I like.'

'Christ, if you don't stop...!'

'And if you don't stop, I'll tell your supervisor. How you messed around on the job all summer.'

'You can't prove it.'

'I'll give him dates, places, times.'

Facts. Details. She knows how to get to him.

'I tell ya, I'll get the police out on you if you don't stop!'

'What, can't handle it yourself?'

The leap in his eyes shows how right she is.

'Discussed it with my wife already. Getting a restraining order.'

'You mean your wife discussed it with you. She put the idea into your head.'

He startles, reverts.

'What were you doing outside my house the other evening?'

She steps closer still; she can feel the warmth coming off him, and the fear.

'Oh? When was that?'

'Last Monday. About 6pm it was. Looking over my fence. I saw you.'

'Remind me: where do you live again?'

He hesitates again, diverted by a fact. Tells her, literal as ever, house number and all.

'Is that near the station?'

'You should know.'

Right up to him, aura to aura. 'I don't know.'

'Don't fool with me. Wasn't just me saw you. My mother-in-law saw you too, snooping around. She lives opposite.'

Closer still, and her much-memorised fingers slide along his arm, and up to his neck. She knows he dare not bring his own hand up, to touch them.

'I could have been walking down your street for any reason. Why shouldn't I be outside your house?'

Her fingertips tracing his stubble and his lips and down to the open neck of his shirt, undoing his shirt buttons, pulling it out, to get to him, his warmth, his thudding heart.

'Outside! You were practically inside. Hanging over the fence. I saw you! —Get your hand off!'

Her long sleepwalk round his place, as he sleepwalks the streets. Not looking for a way in, so much as a way to understand him. Who he really is. What keeps him here, on Waste Island. Her hand's on his chest and neck now, keeping him there at the wall, turning him giddy. He stands helpless, back to the wall.

'How did your mother-in-law know it was me?'

'Knows you by sight, all too well. She knows all about how you follow me. Get off me, I said!'

But he can't move. Her well-remembered hands are on him. Already he's stiffening, all over his body, at her electric touch.

'Well, bully for her. Why didn't she come out and tell me herself? Film me on her mobile phone to prove it? Why do I have to account for my movements to you? Never mind your fucking mother-in-law. Would you like me to give you both a daily schedule of where I'm going to be?'

Her thumb sliding into his mouth, tippling his tongue. Her other hand easing into him. He turns away, shivering, spitting her out, edging sideways. Only he can't move.

'Did you go into my house? Did you?'

'Why don't you ask mother-in-law?'

'You did, didn't you? I know you.'

'Don't be ridiculous. How could I? It was locked up.'

'Oh, so you do admit to being there.'

Her first kiss drifts up to him, their lips meeting hair to hair, electrifying; then closer, feeling the tremor in his. Feeling him poked defenceless into her hand.

'That was ages ago, Dominic. In the summer. Cherry season. I brought you some cherries. Remember? It's nearly autumn now. I haven't been back.'

'You lying bitch... You did go in, didn't ya... I saw you... I know you did. You went upstairs...'

He doesn't know whether she's gone or in the house, in London or in his bed. He doesn't know who's after him, Bonnie or his epilepsy. but it's the same thing, he can feel it, got him by the balls and won't let go. Quivering and startling against the wall, unable to move. She laughs, delving ever closer and closer. Watching his eyes darken. But in torturing him, she's torturing herself.

'Wasn't mother-in-law out there? In on the action, giving you a bit of support? Don't tell me she stayed behind the net curtains, with so much going on.'

'She did come out. Followed you round the corner... You didn't see her, did you? She was about to call the police...'

'For looking at someone's house?'

'She knows what you're like. Told me she's been waiting for you to turn up.'

'I guess the police would have had a good laugh. If they hadn't cautioned mother-in-law for wasting their time.'

Shoves at her, with an effort. Fighting like a madman for clarity, for an inch of space between them. Pushes her back, to arm's length.

'She's a witness. Saw you plain, standing on that pile of grass cuttings we throw over the fence. Too high to see over otherwise, isn't it?'

'Yes.'

His hands fall to his sides; his mouth works, voice a dry whisper. 'So you really did...'

He backs away again, rearing and startling, with deep, snatched breaths; again she steps up close, pinning him up against the wall, feeling his trembling, his quick breathing. She clings closer, her leg between his; feels his resistance sag. Covers his sea-beaten face with kisses. Her hands travelling him again like an unexplored land.

'Jesus, get *off* me!'

'Yes. I did. I was there. I had a good look. Your utility room, with all the junk your wife leaves on the windowsill, that she's always going to clear up some time, that you nag her about. Your garden table and chairs, so neatly laid out. Your beautiful flowers, that you never talk about. And maybe I went right into your house, had a good snoop around that as well. You'll never know.'

She laughs, fondling him, while he stands splayed against the wall, the lights all change in his eyes. Like a man in a dream, he can't move. Didn't he know it, that she was there. Doesn't he check the floors for her footprints every day, for her ruffles on the bedclothes. And one of these days he's going to give himself away to his wife by saying the wrong name at the wrong time.

'No, leave me alone... not again... What have I ever done to you...?'

'Don't worry, Dominic.' Her mouth at his ear, her breath shivering him into a thousand pieces. Her hand picking up the pieces, one by one, somewhere outside the world.

'Like I said, I'll always be there. Tailing you in my car. Hiding in the car park at 6am, waiting for you to start work. Following you down every street, as slow as you like. You can't lose me. I promised. I'll follow you to the ends of the earth.'

'Too bad I don't go that far,' his voice softened and crusty with terror.

'And beyond. I told you, I promised.'

His head thrown back, arched and stiffened against the wall, her fingers palpating him, soft electricity on his most sensitive parts. Eyes up over his stiff shoulder, whispering into the void.

'Christ, no more... I'm going to fall in a minute if you go on. Oh, Bonnie, stop, I'm falling – if you don't stop – don't stop...'

With a last effort he pulls her hands away, holds them out, at arm's length.

'Can't you take it, Dominic? Can't you take a bit of real love?'

Something breaks suddenly in his mind, at the impossibility of breaking his routine. Wherever he goes, in this small town, she'll be there.

'I'll kill you!'

'Go on, then.'

She's safe with him, back in his arms as his hands drop again, her lips up against the hard-thudding pulse in his neck. If he could take that first step forwards, she'd be for it, but he can't take that first step, he can't. It's what's held him back all his life. He's never been in the competition; outside the game, without power, money or intellect. If he could have taken that first step, he'd be far away from here, doing another job, living another life, an architect in Montreal, an artist in Barcelona, a draftsman in London. If he could take that first step, he'd have braved Bonnie long since. He'd be fucking her into oblivion in the lift now, would have pulled her in there on her knees, be waiting for her mouth to hug the life from him, he'd cry out to God how she's killing him, the tears would course down his rough face, everything in him would explode into sobs.

'I'll *kill* you if you don't leave me alone!'

The lift doors open with a buckle, releasing some people, who flounder out, gaping at the aftermath of his words.

'You leave her alone, you jerk!' says one of the women.

Dominic blinks back into his usual distance, of being insulted by the public. It's what he's used to. Sticks a foot in the open lift door, shakes Bonnie off, steps backwards into it, pulling the barrow quickly after him. The doors hesitate, waver, close. Bonnie pushes them apart at the last moment, joining him. The descent in reality not long enough for her to feel how he's still hard under her lingering hand, though he shakes her off again, how he's still trembling with fear as much as rage. Well, the poor lamb. She accompanies him into the depot, the basement with its two sinks, the fluorescent strip not amplified by the feeble light from the window with broken panes, the spare barrows lined up, chariots at rest. He brings his barrow up alongside them, bangs it forwards into the wall, where it reverberates gently. Washes his hands, thoroughly, to the elbows, while she watches in silence. Listens to his heaving breath settle. Watches him start unlocking his bike, hand shaking. Still thinking he's going to escape. She hears the whine of the lift again; the others also returning. The halt, the maimed, the poor, must all return home too.

'I'm pregnant. Yes. You heard. How did it happen? This is how it happened. I'll show you.'

She takes his litter grab from his barrow. Gauges her distance a second. Brings it hard across the side of his head; the cap goes flying. Slashes at him again and again. He takes the blows as if attending to see if they're real or not. As if it's beneath his dignity to evade her. Eyes wide, as if listening. For those moments she sees herself as he's always seen her: intrusive, inflated, female. Taller than the cliffs, soaring above the prom. More powerful than the sea that sucks the land in. Giving him that much-deserved thrashing, the one every woman wants to give the bastard who's impregnated her. Hitting him with the furious abandon of the woman who's let her man shoot his fruitful seed into her, who knows she's on her own for the next several months now. What she should have given him in spring; and another, and another. She'll have his child, but she'll have his life first. He's half-smiling, as if embarrassed for her, that she should make such a fool of herself, despite the welt across his cheek; that'll take some explaining away to the wife. Reaching up to take the stick off her; easy, easy. But it evades him, like so much else. Out of the depot, up the malodorous stairs, scattering a dozen other road sweepers out of the way, tipping them backwards into their barrows, out of the car park she drives him, back up the hill, the harbour falling away beneath, the boats diminishing, right back up to the esplanade, to the bandstand where they met, there in the open air where she can really lay into him. The blows echo to France, to Dover. In the bandstand she sends him spinning round and round, the sea whirling around him in the opposite direction, the sky cascading sideways in slow motion in a third, outermost circle. It started out slow at first, his life, but now it's going by him in these three circles, faster and faster, and now he's coming to the end he can really say he always knew it was going to be like this. You spin and spin, and then you die. Trembling, he drops to his knees, gives the old fish's bark, the protest of the sea animal forced to come once more onto land, his head jerks up, eyes upturned, round and blind like those of the fish. Goes rigid. She lashes him round and round, round and round. Sea spinning into sky, sky spinning into sea. He goes ricocheting round the harbour, from pole to pole of all the yachts clinking together. Round and round, she drives him, round and round. Right round the world, to Canada and back. His grand gestures fling him across the skyline, turning, searching, with blind eyes; his turning is the turning of the moon as she flings out across the sky, spinning in slow motion halfway across the night, and halfway across the day. And she's the sun, wheeling round him for ever, a stream of unbearable light. Though she's got nothing like his strength, she draws blood from his ear before collapsing on top of him. His blood patterning the white skirt of her dress, his last jerks subsiding beneath her. She lies on top of him, eyes closed to the spinning sky, feeling his breath on her ear, his hand closing round hers on the stick. The white sky spinning into nothingness.

His cyanosed, unconscious face close to hers; she watches the colour slowly returning. Waits for her heart to cease rebounding. Lies there, next to her man. So warm, so close, so absent. Their breaths mingle; she snuggles her face into the crook of his neck, and sleeps too. Faint snuffle of eau de cologne overlaid with the day's work. Ten minutes go by; no one takes any notice of two lovers dozing on the grass by the bandstand. His eyelids flutter; and like lovers they gaze into each other's waking eyes. An infinity of hazy ocean. Smoky with possibilities. Come into focus; he pushes her away. Sits up, hand to head. His face like sand. Rises to his feet with a stagger. Bends to pick up his bike key, which got dropped in the scuffle, picking at it repeatedly before he manages to grasp it. Then he's walking away, veering a little towards the railings. His footsteps fade slowly down the esplanade.

*

She gets to a bench. There's a slash of pain across her abdomen as if she'd just laid into herself. She shouldn't have hit him; he's not the type, he's not the type. Hasn't she learnt anything? She's gone too far; again. What's she done? Struck him, and caused herself agony. How could she? How could she have done that to herself? Sent him spinning down the esplanade, a yellow blur receding into the distance. Sent her heart after him, scattering blood and shreds of flesh everywhere. Scalding silver tears sending him ever further and further off. He'll never forgive her, not in this world, or the world to come. Her tears flow all down her front and onto her hand where they coalesce into a hard small round: the ring. She's feet away from the cliff-top railings; the entire sea below, ready to swallow it up. But no. That's no choice. Nothing else to do but slip it back on. This time her hot tears seal it on for ever. A long, dragging walk back along the empty esplanade. How can he stand it here?

Bonnie goes daily to the empty beach so the baby can hear its ancestor, whispering promises as it rushes up the shore. Fingers sinking into the sand before it can grasp the land. The endless inability of love, rushing blind up the beach, hands outstretched, to sink headfirst into nothing. But here on the friendly sand, still warm from summer, is one place she feels less unwell, even with Finbar's summer ghost playing down by the water's edge. The air, straight off the sea, is that much easier to breathe.

What's she living on? Sea air, mostly. A few piano lessons, scattered across the isle; one morning a week at a school for disabled children; the odd music workshop. Austin's said she can have the house; for sure, no one else wants it. Sally will buy it outright for her. Nothing else, though. Access to Finbar at weekends, but only in London; too unsettling for him to come down there. Not to mention the rubbish man hanging around all the time. Austin'll pay the fares; otherwise she can starve as far as he's concerned, or live on the crusts her lover picks up off the streets. That's fine with her; wouldn't take a penny of his money or Sally's; will buy the house herself, out of the small legacy left her by her parents.

The travel's difficult for her, she's so ill, the weekends hardly a success, she mured up at Sally's place, that heavy Chelsea nightmare to which she vowed never to return, and then in the Hammersmith house, neat and claustrophobic with its little rooms, its curtains like frilled pinafores. Finbar elusive and remote, hiding away his new school uniform; Austin away with his new girlfriend, the black Texan princess he met in America. Sally came down to talk to Bonnie, crying, saying Austin's gone so hard-faced, her son, so hard-faced. But it doesn't move Bonnie.

The baby goes out with the tide; rock pools of blood and pink foam. Starfish hands, sea-anemone nose, seahorse tummy, magic round black eye, all washed away. One translucent possibility squabbed out by nature's blunt, salty fingers, reaching up into her womb. Seawater's the only fluid could penetrate up there, washing out the firm mucus plug that sealed the foetus into place, rinsing and swilling it all away.

Cerebral hemispheres in place, thin membranous sacs distended with liquid. Nerve cells multiplying in the cortex. Vestibular canals and cochlea forming, seashell labyrinths, the spiral, commonest shape in nature, that can turn a man dizzy when it starts spinning. Small enough to feature in the double helix of DNA, large enough to form the spiral structure of a galaxy. All that cerebral potential, that twelve-week grape of veins in fluid, wrinkled and squashed. Jokers; sports of nature, collected with all the summer things. Gone on its way on the great journey, was just passing through.

Last salmon oozings; a coarse, sympathetic blonde nurse, offering mighty sanitary pads, full of how Bonnie should have attended earlier. Not that there's generally much they can do about it. Happens so often, a third of all pregnancies. Never mind, dear. Plenty more chances, at your age. Too bad about this one, too bad. It just wasn't meant to be.

PIANO

Twilight states. Twilight at noon, eyes darkening against the sun. October blazes which no longer reach him. Out of it. He's gone, eluded them all, even his wife. Epilepsy, mean and seasonal, has him in its grip. His true-love, against which there's no real competition. Consciousness fluctuating, held in check by drugs which dampen him further. Which every winter aren't as effective as they were in spring. Remote as the moon, he stares through the crowds in the precinct. Blank, vacant. You can pass within two inches of him and he won't flinch; won't even register. The cars shaving past him. Barely nods the distance to his old acquaintance. And all his summer friends have dropped away. The bench people, the over-eager, the over-ambitious, gone. Gone to day centres every one; homeless shelters, prisons, to await the spring.

Bags at street corners, filled with sodden leaves. Trundling the old barrow back and forth. Coming home, eating tea in silence. Like any middle-aged workman with little to say for himself. How was the day? Oh... same as usual. Meet anyone? Nope. Anything happen? Not so's you'd notice. Water hot? Of course. Okay. He'll take his bath now, then. Unrousable. Puts his uniform to be washed in the basket, as usual. Cleans the bath meticulously afterwards, puts the soap back in place, hangs the white towels, leaves not a drop out of place; sets the window ajar. The October nights reaching dark fingers through earlier and earlier. Doesn't bother him. He'll go out to the garage, look over his carpentry stuff; maybe get the bench out. Might sort through his stuff; the shelves are full of his pickings from the road, ten odd shoes all lined up, dozens of beer glasses, a rag doll or two, sunglasses, broken and whole. Yeah, he should go tidy them. The wife's hand on his shoulder as he goes. Does he want his sketching stuff out? Gallant as ever; ever concerned about him despite her family milling about the place, father-in-law hogging the TV, mother-in-law his little daughter. Clear the table in a jiffy if he likes, been a while since he... No. Like he said; he'll go out. She watches the connecting kitchen door close behind him, into the garage. He's a man held in a glass mountain. He won't fall, but he'll never dance either. In the street lights, the light streaming from the open garage, his boys circle the street on their bikes.

In the kitchen, the wife pours a glass of red wine for herself and another for her mother, thoughtfully. He's been kind of quiet since the surgery, almost depressed. It's helped the night seizures and the morning falls to some extent, but seems to have left him in a kind of neuronal dusk, a numbing. His moods are better, too, but at the price of him being not down all the time exactly but... it's like... he's gone. His personality, his grain sanded down. There's no reaching him. The days they used to take the train up to London for the day together, to galleries, to shows, infinitely far off. Always finding something to laugh at, both of them mocking his condition: You all right, darling? You all right today? Is that a little tremor I saw there? Why don't you fuck off! Yeah, I'll fuck off all right and then where will you be? And now. He's just not the same. The only thing that livens him up is this same wine, which he's not supposed to drink. He's a shell of himself.

Oh, come on, love, says her mother; it's not that bad. Quiet he always was. Main thing is, he's out of the house during the day. Earning a crust. Counts for a lot, in my experience, take it from me. Not to have them underfoot. Who cares if he's the same man or not? Know what? I'm going to tell you the secret of life, babes. The thing with men is, they're a waste of space.

*

October takes easily to Bonnie's cliff-top house, the loose windows, which she stuffs with newspaper; loves the wood floors, the cracks between the rough, sanded planks. Comes dancing in through the sea-warped doors, up the stairwell and straight out through the attic. The ceilings so high that any heat shoots up above her head. The plink of rain in the range chimney, the wind battering the conservatory, its whining at the back door. Echo of footsteps in the hall, but nobody ever there. The foghorns coming every minute from different ends of the bay; the whirr of the pilot boat, making the rounds. It's always about, black and orange, up and down around the island in all weathers.

The autumn sea, asking and asking for the land. Echo and lap of the waves in the caverns beneath the house. Swish of black skirt on the landings, a shadow on the stairs that Bonnie can at last identify as the old lady she doesn't want to become. The one who lived here for a hundred years, long enough to put a curse on the place, that the house should never be at rest, should always be moving, towards the sea. Unlike Dominic's home, so safely bounded by the railway line, forty feet away. It's the fact he deprived her of that safety that drives her nearly out of her mind.

The whispers of the house, going out with the tide. You can't just rush into other people's lives, Bonnie. What about their space? The arrogance. That's Concordia's space, not Dominic's. Barging in, just like that, into this house and daring to live here. Though it's not that the house is out to punish you, Bonnie. You just lost protection by playing too carelessly with its edges. By walking into rooms that weren't even there. Did she really think she'd be welcome? And now it's not clear whether there's room for your piano here any more. Takes up too much psychic space. Maybe you should smash it up; you're hardly likely to be needing it again. This house has no sympathy, beneath the charm. Just says how it wasn't meant to be, her music; her shadow baby, it wasn't meant to be. Its eyes looking out from that shadow world that she made but can never visit.

And Bonnie won't break, although she hears the baby crying from the cellar at night, an eerie, jerking, mechanical cry. Goes down the wooden steps by candlelight, slowly, not remembering which ones are missing. Looks up at the old coal chute where the frozen wind is falling, at the yellowed walls where the brick dust is still collecting in little heaps. Finds the naked baby in a corner, arms splayed; a toy left behind by visitors, its mechanism sprung impossibly into action, its plastic body cold, cold. Plugs it with the dummy hung round its neck, rips out the battery. Won't give the baby a proper burial, just stuffs it in the bin.

*

'Dominic.'

'Good morning.'

How do you track down a street cleaner who doesn't want to be found? He has the whole town at his intimate disposal, a myriad of secret passages and pathways to hide in. Why, he spent all September scurrying down alleys at the sight of her, and where he went after that, she never could work out. So why not just let him run? But she found him easily enough today. Just like old times. Thin sun, early morning. Bonnie thin and pallid, bringing no music with her on the quiet street. He barely registers, goes on with the work after his automatic greeting, looking over her shoulder. Except the glint in her hair keeps catching his eye.

'Dominic. I'm sorry about all that.'

'Pardon?'

'Sorry about all that. Last time we met.'

'I don't know what you mean.'

Stops work, stands looking at her. Yellowed, eyes dark. Lines rounding across his forehead. Civil, formal. She's ashamed, bothering this inoffensive middle-aged man. In his green army jumper, the protective trousers from a prison that excludes her. Sleazy, with his beaten-up skin and coat, face like a crumpled paper bag, his rings, his medallion with I *have epilepsy* inscribed on the other side. This two-inch pool, that she thought was a fathomless deep. Looks back at him; at the end of her exhaustion. She knows him, that he doesn't lie. He's not playing dumb, to stay uninvolved. He doesn't know what she means.

'You know… You were rather upset last time we met.'

Still he looks at her, waiting.

'You know. You must know. I hit you. Told you I was pregnant.'

'Oh. Yeah,' but as if recollecting generalities, rather than particulars. 'It's just that… I'm married… and you keep on…'

He sounds dignified, helpless in his integrity. Lying isn't in his scheme of things.

'Not any more. And – and I'm not pregnant any more.'

He nods, remote, remote. Letting her quick words evaporate. Turns his head up to the branches of the tree above them as if calculating how many more leaves must come down for him to sweep up. He looks older, yellowed. A new line beneath his right eye, a slice from a razor that cuts her to the heart. She hesitates. She's got to make contact somehow.

'How's it going?'

'Oh… 'bout the same.' His slow drawl. Weary. 'Leaves coming down…'

'Yes.'

He has more to say. Points up the street. 'You can see for yourself the state of the sidewalks.'

It's important to him.

'Yes.'

'With all the leaves...'

'Yes.'

He's got still more to tell her. Gestures up the street again. Something else important he's got to say.

'It's taken me an hour to do just from the park to here.'

Her heart quickens, contracts. There must be some way of getting in touch. But no one's at home. And maybe the lights aren't even on.

'And... how do you find the weather?'

'Eh?'

'Do you mind the wind, the wet?'

'Oh... maybe...'

'The cold...'

'Doesn't really bother me...'

'Do you ever fancy a change, ever want to work indoors?'

'Maybe... now 'n again...'

'Be hard to adapt, I suppose, now. You're so used to being out.'

'Guess so...'

He turns away. Props the broom.

'Ever find anything interesting these days? On the streets? Or don't you look?'

'Oh... like I said. I'm always looking...'

'And?'

He thinks about it a moment. It's difficult for him to put it into words. Flexes his fingers in the thick ivory glove, on the broom handle. Sums up, slowly.

'You never know what you might find.'

Again her heart stirs, like the hairs on her head. Where are you? And when she puts her hand on his arm, he's even further away. She's missed him so much. Or is it him missing her? Almost more now he's in front of her. Because there's no one there. She can stalk him all she wants. He's found his way of escaping her; is gone, right out of reach. Resumes work as if on a ball and chain, swooping slowly along the pavement and back to his barrow. Works slowly, slowly. The words wandering out of him, as if he's too tired to resist her. His innate honesty remains also; when she speaks, asks, he has to answer. The surgery couldn't excise that.

'I came to say goodbye, Dominic. I'm going back to London.'

Where else.

'For good, I mean. Moving right out. My little boy – you're right. He missed me too much. And it tied down my mother-in-law too much, looking after him. She's a free bird.'

'U-huh.'

'I'm going back to share our old house in Hammersmith with my husband.'

Not a tremor. Pushes the broom on, into the thin, uncertain day. Diseases exist to remind us that we are not made of wood, as Van Gogh said. But don't seem to be doing their job here. It's clearer further off. Great flocks of birds circling the sky in the distance. Some kids trail by en route to school, recalling Finbar, his uniform still spruce and stiff and too big, at a school so far away. She's allowed to resume the school run now, now she's promised to return to London for good, though she doesn't talk to the other parents at the school gate, waiting for this vast, lost fragment of her heart to come out.

'Thought you were doing that already.' Profoundly disinterested. Why wouldn't you share a house with your husband?

'Well... I've been down here, if you remember. Just going up at weekends.'

'Oh yeah?'

'We've come to an arrangement, Austin and I.'

'Who's Austin?'

'My husband... so I'm moving back in, to look after our little boy in London, but... well, not as a couple any more. Separate but sharing. Austin has his friends. I have a room downstairs...'

'Yup... why is that... don't they let you use the rest of the house?'

Almost complete indifference tinged with cynicism. She can't tell him about the neat little house where she wants to pull the curtains down from her window every night against that intense claustrophobia of street lights; the sullen, silent mornings avoiding Austin in the narrow kitchen, making Finbar the porridge he won't eat. Finbar chattering away to her in his own little London language, a local patois that goes right over her head. The dining room empty, waiting for her piano.

'Well, the idea is I look after our child. You know. Continuity. Convenience. So I'll be right out of your way. Up in London. You won't have to avoid me any more... we're going to sell the house here...'

He has no ears to hear the misery in her voice. Doesn't she understand, after all this time? Not his business to avoid anyone. He just works the route he's given, preordained. Glances at her, no trace of bafflement in his eyes.

'The poor kid. Seems like he's getting a bit of a rough deal, eh?'

'What it's to you?'

'Well, nothing. Just seems a bit rough on the kid. Being pulled from pillar to post.'

'But that's it. I've just said. I'm going back to look after him.'

'If you can look after him.'

'What do you mean?'

'What I say. If you're looking after your kid in London, what are you doing down here?'

Speaking with the baldness of the simple, as ever, and more than a little threatening in his directness. Won't be moved from his stance, that she shouldn't be down here. At all. She's frightened, that he sees something she can't. But he still seems only half-connected. Aloof.

'I've just come to pack up for a few days. I hope that's all right with you. I'd hate to disturb your routine.'

Even that doesn't get through.

'Dominic. Don't you remember?'

She's calling from some far-off place. In her navy bodywarmer and cream jumper, short navy skirt and leggings and cap, the necklace of big blue beads, she retains some of her London difference; the islanders would still spot her a mile off, as being not from here, a casual-smart, inland evocation of *marin*. A ridiculous gulf, the rough, elusive man before her. He glances at her again, sideways, bent over the broom. A shade more alert. A shade of the old irony.

'Don't I remember what?'

'Well, if you don't, best I don't remind you of it, maybe.' But she does, of course. The day she sent him and her heart spinning down the prom, and neither's come back yet.

'Do you really not remember?'

'Nope.' Still with the same shade of irony; it's she who's the crazy. Imposing her whims on him. The stolid man of work. Switched off, a man of concrete. Impervious, limited. Not open to middle-class fancies. Irritating women of this town.

'Nothing to remember.'

How it caricatures the normal conditions and changes of life, this epilepsy, as the Punch and Judy did in the summer. He's forgotten already.

'So you did that, eh, you reckon? Drew blood and all?'

'Dominic – can't we be friends – go for a coffee or something?'

She's sad, knowing she can't have it all. But her sadness is her sanity. She knows he's a gentle nonentity she's driven into an impossible position. As she drives him into a moment of presence now; straightening up suddenly, eyes snapping.

'How could you and I be friends? What,' – with more open mockery – 'you'd bring a little sunshine into my life, eh? Stop and pass the time of day, cheer the poor old road sweeper up? Be there for me when times are tough, when it all gets too much, with the old health and the family? How nice for me, eh, to know that someone's thinking about me.'

Utter impossibility of any social normalisation here. Does he even know who she is?

'Maybe even give me a free ticket for one of your concerts, donate the fare up to London, because you know it's a sizeable proportion of my pay cheque? Very nice of you. —I've got to get on, Bonnie.'

Leaves the pavement half-cleared, the brown mat of leaves ending abruptly; slings the brush into the barrow and is gone, crossing to the other side of the road and along, round the corner.

*

Dominic saw it, Dominic foresaw it, with his cynical insight. Saw right through her, as he always does. Come end of November, Bonnie's left London again, because if she stays another night between those walls that are like a skin she's bursting out of, she's going to pull the entire place down on them all and go screaming down that quiet urban street that Dominic will never walk. She left quietly, at 4am, to the bobbing and padding of silent foxes down the empty street, couldn't bear it any longer, his absence, that he would never be on any of the streets here, that she'd never bump into him on any station concourse, never see his figure disappearing in a crowd. That he's so familiar, or her familiar, an integral part of herself. He's the shadow that's always been accompanying her, right back from childhood, from her pre-memory days and before. He's the unresolved grief for her parents, who fled into death rather than stay and look after her, his deep nurturing is what she can't live without. There's no one like him in London; they all look of another race. Why couldn't he take a train up and find her? Why didn't he come looking for her, along all the anonymous London streets? If she stays any longer she's going to die of homesickness.

It's like she's under a spell, says Sally in exasperation; she's never known her this bad before. It's driving Austin and Finbar mad, too. They're fed up of Bonnie jumping up at meals she can't eat, fed up of her jumping up to turn the radio off in the middle of a fine piano concerto because her malady's returned and she's unable to bear the sound of music again. And when Austin tries other stations, it's torture, the autistic drumming of pop songs and their one-liners for the simple, full of secret messages for her, songs that tell her he's waiting. She knows Dominic's expecting her, calling her. It's a draining, dragging feeling that noise gives her, like a sickening, a failing. So many noises she can't bear: the rumble of dogs barking, the cooing of woodpigeons like a solitary nightmare, two ends of the same sound, a great bruise waiting to press through her skin. The humph of Austin's breathing, the grate of his voice. The confident sound of media megaphone, the insidious voices of the radio presenters, announcing reality. Even Finbar's little vocalisations.

Dominic saw somehow, how she wouldn't be able to connect with her son, but even Dominic wouldn't understand how she's gone tone deaf with Finbar now. Not in tune. Increasingly unable even to hear what he says any more, in his little ringing voice. Like some strange little cub, singing in an unknown language. She's heard the young foxes round Concordia at night, their quavering and yammering that builds to demonic squealing. Something in the timbre of Finbar's voice reminds her of it, the uncanny snuffling at bin bags in the street, the long, black, sleepless nights, and the harsh, high screeching, like a wounded child screaming for help. She could never tell Dominic, how the eerie, otherworldly pitch of her son's voice makes her feel unwell. How she can't bear to be in the same room as the sullen father fox Austin, can't breathe fully when he's around. The little house is full of the unbearable oppression of two egos in full collide.

It's hard on them both, father and son. They're fed up of her wrestling at doors and leaving, always leaving, disappearing and roaming, like a shadow of herself. Leaving meals, leaving Finbar's bedtime routine, leaving the interminable talks with Austin, about what they're going to do, how they're going to manage. And in the end, Austin tells her, Bonnie, the front door isn't locked.

And when Bonnie gets off the train at the end of the line, she smells the air of the place, a waft of freezing coal and salt coming off the black sea and gusting along the black streets, and she's back in a place where she can breathe. It's the long, dark slide to midwinter. And quiet. So quiet. The house is a cold, dark ship, a massive, empty ark, the endless stairs like a series of ladders up to the top, where snow freezes on the attic windowpanes. The electricity fails the moment she walks through the door, the tiny whitish light from her mobile phone lighting her through its great dark spaces, down to the kitchen and candle drawer. The heating's broken down, the boiler won't light, the tiny, obstinate blue flame refusing to fire in the darkness of the kitchen. She moves down from her airy summer bedroom, her attic refuge, and into the living room, where the open fire, tended, keeps the place bearable. Goes totting for wood in skips, for bare knobs of sea coal on the beach, following the trail of black dust along the sand, dropped by steamers en route from Newcastle a century ago. Her gloves freeze into five-point stars, the wind flings iced sand into her eyes, pulls her by the ear back up the long hill to the house. The fire burns soft and tarry, with a blue light. Whose flames she never can read. They burn at the limen, the trail of spume between water and land: place where trees become rock, rocks break down into grains, and bones become sand. My thoughts sailed over many seas. I dreamed of the ghost house condemned to be on the move for ever. To inch over the cliff-top and sail the seas. The one spotted from afar, light glowing ghostly. Whose crew, if hailed, will try to send messages to people long dead. Sailors drowning not in water nor on land but in sand.

Listening to this house of winter storms. That now possesses her with a hold as tight as that of failure. The music she hears is different to that of summer. The flamboyant staccato from downstairs where the piano's beaten up every night. An atonal arrhythmia, dustbin lids and cans rattling and rolling, the howling from an attic heaving and rocking in the tearing winds. Every window encrusted with salt inside. Gusts and eddies on the stairs, breezes in the corridors, flags snatching and flying on the landings. The geese flutter in the wallpaper with a noise like the ripping of silk.

Open all the windows, right up to the attic. Let them out. Drifts of light snow and cold air falling softly throughout. A ripping of wings she hears each night, as she dreams of birds preparing to fly, up and out through windows and walls. But the geese are still clinging to the wallpaper. Svelte bellies curved for flight, dulcet black dits of eyes that flick towards her. Wings half-out, tails streamlined behind them. She's afraid of touching their black clammy feet, their tail feathers like tight grey combs. The house dreams its dream through her, of birds flying. Of sudden multitudinous rippings, like many silks tearing. A bird shape perching on the banister, hesitating, adjusting. Its heavy goose waddle and slither of webbed foot on the wood, about to plunge down to the wrong element. Spreading its wings. Its long neck, poignant and brown, like a baby's. Then another, and another, all the way up the stairwell, a heavy fluttering. Exploding into motion like so many soft brown-grey bombs, their heavy streak up the stairs. Banging into the landing walls, leaving them spattered with brown stains. The air filled with beating wings, wings through her hair, feathers brushing her forehead, the soft punch of a webbed foot onto her cheeks and lips, birds rebounding from wall to wall, from wall to window and out, above her head. The calling and yarping in her ears and then in the sky, as they stream finally out of the attic window. But when she wakes up, they're still there, bulging and enmeshed, and she doesn't have the magic to release them.

*

December, Austin's birthday. She sends no card, but he rings up. Can't get through on the landline, because she's had the phone cut off. Can't afford it; in that island way. Catches her on her mobile finally. Comes to see her; says he's got to discuss Finbar with her. And everything else. Stands looking round the room in disgust. At Bonnie, pale and blonde on a winter's day, thin in her navy leggings and long cream jumper, grey shadows beneath her eyes, looking indefinably chilled, as if she'd washed in cold chalk water; which she has. Boiler's expensive to run, old, irregular; unlike Dominic, with his regulated life, she doesn't have a constant supply. And the heating won't work at all. The house is out to break her spirit. Austin stands in the middle of the room as if avoiding contact with the walls, bringing the foreign, wealthy smell of leather from his jacket, jingling his car keys. His large, dark eyes flicking round, that always see so much more than they should. His voice wary, peremptory.

As she knows – or should know – they're having a hard time with Finbar. He hasn't reacted well to her walking out again. Gone very quiet. Very picky with his food, impossible to put to bed unless someone sits with him for hours; even gone back to bedwetting a few times. Asking for her all the time. So it's not working, big time. She's constantly reneging on the deal, all this coming and going. It's not really about her any more; she has a son to consider and responsibilities to honour. —What the fuck does she think she's playing at? The child's confused beyond belief, and her husband's not far behind. He's had enough, and he's going to protect his son. So here's the ultimatum, well overdue: that's enough seaside life, enough allowances made. One last chance, Bonnie. She's got to get her act together, cut it here; either she comes back for good, and looks after her son, or it's time for a divorce. And it's not just Finbar who's affected. Sally's had enough, too; her tolerance pushed to the limit. He can't believe how it's used her up, aged her, even. She's aching for Mexico, the old depression threatening in the London winter. They've got to get her out soon, into the harsh bright lights of Mexico City, or she'll be incapable. As it is she spends the day crying once Finbar's gone to school.

'Why can't Finbar come here? There's that nice little primary school just up the road, with plenty of places.'

'Down here? You must be out of your mind. I know you're with some old dustman, but does it have to so look the part?'

The heavy grate spilling ash, the brass lamp holders coming out of the walls. Ornaments crowded into the dust along the mantelpiece. The warped piano in the corner with its dulled, curlicue brackets, the tangled, lumpy brown sofa, the French window onto the garden, the red velvet curtains lopped untidily across; the dank yellow sea air coming through the warped frame.

'I'm not, actually. And anyway, his place isn't like this.'

Very different from his snug box, radiating its intense, clean privacy. His warm living room with the shiny parquet floors, the effective radiators and imitation coal fire, the rugs, the solid, capacious cream sofa and armchairs, clean white walls, the hatch through to the spotless kitchen, his sketches, the gentle orange and umber nudes, the ethereal city buildings. The sparse, modern ornaments, the silent, smiling clean family photos. The Neil Young CDs he refuses to throw away, the collection of thirty-three records all neatly stacked in the plastic storage unit; he's vinyl man. All vibrating gently to the passing of the trains at the foot of the garden, two an hour, to and from London. Up and down the line, up and down.

'So it's all over, is it? Well, that was predictable enough. Sad for you, of course.'

'If you've just dropped by to be insulting...'

'I dropped by, as you put it, because I need to talk to you about our son, for whom you're still responsible whether you like it or not; and because you don't answer my emails, and you don't switch your mobile on until after sundown, or whatever it is. We had a workable arrangement, for Finbar's sake. I need to know when you're going to honour it. When are you coming back?'

It's liberating to see how little he wants her.

'Whenever.'

'You don't want to come back either, do you?'

'No.'

'Well, there are other people to consider apart from yourself. Your son, as I've said, who would appear to be missing his mother. You can't rely on Sally to babysit for ever. Can I ask why you're not available on the phone?'

'Too many nuisance calls.'

For the phone's still ringing at odd hours of the night and day.

'Doesn't it strike you as slightly irresponsible, when there's a child involved? And your mobile?'

'You know there's no signal here. I have to go out of the house. People can text.'

'And do they?'

'No...'

'Doesn't he call? Keep in touch?'

She turns away.

'Miss him, do you? No one else will do?'

He walks up to her, tilts her chin up. Her blue eyes, long cheekbones, that have acquired that island shade.

'What did he have in the end?'

'Epilepsy. But—'

'So much for existential choices. I bet the epilepsy was only part of it, too. The tip of the iceberg. Don't you miss your son, down here?'

Nothing moves in that long, dingy living room. Unless the house just lurched forwards a few yards. Bonnie barely moves either, just drifts, barely perceptible, barely eludes Austin, standing there in his jacket like a street tough, makes sure she's between him and the door. Opens it casually. Clocks her handbag, in the hall. Intent on her, he doesn't notice.

Again he looks round the room.

'I'd forgotten how awful it was down here. Smells of cat and coal dust. So dank.'

Hand on curtain, he looks out into the garden, filled with yellow sea-mist. His face harsh; new lines beneath his eyes, the same process as with Dominic. But it doesn't hurt her, with him.

'It's fucking freezing. Don't you run the heating?'

'It's broken down.'

'I had a terrible time getting over the causeway. Tides and high winds. Waiting for ages.'

'Yes. It's bad. One's almost cut off here some days.'

'Isn't this all rather stupid, then? You living here like a tramp?'

'Perhaps.'

'Sally has got to be got out of the UK. With her history. I'd give her another couple of weeks maximum before she cracks. If she drinks again, you know, with her liver, that's it. No more second chances. She lives on a knife edge as it is. You know that.'

'And Finbar?'

'You saw him this weekend. You should know.'

'He doesn't say a lot to me.'

'Do you blame him?'

'Does he talk to you?'

'No. No, not really.'

'To Sally?'

He's silent, hand on curtain. Looking out into the yellow and grey garden where the shadow of a fox stands sniffing the thick winter air.

'Do you know he hasn't said a word since you left on

Sunday? Not at home, not at school. His teacher called me in. Sally's utterly distressed.'

'Yes? What would you like me to do?'

'She keeps going on about time.'

'I remember. The old complaint.'

'Depression isn't really the word. It's as if she's physically terrified – you know. Even more than mentally. She has these fits. Shaking and sweating. Comes out drenched, her whole blouse soaked. Like DTs without the drink.'

'It's probably just menopause. Tell her to go to the doctor.'

'She's been. You can't reach her. I wish... sometimes I wish she'd managed to hold onto one of those husbands of hers. It's always taken a lot of work to keep her steady, but now... As I understand her... She says the terror is not that it doesn't happen, but when you do get it – whatever it is that you want, I don't know what that is – you find that time is the price you've paid. She seems to have an absolute terror of the passing of time. That's why she needs to go back to Mexico. They don't give a toss about time there.'

'It's the same down here, you know, Austin. Only the weather isn't as nice. Or the people. I thought you'd come to talk about Finbar.'

He looks at her, startled, like a man who's been talking to himself. Gestures at the piano, not observing it.

'Keep it up?'

'Every day.'

'Not a lot else to do down here, is there?' Then he looks at it. 'But surely... what happened to your piano?'

'I traded it in with Dudley at the music shop over the road there. He's going to hold onto it for as long as they can.'

'For money?'

'For money.'

'And he kindly gave you £200 and a mouse nest?'

How tell Austin that the real reason she gave it away was that it was haunted, that like Chopin she was still afraid of what might issue from within. Terrors and ghosts. That she deliberately chose a dead piano. He raises the lid, tries a few chords.

'But it's completely out of tune.'

Slams the lid down, gives the piano a mighty kick. There's an off-key resounding and rumbling from within. Austin kicks again, and again, evoking the same growl of off-notes, the piano acquiescing in its own dissolution.

'Stop that! It's all I've got!'

He takes her by both hands, looks at her fingers. Their fine whiteness gone. Dingy grey, grime clinging in the cracks, from the coal. Roughened by the wind and by totting. Chilblained, the gentle swellings marring the slim straight lines. The nails still manicured, short, but ridged with coal dust, and chipped.

'What the fuck... Think you can play with those?'

She snatches her hands away. 'I do play.'

'No. You're outside the game now.'

'Don't write me off, Austin, just because I'm not in London. There are other worlds than London.'

'No, there aren't. You think there are, but it's an illusion. London's the real world. The only world. Anything else is a waste of life.'

She hesitates. He has his old power, of being always right. Dominant and smelling of money, in his leather jacket, his dark mustard and green scarf, his good, foreign clothes. The underlying London savagery that makes her glance again at the door. Bonnie wan in her cream and navy. Woken by seagulls, mice, ghosts, winds, cold, she doesn't sleep well. Her elusive, cool beauty is worn, shadowed, her face tinged now with the wariness of Dominic's wife, who picks her steps carefully across the car park ground floor. Taking him his snack at break, some awful English hot snack in a yellow plastic carton, she silent, valiant, looking everywhere, the steady, firm-slung jowl, the ash-blonde curls, her dimple and capable irony masked by the careful make-up. Alert, light-footed, clutching the carton warily in front of her, looking this way and that as she treads across to the break room. Bonnie another race, adult beside this strong, capable girl. Austin too has matured, his shoulders tougher; but she doesn't like the new edge to his face. The way he swings round to her, seizes her arm.

'Come back to London with me now and I'll buy you a baby grand.'

'*No*: no, not London, no.'

'You could leave now, this minute. I'm parked right outside. Just walk out. Leave it all.'

'No.'

'You need therapy, Bonnie. Sally knows some good people, we'll set you up. You know Sally adores you, she'd pay anything to have you back again. You can't be serious about him. That fag-end.'

'I know.'

'Will you come, then? Now? Back to London?'

'No.'

Austin whirls round, back to the piano. The wood splinters under his foot. Kicking until the lower front board breaks out and falls forwards, the strings exposed beneath. True enough, a strong smell of mouse emerges. Rust furred around the tuning pins where the strings are wrapped.

'Fucking bit of rubbish. Look at it. Look at how you're living. It's sectionable.'

'I'll never come back, never! And your mother's a raving neurotic. Just like you!'

'Fucking stupid bitch! Wasting your life! Destroying our child! When we had everything!'

He sweeps the piano top clean of music and ornaments, the photo of Finbar, rips the top board off from its rotting hinges. Smashes it across the yellowed keys, which break, jar, stick. Their twangs forming a broken accompaniment to Austin, smashing and smashing.

'You're into auto-destructive art, aren't you – Western culture burnt out. Well, listen to this for the ultimate work of art. This is art in practice. A real performance. Art in progress, art in destruction, the same thing. Smash out the swan song. Art heading for destruction, where it belongs. You trashed your talent – your life – why not do the instrument as well – do it like this – and this. How does it sound? Best music it's ever played in its life. Keep going. A finite performance. A final performance. A kindness to destroy it. Outlived its time. The whole London thing of listening politely to pretty piano concerts – pretty women playing. Pummelling the keys. Keep going to the limit of endurance. No going back. With a hammer well-aimed, try to destroy the whole at a single blow.'

It's not that easy to trash a piano, the original inde-structible object. The damage is more psychic. A violence done to the spirit of the instrument and the player alike. Both standing aside, watching aghast. But this one's so old and fragile that Austin manages to crack the soundboard, which splits right across. Austin kneels down and with his bare hands pulls at the key strings. Some come out. Picks up one of the heavy old brass candlesticks on the mantelpiece, lays into the instrument with that, tugging at the case. More twanging and splintering, and the smell of snapped wood on the air, a dusty, muted memory of when it was fresh. Attacks the front of the case. The brass candleholders pull out easily enough, sling right across the room and through one of the French windows, with their thin old glass. A neat hole in the glass; then, after a hesitation, the whole big pane quivers, drops out. The air gushes in, finally, quelling the faint warmth of the room. Raw as selfishness itself. Savage, savage sea air, yellow, ferocious with spray, unforgiving. It's as if the house, after taking so many quiet steps towards the cliff edge, so many imperceptible lurches, has finally gone over.

Austin's performance continues but the audience proves elusive. Too terrified to engage, slipping breathless towards the door, back to the wall. If she didn't have the spirit of the house to support her, she'd never get through that door. The ghost of the metronome beating out the last of their time together after her.

Wiping his bleeding hands down his trousers, Austin turns to Bonnie. White-faced, lines heaving down either side of his mouth. But the front door's open and she's gone, fled onto the streets where she knows she's safe.

REST

I'm waiting. Outside the multi-storey car park where flying grains of sand sting the eyelids. Snow thick and white on the beach, crowded in loops along the water's edge, soiled by the frozen yellowed foam. Waves of heavy grey liquid ice, freezing and unfreezing into movement. Snow weighting down the lavender bushes on the prom, drifted onto the steps down to the sands, making new white steps. An utter malignancy of winter off the sea. Put up a hand to shield your eyes, feel the hand go frozen, immoveable in seconds. This isle with no trees lies open to all seas, all winds. In London, in this day and age, it's not easy to cry with cold but it happens here. People pass each other, shuddering and sobbing openly on the streets. No one takes any notice. You can cry all you want.

I'm waiting.

Here they come, spilling out from the car park, top to toe in the yellow protective winter gear, faceless in swathings of scarves, hats beneath the anonymous fluorescent, shiny hoods pulled tight round heads and coming low on foreheads, like Inuit seal hunters issuing out to the front, hakapiks stuck into their sledges. Chewing their whale blubber against the cold, the last of lunch. There are seven of them but there seem to be more, trundling in different directions across the road. Dominic's last, striding out bareheaded. She hates the sullen streak of gold in his hair, dull memories of summer. Even as she looks, he feels in his pocket, pulls out a navy wool tuque, puts it on. A white silk and wool scarf that looks new, a Christmas present from the wife perhaps, looped loosely round his neck, like some battered Gallic dandy. Sees her, his regal lope arrested, just about lifts a guarded hand, vigilant. Eyes pulled down at the corners, face broken up into a hundred pieces. Shows every sign of this rough winter.

'How are you?' she says, temporising, trying to make contact even now.

'All right,' sturdy, testy, walking on.

'Dominic!'

He walks on. She stands there a few moments, dodging the idle eyes of shoppers, the smiles hidden beneath the scarves of the other road sweepers spilling around and past her. Still a conspicuous figure in her London black, jacket drawn tight around her, collar pulled up, black skirt and thick leggings, thick pink socks pulled over, pink scarf wrapped tight to the chin, blonde hair beneath the mohair cap, black boots set to the ground, eyes steady. A figure set for final combat. He crosses the road, goes round the corner, to the foot of the hill; she strolls after him, stands there, watching him start up. Up he goes, yet again; the old Mount Royal; and there's the house, Concordia, at the top, watching through the blowing white veil, as she's watching. Both of them seeing him up the hill. The house urging her on.

Must she, yet again? Why not just let him go? Let him continue on up the same old hill, ad infinitum? Walk the same streets, work the same set hours, pick up the same litter, go home to the same wife, eat the same tea, have the same sex; have the same routine worked out to the last particular against events which would otherwise confuse him utterly. The winter picking at her soft face as she gazes up, his yellow coat cutting through the white and pewter day. Must she? But if she doesn't do it now, she never will. What's between them is passing; all but passed. A day more, a few hours more even, and it will be too late. January, his birthday; end of the road. He progresses on up, in his steady way. She lets him get well ahead, the cold reaching into her. Hopes he's got his thermals on, her man. If he can do nothing else, let him keep himself warm. Follows, her footsteps in his.

He turns off, down Acadia Street. They both walk down the little side street, he ahead, hasn't seen her yet. His straight back that looks vulnerable and lonely. Doesn't know she's there. Her footsteps silent on the packed, white pavement. She could still turn round and flee. Back into the warm. Back into sanity. With sudden urgency she walks on down the street, against the picky wind, after the minute itself.

'Dominic.'

He stops, half-looks over his shoulder in his old way.

'Please, don't get angry.'

He turns right round, stares at her. She approaches a few feet, halts. She's walking on a sea-lane of thin ice. The surface lunging and creaking. And beneath, all sorts of strange sea creatures.

'I just need to talk to you a moment.'

He stares in silence. Face and eyes dark. Waiting to hear what she has to say.

'I came back to get you. To get you out.'

She struggles on, like snowflakes struggling to land. To say only what has to be said, without embellishments. Literal. Just the facts. With anyone else it would sound stark; melodramatic. But he's sifting it for fact, fast. She can tell that by his blank, frozen eyes.

'Off Waste Island. To take you home.'

But where's home? In this heartland of white wraiths drifting by? The snowstorms of winter, which turn his town that strange pink light. Pink snow drifting through Mount Royal Park as he cycles slowly to work in the dark, the trees ghostly gleaming mauve in the lamplight.

'It didn't work, that arrangement with my husband. I had to come back, to Concordia.'

And she isn't going to tell him what nights she's had, listening to the house's whispers.

Still he gazes, intent, as if listening. Impossible to say if he even recalls the event between them or not.

'Will you come with me? Come to London with me? If we go now, we'd make it. Just. It's settling fast. But I think the main roads will be okay. Car's in the multi-storey.'

Eyes dark and blank. Impossible to tell if he even hears her. Still fixed on her. Her face looking out of the spirals swirling thicker round them. In her black mohair cap, her black jacket, where tiny bites of white keep landing and disappearing. Eyes concentrated with all the solemn blue of summer.

'I've got some work. We could go anywhere, travel round.'

Poised, balanced. To give only facts, the bare minimum. Now that she knows what she does to him. Not to say a word too much. Not to say the word that will trigger him, send him away, into that hinterland of the brain. To reach him. She's got a lunchtime concert tomorrow, a recital in a City church, the first cautious step back onto the circuit. But this she doesn't tell him, knowing how little it will mean to him, how it will overwhelm him. She keeps her distance, several yards away.

'I've got a room we could go to, at a friend's, in Hammersmith. I reckon we could make it to London, if we leave now. If you come with me, Dominic, I could leave the house. I can't – don't want to go back in there, ever again.'

But the house at least has claimed her. And she has nowhere else to go. There's no friend would receive him; they've all said so, unequivocally.

'Have you – have you been all right?' as though his appearance didn't answer her question. Face battered as if he'd been in a fight. Aged ten years, face like the snow on the beach, caked and cracked; arrested, he stares, bare, half-human. Great lines pulling his eyes down. But the old green gleam is still there, green eerie and ethereal, northern lights. The leap of fear, that she's always mistaken for love. A gleam that seems to grow and spread through his weather-beaten features, although he moves by not a muscle. Eyes fixed. As if staring into the very source of the snow.

'Once we're over the causeway, we're home and dry, on the dual carriageway. We've got low tide for an hour more...'

   She's very thirsty. Dries altogether. With every breath comes the plunge of exhaustion. Her legs keep beginning to give way beneath her. The run down the street, a few yards, used up the last of her strength. The street is empty, quiet. It's a myth that the Inuit have a hundred words for snow. There must be a thousand, one for each kiss that drifts down from the sky.

Here at the end of the world the grey wind blows in from the sea. Spring far, far behind. The street cleaners are out as usual, labouring in all weathers. A freight ferry waits in the port, grey and anonymous; two unmarked juggernauts snaking down the hill to the port, the paint blistering off their sides. And atop all the house, Concordia, looking through them.

Bonnie's so thirsty. Wishes she were in the warm, eating lunch like a forgetful human being. She wants to go home. That desperate homesickness for a home that no longer exists. To do the ironing for an hour before picking up Finbar from school. Put him to bed, the story book, the nightlight with the man in the moon. To practise until her fingers bleed. To prepare for recitals, in her black suit, crisp, sharp and nervy as a winter's day; to have her hands manicured. To answer the phone to the middle-class friends, after the months of silence in the cliff-top house. Not to feel crazy, outcast. Not to feel she can only bear people for two minutes before needing solitude again. To see Austin screw up the evening paper and feed it into the fire where it belongs, refusing to recycle because recycling's just a propagation of our rubbish society. Going round the corner for a curry. Acutely homesick she is, but not for any of this. She knows that if she persists, cajoles, licks down his injured pride, Austin will take her back again, they'll both be sadder and wiser for the rest of their lives together. The rest of their lives! If she goes back to Austin tonight, her young bridegroom (he's waiting by the double bed. Folding down the duvet with wiry, white, uncertain hand). But Austin won't do.

'It's been hell, Dominic.'

He looks at her still. As if attending; as if waiting for the words that were going to involve him. His shoulders rise, the mist of his breath streams out long. Still fixed on her, the snowflakes dashing inconsequent across his face. Terrified, she wants to run. But it's the terror of herself and her own pain, rather than him. The agony of staring into him, naked.

'Just hell.'

She can feel him breathing, gleaming and unreadable as the sea. Arrested, still seeming to listen. With the utmost intensity of attention, as if for the tiny plink of flakes landing on the parked cars. As if waiting for the terror that stalks these little streets to show itself at last, in the open. She stands her ground.

He's the finder. Found her one day on the prom, and kept her. Diligent, conscientious, picking up everything he came across. Now standing stock-still, his work suspended along with his consciousness. A thin layer of snow already on his wool hat. The white feathers also gathering on her black cap and shoulders. Standing as still as him, waiting. She belongs to the finder. But he sees none of that. He's gone, sent by her again, into his old dream.

Where are you?

Find me; come find me if you can. I'm waiting. Somewhere in this dreamy state, somewhere behind these empty eyes. Inside the thick protective jacket, gathering drifts in its fluorescent creases, which stands as if empty, in the gloved hand closing and reclosing on the air, in the mouth quivering with its slight drool. I'm in here, waiting. Behind where the wind blows, in all memories drowned at sea. In the silence of this little street, in the newspaper frozen in sodden folds in the gutter, in the malignant sea cold. Only you've got to come and find me. Come right in, because I can't come out. Take the plunge; go backwards. I'll never move forwards, never come for you, because I can't.

No place to run. Come and find me, if you dare. If you love me.

It takes all her courage and more, to approach him. But she does, step by dragged step. And once you've gone so far, something else takes over. Something else dragging her over to him, across those last few yards of road. She pulled along in its wake. And now they're aura to aura again. She taking off her gloves, flexing her half-frozen fingers.

How do you call someone out of that dream? But the touch of her hand on his wrist maybe coincides with his slow return to consciousness. His forearm beneath the coat is like wood. He gets cold, cold, doing this job, if he stands around. Got to keep moving. Her own cold hand pushes on, beneath his jumper sleeve, seeking out any warmth further in. With her fingers, with which she does so much of her seeing, picking out surfaces that others would miss, she feels the long ridge of his scar again. It's like coming home.

He sighs, coming to, as if weary with winter; wipes his mouth automatically, pulls at his coat. Half in that other place still, patting down his coat pocket, searching for something, confused, eyes clouded, clearing.

Her hand closes on his arm.

'No,' he says. 'No. Not again...'

At the end of the little road, just behind them, is an alley onto the cliff-top, and here she leads him, his eyes dulled, docile. He knows the place, of course. How many times on a summer morning has he explained its name to visitors. It's called Screaming Alley because 200 years ago a couple of horses and a carriage drove straight down it and over the cliff, and the screams of the horses can still be heard on wintry nights. And maybe days, too. An odd kind of whinny coming up from the far-off, white-ridden waves. The alley slopes rapidly down to the land's edge. There lies the bare, bold sea, separated from them only by the bleak, thin strip of prom. The cliffs eighty million years old, chalk-white and carved by the sea into a myriad of hollows and bays. On this stretch they're as they always were, left to crumble gently onto time and the natural air. It's the only undefended strip of coastline in this part of the world, simply because there's nothing here considered worth saving. Some 100 feet below, there's the black glint of rocks and the waves spreading over them like icy lace, but here's shelter, here in this little path that leads down the cliffside a short way. It goes nowhere, nowhere but a small hollow, screened from the prom view, only used by the most daring of lovers, a lip of sand right out on the edge. Beyond it, the path continues a little further, goes round a corner, and gives out.

'No,' he says again. 'Don't take me away... please don't take me away again...'

He pulls away from her, stands back, in his confusion. Dipping in and out of consciousness, in no fit state to go with her, and anyone else would have pity. But she pulls him on, past the *Danger* sign and down the little path to the ledge, their sharp, dark footprints blurring whitish even as they go, with more, fast-falling flakes. No one says, be careful Bonnie, don't go there. All her protectors are gone and there's just silence apart from the hoarse acclaim of the waves and their constant, eerie, secondary echo, going round the cliff base. And there it all is, as in spring, the bare-twig bushes whistling above them, him putting her up against the cliff face, taking off his gloves, taking off her hat, grabbing her hair in two fistfuls, thumbing her chin up to meet the falling sky. His cold lips, frozen stubble; her soft, cold cheeks. His fingers burn and bite like snow, pulling at the zip of her jacket, she can feel the unbearable longing in the cold, sharp movements of his hands into her clothes.

'Warm me.'

He's got his thermals on. She feels beneath the green army jumper, pulls out the thick shirt, the pale blue vest, slides her hand down his buttock, easing the long johns down, exposing him, as she's always exposed him. Feeling the goosebumps on his buttocks, feeling for the flying goose tattoo at the small of his back. Knowing by his sigh when she's found it. Pulls him into her, to meet his demand. He has the right to make it because long ago he gave her something, he can't remember what, a soul or a route or a promise, something that would last, and she accepted. It's all preordained, destined. And she can't go home because he is home. His smell of salt and freedom, his neck, his limitations. A long snow kiss, her tears freezing into spirals as they emerge. His hands are cold blocks on her ribs, feeling for the warm and beating source behind. Cold powder falling into her eyes from the little gorse bushes branches shaken above them, down the back of her neck. Their feet slipping and colliding on the virgin snow that turns swiftly to a scuffle of mush. Life with him: untenable. Life without him; unbearable. How do you make love out of the rubbish of human emotions? How transcend those torn and ragged bits of litter, blown this way and that, that make up a heart?

Desires without name, that can't be fulfilled. Snow kissing their lips, their exclamations and ejaculations muffled by snow. He gripping her hair, the savage snow burn of his eyes. She biting and biting at his mouth, with no intention of letting go. They brush the gathering snow from each other's heads, his semen already cold, trickling on her inner thighs. What snow-child, conceived of the *aurora borealis* and the north wind, both unbearably cold on this blue, hostile coast. But he's gone again. She holds him close, someone who's not there, and closer. He's already left her before he withdraws. Turning away, vacant, distant, mouth slightly pursed, fingers fumbling at his coat.

His vacancy looks like anxiety and his activity looks like purpose, but she knows better now. Knows he's someplace else, somewhere far away. Maybe the only place where they can meet. In his seizure shadowland, where consciousness is neither here nor there. There's nowhere else to go. He can only love her in his absence. When he isn't hampered by the life he arranged for himself, all its escapes, the house at the end of the line, the nurse wife who'll look after him for all time, the nowhere job that absolves him on a daily basis.

Unlike him, she's cursed with consciousness. Can't leave him like this, in the world between the worlds. Makes him decent; cold, wet and soft against her hand; tucks his vest in, wipes her palm on it, feels what's left turn to crinkly rice paper in the wind; pulls his shirt back down, his jumper. Does his coat up swiftly, dodging his inept, stumbling fingers that are mechanically pulling at its front, retrieves his wool cap from the ground, shakes it. Slips it onto his head easily enough, while he's still pulling at his coat. The gloves are more difficult, but he fumbles at them automatically, and they finally go on. Then she'll die if she doesn't give him one last kiss, but it doesn't wake him.

Only just decent herself, tousled and scarf awry, skirt
scuffled, coat still undone. Her face smoothed, full of light
and rest. She knows he loves her at some level, that she got
through. That he'll keep faith, simply because he can't help
it. They're going to be together for all time, she'll follow
him for ever. She it is who sends him spinning through this
town, who trips him up on his morning road, watches him
fall; she's his condition now. Condemned to a lifetime of
visiting on street corners. Her soul's the exact shape of his
scar. She's going back to Concordia, to build a fire and sleep
all day and all night, to wake to dawn over an empty sea.
She's not afraid of the house any more, its bleak, off-white
winter views and sounding rooms. Even if she has to cover
every mirror in the place, smash all the clocks and throw
the phones into the sea. She's going to go back and open
the attic windows wide to the winter sky and rip out the
wallpaper for the wild geese, trapped in the arabesque and
watched by Death. And tomorrow she's going to play like
she's never played before.

'I love you, Dominic.'

This she has to say to him, that he might not think of
himself, being so literal. His arms tighten round her. It's all
she wants, to have his arms round her, like any girl in love.
She'll stand here for ever, resting her cold face into his warm
neck. But a sudden intake of breath, and he pushes her away.
Passes a hand over his eyes, pulls at his ear. Pats himself down,
all down his coat. Looks at her blankly. His face wakes up
suddenly, as if seeing her for the first time; gathers in its old
hostility. Her heart sinks, it's the profile of the bin man he

turns away from her, the rough, tough bin man, shoulders set, hard, impermeable. Returned from wherever he was, and ready to fight for his consciousness.

He turns his back on her, an instinctive, protective reaction, denying her existence. Looks out to his vast dominion of air.

'But I don't love you,' he says, with his devastating bluntness. The whole sea hears him.

She laughs, reaches out a hand to his neck, feels it quiver. 'You did a minute ago! Darling... you do, you do...'

'Nope.'

Still with his back to her; his stiff, yellow, thinking back. She can hear his breathing, slightly raspy.

'But... how can you? How can you go from...'

Of course. Of course she knows. She's up against her invisible rival again; the wife's nothing to this. His condition. The other obsessive lover who haunts him. Another twilight encounter. Where their relationship always took place, in the hidden corners where both can be invisible. In his seizure trance he acted without knowing. The immediate past's gone, into his broken memory. The encounter's simply dropped from his consciousness, like dropping a pebble into the sea. He's got no awareness she's just dressed him. And he could dip out of it again any time, in his wavering, post-seizure fragility. The epilepsy's still circling his brain, massaging his neurons with delicate fingertips. But for now he's lucid enough.

'You don't love me?'

'I told ya.'

He thinks on, turns round to her, slowly. 'I'd walk over this cliff to get away from you.'

Bleak, sane, regarding her steadily.

'No... I mean you can't say that. Don't you realise what you've just...'

Doesn't he realise? The consequences? Doesn't he know there's no freedom of speech on this isle today? That it's punishable by death? You can't just say what you really think. Be careful, Dominic.

'Oh, darling... Come back with me – come back with me now... We could go anywhere, do anything. Come to London with me. Get off this bloody island and have a life.'

'No.' Not even so much that he doesn't want as he can't envisage it; that anyone should live off the island is inconceivable to him. He doesn't even know the train times from the station now, nor where the routes go.

'Come and live in Concordia with me then.'

'I live at home with my wife.'

The wind of pure ice comes off the sea, the cruel cold spreads through her, an utter, callous desolation of chill spreading through her. She's frozen, frozen, always has been, a girl held in a globule of ice, held in frozen trauma. The airbag blew out to ice in the car crash, a bubble of ice encasing her for life. And suddenly it's as if she can only just speak against the ice packing round her heart, her lungs, her lips.

'I can't stand this... This is going to do for me, I know it is...'

He looks at her, a young snow queen with hair of fine, friable sprays of white, eyelashes of frost, eyes of deep blue ice. Her heart stabbed with a hundred icicles.

'Well – you shouldn't let it.'

'Do you really think I have a choice? That feeling I get

with you, I don't get it with anyone else. It's something completely apart from the rest of my life. I never knew it existed, before you.'

'Yeah, that's right. I never thought of it either, for sure,' with jeering insolence. 'I sure never could've made you up.'

'And once you've felt it, you can't go back. You can't close that door once it's been opened. You feel it, too. I know you do. It's like water in the desert to someone who didn't even realise they were thirsty.'

He stares at her. Glances back up the little path to the prom.

'Dominic... I feel like I'm going to die... I'll die without you, I know I will...'

'We all got to die some time.'

The same old stolid irony, dour. There's no reaching him, this block of wood. He has no compassion, no empathy. She's made a fool of herself, but there'll be no pity from him, no extra effort of kindness. He can't; he doesn't have the capacity. Generosity, emotional largesse, are luxuries beyond his grasp. His emotional meanness is the other side of his rough integrity. All he knows is, listening to her is like listening to his epilepsy and the more he listens, the deeper he goes into that no man's land. He wants to stay here. Here out in this fresh, keen wind; to walk free along the cliff-top. He doesn't want to go where she takes him. The lamp posts are shaking in the wind, strung out at intervals all along the prom, as if they're shaking out the snow in long, slow streamers. They're of the island, bleak and bare, with peeled, lizard heads. London doesn't have street lamps like that, naked and prehensile, sleek grey-green, but solid, orange, concrete chunks.

'So that's your final word.'

He doesn't bother to repeat himself. What's spoken is spoken. He regards her in silence. A seagull floats past, sideways, like a lump of snow, grey and white and delicately packed. Bonnie looks down onto its quivering shoulders.

'So what was all that about, then, just now? Just a fuck?'

He shrugs. He won't even engage with her long enough to know what she's talking about.

'You wanker! You've just fucked me, do you realise that?'

He does, suddenly. So that's what he can feel on him. So that's what happened. Again.

'Or did you think you'd just come down here to admire the view?'

'What – you…?'

Perplexity and fear as he glances round, as if realising his surroundings for the first time. The little alcove atop the sea, the dangerous footpath.

'Yes, I took advantage of you. But you enjoyed it.'

His face goes white, nostrils flaring.

'You bitch. You did that to me…?' Furious in his impotence, but not so impotent he can't throw her off the cliff. He grabs her by the arm, shakes her.

'What, brought me down here when I was…? That's no love on your part. That's just selfishness.'

'Oh yes. Convenient. How convenient epilepsy must be sometimes. Tune out when it suits you, and then blame other people.'

'It's not like that!'

He holds her pinned to the cold chalk and his cry seems to go right up and down the cliff. Face still white, contorting in and out, breath gone creaky. If it wasn't for the human warmth coming faintly off him, she'd think it was justice come for her, pure and impersonal. The sea heaves at her feet. He bangs her against the cliff wall.

'You can force me to fuck you but you can't force me to love you!'

'You… I thought you had a heart.'

As if he's broken her own heart against the fragile chalk. Something cracking in her as he rams her up against the cliff wall again.

'I got a heart all right. It just doesn't belong to you.'

'If you're too unsophisticated to understand love—'

'I *am* unsophisticated. That's why I'm a road sweeper—' with infinite bitterness and grief. Lets her go.

'Oh darling—' laying her hand on his forearm. He grabs it convulsively, as if grasping safety; stands with his breath heaving, beside himself. For a moment their hands clutch, gloved fingers clumsy and cold. He's broken her heart indeed.

'For God's sake come away with me. It's hell without you.'

'It's hell without you – worse hell with you.'

They gaze at each other, breaths mingling. His eyes with that green light and no depth. Her eyes gone deep blue, almost navy. He shoves her away again, into the unyielding chalk.

'You're not going to get me, d'ya hear!'

'I don't want you. You're just a loser. You'll never be any good.'

'Yeah. I know.'

A sudden, fatal acceptance; he's been hearing this all his life.

'You're just simple. A broken doll.'

He pulls himself back, a thousand miles.

'You can think what you like. You've the right to your opinion. You're the public... the public...'

It's too much; his brain cuts out again. He's only just been holding on. Now her tears send him, he can't stay here and watch her cry. And he's gone again, gazing at her vacantly. His eyes cloud. A tremor spreads up his right hand to his shoulder, he jerks his head twice.

He turns away, to the other side of the world. Stumbles slightly, goes slightly wayward. She doesn't realise how far away he is until she sees him take a step or two towards the cliff edge.

'What road do I go?' he says, to himself, not her.

What road do I go, which way take? When I leave love behind, what path can I walk? Is it far – how many miles? Must I tread on thin air or just on water. Will I fall. Will it be a lonely road, far from home; what chance of a companion along the way. Will an angel walk beside me, will the evening star light me when day gets dark. Will I ever get as far as three score miles and ten, my allotted time. Can I get there by candlelight. And why would you ever want to come back again. He looks out, to the sea lane created by a glimmer of winter sun, a thin white track out to the horizon. She can see his path much more clearly, at his feet in their thick, black working shoes, that narrow torque of snowy shingle that goes on round the corner and then steps out into nothing.

Fumbling at his pocket again, he brings out the piece of paper with his route for the day and scans down the printout with his forefinger: The Plains of Waterloo. Meeting Street. Acadia Street. Belle Province Road, Quebec Avenue, Penfield Avenue, Michael's Road, Mount Royal Avenue, Royal Esplanade, Royal Road.

'I only done three of them.'

'Dominic...'

He folds the piece of paper, puts it back in his pocket, carefully.

'I got to get on.'

'Kiss me before you go.'

'Kiss you?'

'Please...'

He pauses, arrested, eyes alight, half brought back, standing alone on the little path with the sheer drop at his side. Looks round once more, to the icy glimmer of the grey sea, the claustrophobic tangle of snow and bushes that's the land. Looks back down at her, through her. He can grasp nothing, he's not with her. Where he is, God only knows, but she hasn't got him. His wife would maybe say that the angels have got him, in a neuronal swirl of white wings and protection.

His breathing is coming unsteady, with its slight wheeze. She takes a few steps towards him, down the treacherous little track, and they balance on the edge, facing each other. She holds out her hand to him. He looks down on her in disdain and cold dislike, aloof.

'I don't want to kiss you.'

He moves forwards. A slight fall of sand and loose scree at his feet scatters into the space below but neither of them take any notice.

'Get out of my way. I got to get back.' And with strange, pathetic dignity, a final grasping at firmness, 'I'm here to work.'

She doesn't get it, she'll never get it. That all he's got to ground him is his routine. That he mustn't linger here, on this crumbling cliff ledge. That he's got to reach solid land before he's overtaken by a growing light-headedness and the faint stirrings of music coming in over the sea at his back, ripples and tinklings like wind-chimes of ice. That she's standing in his way on this narrow footpath, barring his route to safety.

'Just one quick kiss... You won't even do that...'

One rejection too many. All his rejections tipping her over the edge; she dare not look down, to the black and foaming waves. Again she reaches a hand to his arm. He bats her away.

'Let me pass, I said!'

Time's running out for him. She's looming over him, and the slow striding of the harp at his back, slowing down time. It's music she's played before; he's heard it before, a thousand times. She seems to be inching him ever further down this fragile thread of a footpath, the shelf where they made love infinitely inaccessible, far above. The minutes spiral down to long seconds, the snow whirls, spiralling round in a slow whorl to the vortex in the middle; he being sucked into the centre. And now he can't tell where the music is coming from, the infinite ocean beside him, or her, standing tall and numinous in front. He just knows that it's about to catch up with him, that any moment now it's going to trip him up, take him off his feet again, send him spiralling into its centre.

'You'll never get past me. You'll never escape me.'

He seizes her lapel, pushes her back.

'I tell you, I'll fucking throw you over if you don't get out of my way!'

It's the last of his great battle for consciousness. She presses herself back, and he thinks she's going to let him pass. He doesn't see how she's looking at him, an odd, speculative, calculating look. Infinitely distant. She's gone, too, into the snowy void, she'll never come back. She gauges where he's shaky on his feet, as he tries to advance. Gathers herself. Raises her hands, once so magical, that still have power. Then she smashes him across the face, an almighty blow that takes him off balance, the third time she's hit him, she's learnt nothing still, and now she inherits her fatal lack of restraint; again she sends him spinning, he folds easily, lightly, the way a child does, goes turning, searching, curves round, in slow motion, staggers away down the path. She turns away and is gone, pell-mell back to the land. He stumbles on, down the slippery track to where it gives out at the end of the land, and he falls. His arms fling out, his body arches, he gives a hoarse cry, and he falls. Eyes rolled up, head thrown back. Turning, spinning ever faster. Jerking into the vortex, a land animal becoming fish again. His clonic curvetting imprints itself on the air: I'm falling, oh Bonnie, I'm falling. He's falling with most of his work undone, and no more chances now to make good, a great fall into that other place. He didn't realise time would run out like this; thought he was condemned to sweep the streets for ever.

*

Atlantis, lost isle. Place of burial for all broken hearts. What road can I go, what way take, when I've thrown love away, when I've done the one thing I'd have given the world not to do, destroyed love, just by being myself. There are no roads I can go, no seas I can sail. This is an island there's no leaving, and no home now, just the house at the end of the road, Concordia.

The only place that'll take Bonnie in. When time runs out, there's no intervention, no one to catch her, and no music, only a sickening anonymity of snowflakes, coming from all directions, dizzying, incessant. She even breathes snow as she hurries on, an inhalation of fluttery cold. She doesn't see him fall. Maybe doesn't want to. Maybe when faced with the unthinkable, it's best not to see it. Like him, she cuts out. Ready to fall to her knees herself and freeze to death. It's the end. She can follow no more, no more. The snow drops away, a clean spring comes to her disassociated mind like holiday, fuzzy and fizzy with pink blossom and champagne, and all she can hear are the minor notes of some unknown nocturne playing somewhere, and his voice beating time: Find me; come find me; I'm waiting. It accompanies her as she struggles back up to the top of the cliff where the house is waiting for her.

She looks round, sets out to find him for the last time. The prom stretches left and right, a white road criss-crossed by a few tracks that become clearer as the snow ceases. She walks along to where the harbour lies below, a confusion of static cars, frozen yachts, the odd forklift truck moving like a slow toy, with its faint spitting. A great bleak grey and white spread. The sky pressing down, leaden and low. He's not there. But it's spring to her as she drifts along, some scent keeps coming to her from beneath the snow, a sweet, elusive waft. She goes back to the alley, finds his barrow still waiting, and also drifted with snow. Opens the little front section, finds a local newspaper, the bottle of water just tinged with squash, a spare pair of gloves, a chocolate bar, four tangerines, some hand sanitiser, a small pack of plasters. She looks along, waiting to see his figure in the distance, walking towards her. Stands there waiting. He'll be along. He's at his break, or chatting to someone in the town. Still she waits. Wanders to the edge of the alley for another look along the prom. Sees the small huddle of dog walkers looking over the edge of the cliff without registering; without allowing herself to register. Surely she can catch the faint tang of the wild wallflower on the breeze. When he comes back she's going to make it up. Give him handfuls of daffodils from the flower stall, dim and blind and sheathed. They've got the entire spring before them. She waits until she's so cold that her entire body feels as if it's encased in a layer of ice, as if she might herself be a frozen, sodden body in the sea. Eventually, she has to return to Concordia.

As she reaches the door she hears the sharp puttering of the helicopter right overhead; hesitates. Somewhere she already knows. But Bonnie doesn't follow; she'll follow no more. She's broken her promise, won't follow him to the ends of the earth. She won't even follow him over the cliff. Shutting the door, she shuts him out, for ever. Doesn't see the yellow Sea King slowly descending, though the entire house vibrates with it, nor the black-and-orange all-weather lifeboat veering slow and fruitless over the winter waves. A row of ambulances lines up along the cliff-top. The kind of last escort Dominic would have hated.

But Concordia lets Bonnie in. No one connects her with the event. The police put out an appeal for anyone who saw Dominic before he fell but Bonnie doesn't respond, doesn't see it. That's the outside world, from which she's exiled now.

The postman tells her what she already knows; shocking, isn't it. A real loss to the community. Bonnie hears the news in silence, has nothing to say in return. She has no confession to make, no one to tell, no one to talk to. Just the silent hall with its dancing shadows, the footfalls on the stairwell that she can walk into now, the ghost in the attic she's ready to become. Concordia closes round her. Tells her that at last they're ready to share their memories. Now she knows the secret of the house, how easy it is to kill what you love. Together they're left with her solitary experience, which replays itself every day, as she plays the same tinkly, faint notes on the broken-down old piano. To wait for her own fall; she'll go over some day, with the house, as the cliffs continue to crumble. That evil old house, that's witnessed so many heartbreaks, edged so many lovers over the cliff. But her fall happens by inches. Bonnie's left with her array of ghosts, from the life she should have had; her child, her talent, her husband; herself. The woman who walks from room to room at midnight, who sees the silver moon-streak across the encroaching black sea, who never goes further than the back door, where she can look out onto the garden and the visiting foxes. Dominic's ghost doesn't visit.

You have to go back outside for that. Maybe catch a glimpse of him along the prom. The finder. Picks up all the wind leaves behind. All that's been lost and dropped by the heedless. Picking up lost girls on spring mornings. Picking up all human rubbish. Broken promises and hearts, damaged brains, malformed babies, love born before its time, discarded treasure, forgotten tantrums, old kisses. Half-lived lives, half-told fortunes. Dreams, dreamlets, other years. Harmonies from the deep. Stepping back along the snowy esplanade. Past the empty bandstand. The sea below a winter harp, strings of silver ice sounding to the sky. The wind raw and savage across his face. Walking on, and on. Little to pick up in winter. Light agleam out to sea, and gone.

ACKNOWLEDGEMENTS

Thanks to Dr Sallie Baxendale, Consultant Neuropsychologist, Department of Clinical & Experimental Epilepsy Institute of Neurology, UCL London. Also thank you to Mandy Little and Soulla Thalis.

I am grateful to Louise Boland, publisher at *Fairlight Books*, and her dedicated team, including Urska Vidoni, Lindsey Woollard, Gabriele Gaizutyte, Laura Shanahan and Mo Fillmore.

ABOUT THE AUTHOR

After graduating from Somerville College, Oxford, Fiona Vigo Marshall started her career at a local newspaper. She then continued pursuing journalism in Mexico, covering news and features for a newspaper. On her return to London, Fiona worked as a publisher and freelance writer.

Her short stories and poems have been nominated for numerous awards, including the V. S. Pritchett Memorial Prize, which she won in 2016 with her short story *The Street of Baths*. Her work has also appeared in *Ambit, The Royal Society of Literature Review, The London Journal of Fiction*, and many other publications.

Find Me Falling is Fiona's debut novel.

Bookclub and writers' circle notes for
Find Me Falling can be found at
fairlightbooks.co.uk/find-me-falling

FAIRLIGHT BOOKS

LOU GILMOND

The Tale of Senyor Rodriguez

A dead man's house. A dead man's clothes.
And a dead man's wine cellar...

It's 1960s Mallorca. Thomas Sebastian, an English conman,
is hiding out in the house of the late Senyor Rodriguez –
carousing, partying, and falling in love with his beautiful but
impossibly young neighbour, Isabella Ferretti.

As the boundary between lies and reality blur, Thomas' fiction
spirals out of control in ways that are quite unexpected.

'A breathless and head-spinning conclusion that
begs the reader to go back and skim through
again to search for overlooked hints and feints.'
—Netgalley Reviewer

ALAN ROBERT CLARK

The Prince of Mirrors

*Two young men with expectations. One predicted
to succeed, the other to fail...*

Prince Albert Victor, heir presumptive to the British throne,
is seen as disastrously inadequate to be king. The grandson of
Queen Victoria, he is good-hearted but intensely shy and, some
whisper, even slow-witted.

By contrast, Jem Stephen is a renowned intellectual, poet and
golden boy worshipped by all. But a looming curse of mental
instability is threatening to take it all away.

Appointed as the prince's personal tutor, Jem works to prepare
him for the duty to come. A friendship grows between them –
one that will allow them to understand and finally accept who
they really are and change both of their lives forever.

*'A gilded cast of characters parades through this
sumptuous tale. A clever mixture of history,
psychology and sex.'*

—Alastair Stewart OBE,
ITN anchor

HELEN STANCEY

The Madonna of the Pool

A collection of short stories, *The Madonna of the Pool* explores the triumphs, compromises and quiet disappointments of everyday life. Drawing on a wide array of characters, Helen Stancey shows how small events, insignificant to some, can resonate deeply in the lives of others.

Richly poetic, deeply moving and entirely engaging, the stories demonstrate an exquisite understanding of human adaptation, endurance and, most of all, optimism.

Praise for Helen Stancey's writing:

'One has a sense of a writer gifted with an instinctive sense of how to tell a story.'
—The Spectator

SOPHIE VAN LLEWYN

Bottled Goods

When Alina's brother-in-law defects to the West, she and her husband become persons of interest to the secret services, causing both of their careers to come grinding to a halt. As the strain takes its toll on their marriage, Alina turns to her aunt for help – the wife of a communist leader, and a secret practitioner of the old folk ways.

Set in 1970s communist Romania, this novella-in-flash draws upon magic realism to weave a tale of everyday troubles that can't be put down.

'Sophie van Llewyn's stunning debut novella shows us there is no dystopian fiction as frightening as that which draws on history.'
—Christina Dalcher, author of *VOX*

'Sophie van Llewyn has brought light into an era which cast a long shadow.'
—Joanna Campbell, author of *Tying Down the Lion*

EMMA TIMPANY

Travelling in the Dark

Sarah is travelling with her young son back to her home town in the South of New Zealand. But when debris from an earthquake closes the road before her, she is forced to extend her journey, and divert through the places from her youth that she had hoped never to return to.

As the memories of her childhood resurface, Sarah knows that for the sake of her son, she must face up to them now or be lost forever.

'This is a clever, sensitive and deserving book.
The journey leaves us, not with the expected
finish but, instead, a master stroke.'
—Candy Neubert, poet

'Atmospheric and resonant, simply and
beautifully told.'
—Rupert Wallis, author of
The Dark Inside

SARA MARCHANT

The Driveway Has Two Sides

On an East Coast island, full of tall pine moaning with sea gusts, Delilah moves into a cottage by the shore. The locals gossip as they watch her clean, black hair tied in a white rubber band. They don't like it when she plants a garden out front – orange-red *Carpinus caroliniana* and silvery-blue hosta. Very unusual, they whisper.

Across the driveway lives a man who never goes out. Delilah knows he's watching her and she likes the look of him, but perhaps life's too complicated already...

'This story unfolds beautifully, with a balance of mystery and wry insight that keeps you turning the pages.'
—Mary Yukari Waters, author of
The Laws of Evening

'With radiant humanity, humour, and spiky powers of observation, Sara Marchant illuminates the wild and enigmatic nature of attraction.'
—Mary Otis, author of
Yes, Yes, Cherries

ANTHONY FERNER

Inside the Bone Box

'As he tiptoed his way through the twisting paths of sulci and fissures and ventricles, he'd play Bach, something austere yet dynamic.'

Nicholas Anderton is a highly respected neurosurgeon at the top of his field. But behind the successful façade all is not well. Tormented by a toxic marriage, and haunted by past mistakes, Anderton has been eating to forget. His wife, meanwhile, has turned to drink.

There are sniggers behind closed doors – how can a surgeon be fat, they whisper; when mistakes are made and his old adversary Nash steps in to take advantage, Anderton knows things are coming to a head...

'This slim novel asks some big questions, with compassion, wry humour and elegant, understated prose.'

—Kate Vane, crime novelist

KAREN B. GOLIGHTLY

There Are Things I Know

Eight-year-old Pepper sees the world a little differently from most people. One day, during a school field trip, he is kidnapped by a stranger and driven to rural Arkansas. The man claims that Pepper's mother has died and they are to live together from now on – but the boy isn't convinced.

Pepper has always found it hard to figure out when people are lying, but he's absolutely certain his mother is alive, and he's going to find her...

'Pepper proves a tenacious, resourceful hero.
Immensely readable and sweetly told.'
—Marti Leimbach, bestselling author of
Daniel Isn't Talking

'A fast-paced thriller which kept me engaged
throughout the entirety of the story.'
—Netgalley Review